RR
Rita

D1089174

ALSO BY SHANNON WORK

Now I See You
Everything To Lose

THE KILLING STORM

A NOVEL

SHANNON WORK

ISBN: 978-1-7354353-6-7 (paperback)
ISBN: 978-1-7354353-8-1 (large print paperback)
ISBN: 978-1-7354353-7-4 (eBook)

www.shannonwork.com

"You do see, don't you, that she's got to be killed?"
Agatha Christie, *Appointment with Death*

PROLOGUE

Saturday, January 8

IT WAS ALMOST eight o'clock, and the approaching storm had turned the January sky black. There was no evidence of a moon or stars, just a frigid darkness that threatened to engulf anyone caught outside.

As expected, the gravel parking lot next to the Nordic ski track was empty. And parking the car just so had the high beams illuminating the trestle bridge that had been abandoned by the railroad decades earlier. The lights cast the area in a ghostly hue, reflecting snowflakes that were starting to fall sideways with the increasing wind.

The abandoned bridge wasn't far from the parking lot, but the area had become overgrown with vegetation that was blanketed in several feet of snow. The hike took nearly ten minutes.

The bridge was sheathed in ice. Each footfall across it was taken with meticulous care. One misstep would result in careening off the side into the frozen ravine below.

The timing of the storm was perfect. Within

hours, the evidence would be covered by two feet of fresh snow. There was a good chance it wouldn't be found until spring. By that time, there wouldn't be any forensics left to collect. It would be the perfect crime.

The wind now howled through the pines like an injured animal. The wooden bridge swayed underfoot. Snow was already beginning to fill the drag trail. Time was running out.

CHAPTER 1

(earlier that day)

It was a cold morning, but there was no wind and the sun blazed in a turquoise sky.

Jack Martin sat outside the Airstream trailer with a New Mexico road map lying on the folding table in front of him. According to the forecast, the day would be mostly sunny until the superstorm rolled in later that night. And then, if what they said was true, by the next morning the entire San Juan mountain range would be covered in a couple of feet of fresh snow.

Several months earlier, Jack had moved the trailer from Shadow Mountain Lake, deep in the Colorado Rockies, to the small campground outside Durango in the southwest corner of the state, where he thought it would be warmer. The idea was to relocate somewhere the winter snow wouldn't be as treacherous, but the forecasted storm had Jack rethinking the location.

The weather was growing colder with each passing day, and he wanted to move farther south. He and Crockett could come back in the spring when everything had thawed.

He scanned the campground. It was quiet—too quiet. When he'd first gotten there in late September, there was still a smattering of activity. A few hold-over summer campers enjoying the fall color change, fishing and hiking before winter set in. But as the weather turned colder, their numbers dwindled, until one day only Jack and an old hippie couple he suspected having been at Woodstock remained.

From what Jack could tell, the couple fished and slept all day and smoked weed all night. He had tried making conversation with them on several occasions and was surprised to find out that, despite all the messages of peace and love plastered across the back of their vintage VW van, they weren't friendly at all.

"We should have gone farther south, Crockett," he told the brown dog asleep on a tattered blanket at his feet.

The dog lifted its head, looked at him briefly, then laid it back down.

"Albuquerque is too big." Jack stabbed a finger on the map. "But what about Santa Fe?"

He rubbed his chin as he thought about it. He had mixed feelings about leaving. His second autumn spent in the Rockies had been even more beautiful than the first. He'd watched the aspen leaves change from a deep green to crisp shades of gold and red before drying up and falling off.

Jack had camped in the mountains outside Aspen the year earlier, but he didn't remember them being this beautiful. The mountains had still been new to him then, and intimidating. When he'd first moved to Colorado almost two years ago, he hadn't been sure if he even liked them. But since then he'd grown to love them.

He would have to leave them soon, head back to Texas or Louisiana to find a job—in construction maybe, or if he was lucky, in law enforcement again—but not yet.

Jack looked down at the dog. "What do you think, Crockett? Santa Fe?"

Crockett lifted his head and yawned.

"It's settled, then."

As Jack folded the map, his cell phone buzzed. He pulled it from his pocket and checked the caller ID but didn't recognize the number.

"Jack Martin."

"Detective Martin, I'm glad I reached you. My name is Alice Fremont, and I need to talk to you about something."

It was an elderly woman's voice. Not kind and gentle like his grandmother's had been. It was short and to the point.

Jack waited for her to continue, irritated by the interruption and her abrupt manner.

"Are you still there, Detective?"

"I'm here."

"Good. I'd like to talk to you. Today, if possible. Where are you?"

"I beg your pardon?" Jack asked. The woman was rude.

"Where *are* you, Detective?"

Jack wasn't sure how much he wanted to divulge, or if he even wanted to continue the conversation. He hesitated before he answered.

"I'm outside Durango."

"Good," Alice Fremont said. "That's not a far drive. I'm just south of Telluride. I have an estate near Trout Lake. If you leave now, you can be here in two and a half hours."

Jack was about to hang up on her. What made this woman think he would drop everything he was doing, which admittedly wasn't much, but drop it, nonetheless, and come at her beck and call?

She must have read his mind.

"Detective, don't hang up. This is not a joke, and I'll make it worth your while. I'm prepared to pay you for your time and gas today." When Jack didn't answer, she continued. "Detective, please. I need to talk to you at your earliest convenience."

The tone of her voice had changed. It was still

short, but Jack detected a hint of desperation. He weighed his options. He could use the extra cash. It was early enough that if he left for Telluride soon, he could be back that night ahead of the storm. But he would have to delay his move to Santa Fe. If they did get two feet of snow overnight, he wouldn't be able to get out of the San Juans for another two or three days. And that was *only* if temperatures returned to normal following the storm and melted some of the snow.

"Detective?" Her tone was insistent, but Jack could hear the strain. "It could be a matter of life or death. Will you come?"

They talked a minute longer, and she gave him directions to her estate.

When Jack ended the call, he turned to the brown dog still lying at his feet. "Change of plans, Crockett. We're going to Telluride."

CHAPTER 2

As JACK WOUND his way through the snow-covered canyons toward Telluride, he thought about Alice Fremont. He was sure he'd heard the name before but couldn't remember where. A quick internet search before he'd left the campground had refreshed his memory.

Alice Fremont was an extremely wealthy woman who'd made her living by writing thinly veiled salacious stories about some of society's biggest movers and shakers, including Hollywood celebrities, politicians, and media types. They were fictionalized accounts of real people and events. And although characters were never identified by name, it wasn't difficult for savvy readers to figure out who Alice Fremont was writing about. Her novels were panned by critics but devoured by millions. *Five hundred million*, in fact, according to her bio on Wikipedia, *in more than forty languages*.

She was loved by readers but hated by those she wrote about and the critics who branded her a "shameless smut peddler." Her books had made her fabulously wealthy, but they ruined lives. The fiction-alized stories exposed the corrupt business dealings and carnal shenanigans of some of the most pow-erful people in the country. Jack read there had been death threats made against her in the past and that she had been physically assaulted at least twice. He didn't care about any of it, but he was intrigued as hell. He wondered why she wanted to talk to him.

He slowed the truck as he made his way through the tiny town of Rico. The forested canyons hugged both sides of the two-lane highway, closing in all but a sliver of turquoise sky. There were still no signs of the impending storm. He would make the meeting quick, wanting to avoid getting caught on the moun-tain highway when the weather turned.

Twenty minutes later, after a gentle rise in ele-vation, Trout Lake came into view. Set just off the highway to the east, the lake was a frozen expanse of white with towering snowcapped peaks set behind it. Several small fishing cabins dotted the shoreline. It was beautiful.

Jack pulled off the highway onto the gravel road. The truck bounced and skidded over rock and ice as they made their way around the lake. Crockett, who had been asleep on the passenger seat for most of the trip, was now sitting up fully awake.

Jack found the imposing entrance to Alice's estate at the far side of the lake, where she said it would be.

Tall standing logs, a single timber resting across their tops, sat on either side of an open gate. Flanking both sides were leafless aspens that stood like skeletons in the winter snow, their branches encased in ice.

Jack pulled through the gate onto a single-lane road. After several minutes of winding through trees, the road opened onto an expansive snow field that sloped upward to the base of a mountain in the distance. It was a breathtaking winter landscape. Presiding over it all was a mammoth stone and wood structure that rose three stories. Two attached towers rose at least four.

The size of the house was staggering. Jack slowed the truck to get a better look. He had never seen anything like it before. Surrounded only by a forest blanketed in snow, the estate seemed hauntingly disconnected from the outside world. Something about it reminded him of the hotel in *The Shining*. But it wasn't a hotel, he reminded himself. This monstrosity was actually someone's *house*.

There were no other buildings in sight—no house or town, not even a barn. There were no overhead power lines to prove the estate was connected to the outside world in any way. The meadow of snow in front of the mansion glittered a soft blue-white in the late-morning sun. Not a single footprint—deer or man—marred its surface.

Just off the side of the house, a small area had

been cleared of snow, and Jack parked the truck there. He left it running with the heater on and got out.

"Stay here, Crockett," he said, shutting the door.

He surveyed the grounds. The landscaping was sparse. A few low shrubs planted next to the foundation were mostly buried in snow. He glanced toward the back of the house, half expecting a crazed Jack Nicholson to come screaming around the corner in a snowcat. But it was deathly quiet.

An uneasy feeling of being watched prompted him to scan the dozens of windows above. That's when he saw it. On the second floor, a head stared back at him. It was the ugly face of a gnarled old woman, and she was scowling at him.

Jack returned her stare for a few moments, and she turned away. He hoped the creepy woman wasn't Alice Fremont, but something in his gut told him it was.

Jack locked the truck's doors and stuck his keys in his pocket, then started up a concrete path that had been cleared of snow and seemed to terminate somewhere near the center of the house, where he hoped to find the front door.

He took in and released several deep breaths, fogging the air in front of him and wondering what he was walking into.

CHAPTER 3

BEFORE JACK REACHED the front door, it swung open, releasing a gust of warm air. A small, stout woman stood looking up at him. She wore a long-sleeve black dress and a white apron. She had a broad, flat face and olive skin, with hair and eyes as dark as night. But it was a friendly face, not at all like the sinister one he'd seen through the window.

The woman made eye contact only briefly, then dropped her gaze to the floor. "Come in, Mr. Jack Martin," she said, pulling the door open and standing aside.

Jack hadn't given her his name. She had been expecting him.

Jack felt like a seven-year-old about to enter a haunted house. He hesitated, then silently chastised himself for being ridiculous. He wiped his cowboy boots on the large steel mat.

"Thank you," he said, stepping into an enormous entrance hall. It was one of the largest rooms he'd ever seen. A cavernous space that opened to a sec-ond-floor landing above. The walls were paneled in dark wood, with art hung everywhere, the floors covered with a deep red carpet that had intricate patterns woven into it like a rug. Two staircases, one flanking each side of the room, rose to the second floor. Between them, a fire crackled in a giant fireplace sheathed in river rock that stretched from the first floor to the timbered ceiling, the opening under the mantel tall enough for Jack to stand in.

The woman shut the door behind him, bringing his attention back to her.

"I'm here to see Alice Fremont."

She nodded silently and started for an open set of doors some distance away. Jack followed, his footfalls silent on the thick carpet. The heads of deer and elk hung overhead, their sightless eyes seeming to follow him as he crossed the room. The house was overly heated and smelled of stale air and old wood. He wondered what kind of person lived in such a nightmare.

The stout woman stopped at the threshold and gestured for Jack to enter the room. "Sit in here, Mr. Jack Martin. Mrs. Fremont will come soon." Without waiting for a reply, she pulled the rolling doors shut, leaving Jack alone.

He took off his coat and glanced around for a place to sit. The ornate, straight-back sofa and matching chairs were covered in a tufted green velvet and looked as comfortable as a concrete bench. Jack decided to remain standing.

He crossed the room to a window. The view was out the back of the house, toward the mountains. He noticed something mechanical in the distance to one side, a tall, rusted metal pole half-buried in snow. Cables attached to the top angled up the mountain and disappeared into the trees.

He turned his attention to the room and felt like he had stepped back in time. The lower third of the walls were clad in the same dark paneling as the entrance hall. Above the paneling, red fabric in a shade similar to the carpet stretched to the ceiling. Small knickknacks cluttered a large curio cabinet pushed against one wall; a set of shelves crowded with books was set along another. Paintings and a giant mirror, all mounted in elaborate gold frames, were scattered around the room.

Except for the rhythmic tick of a fancy clock perched on the marble mantel, the room was quiet—and suffocating.

Several minutes later, the doors were pushed open, revealing a small gray-haired woman wearing a caftan and heavy turquoise jewelry. She was short—not much over five feet—and was frail and birdlike, with a long, unattractive face and small dark eyes that looked like black marbles. It was the same face Jack had seen in the window.

"Detective Martin, I presume." She swept into the room and held out a bony hand for Jack to shake—or kiss. He wasn't sure which. Jack shook it and caught the whiff of something familiar.

"Have a seat." She gestured toward one of the chairs, then chose a spot on the velvet sofa for herself, spreading the extra fabric from her caftan to one side like she was posing for a portrait.

Jack was surprised. In the photographs he'd seen online, Alice Fremont looked taller—and more attractive. Publicity photos, he decided, touched up and filtered for the back covers of the books she sold by the millions.

Jack sat down in a chair. As he suspected, the hideous thing felt like sitting on a dimpled rock. He adjusted, trying to get more comfortable.

"That was quite some detective work in Vail, catching Elliot Banks's killer," she said, pointing a thin finger at him.

"Sometimes I get lucky."

She waved him off dismissively. "I don't think luck had anything to do with it. I met Elliot Banks once—nice man. Such a shame."

Jack had no interest in discussing past cases. "What did you want to see me about?"

His directness startled her, but she seemed to appreciate it. "I have a business proposition for you." She studied him as if waiting for a response. Jack gave her none, so she continued. "I believe I'm in danger."

Jack raised an eyebrow. "What makes you think so?"

"Last night someone tried to break into my house. I heard them. I was in here"—she swept an arm around the room—"reading. I heard someone try to open the front door, so I got up and looked. By that time, they were trying an adjacent window. They were obviously looking for a way in."

"What did you do?"

"I hollered through the window, and they left."

"Did you get a look at who it was?"

"I only saw him from the back. By the time I pulled the curtains aside to look, he was running away. I never saw his face. He jumped into some sort of vehicle and drove away."

"Was it a car or a truck?"

"I couldn't tell."

"Was the person alone?"

"I presume, but I couldn't tell that, either." She frowned, folds of skin creasing her already wrinkled face. "It was dark."

"What time did this occur?"

She took a moment. "Maybe around midnight. I'm not entirely sure."

"Did you call the police?"

"Of course not. What good would that do? It would take them forever to get all the way out here."

She was right. The estate was remote. "You live here alone?"

Alice eyed him suspiciously. "Why do you ask?"

"It's a massive house. I assume there must be family members or staff who live here with you, someone who might have seen or heard something?" He saw her stiffen slightly.

"You assume wrong. There is no one here at night except me."

Jack knew better than to assume anything. He'd made a mistake. "What about the woman who answered the door?"

"Sally? She works for me during the day—cooking and cleaning. Her husband, Johnny, works for me as well—mostly outside, on the grounds."

"Do they have a key to the house?"

"Of course they do."

"Does anyone else have one?"

"A what?"

"A key." Jack was growing frustrated.

"Yes, of course. Both my sons have one, as does my daughter-in-law."

"No one else?"

"No one."

"What about a security alarm?"

"No alarm." She looked at Jack like he was an

idiot. "It would cost me a fortune to wire this old place."

"They have wireless systems now," Jack said, trying to be helpful.

"You assume I have internet, which I don't."

Jack gave up. "Then I'd make sure to keep the doors and windows locked at all times, even when you're home."

"Brilliant suggestion, Detective."

Jack leaned forward in the chair, resting his elbows on his knees. "Why am I here, Alice?"

She raised her chin toward the ceiling. "Most people call me Mrs. Fremont." She dropped her chin slightly. "But you may call me Alice if you insist."

"Why am I here, Alice?" Jack repeated. "You had an intruder. Now they're gone."

"It's not that simple." She fell silent, then got up from the sofa and walked to a window. After a few moments, she turned back. "I'm a very wealthy woman. She paused. "But not very well liked."

Jack didn't know how to reply, so he didn't.

"I write novels that make people angry—very *powerful* people, in some cases. And I've been threatened—several times."

From the news articles he'd read, Jack knew that Alice had been physically attacked outside a posh Hollywood restaurant shortly after the release of her last novel—a thinly veiled account of scandal and corruption at three of Hollywood's largest movie production companies. Alice had spent a week in the hospital recovering from her injuries, and the perpetrator had never been caught.

There had been at least one other attempt on her life. Years earlier, a shooter had tried to gun her down as she walked through the lobby of a hotel in New York City. Lucky for Alice, he'd missed.

"Have you been threatened recently?" Jack asked.

"No. But word has gotten out about my upcoming novel. I'm not sure how. Maybe by some fault of my own—I don't know—but it has. And there are some unsavory people in town who won't be happy when they find out what's in it."

For a second there was a crack in her stone veneer, a hint of fear in her voice before she recovered. Jack realized Alice Fremont was scared.

"What is it that you want me to do?" he asked.

"Stay here, in my house. Just for a short time." Jack started to shake his head, but she continued. "It will only be for a few months—until any furor after the release of the next novel has died down."

She wanted a bodyguard, not a detective. Jack wasn't interested. "Alice—"

She held up her hands toward him. "Don't answer yet. I'm asking you to consider it. You can get back to me tomorrow."

"You don't know anything about me," Jack said.

"But you'd want me to move in here?" He glanced over the room. It was a horrible prospect, but he wasn't ruling the offer out completely—not yet.

"I know more about you than you think." She had a sly look in her eyes. "I know you caught the Hermes Strangler in Aspen, then only two months later solved Elliot Banks's murder in Vail."

"A lot of people know that."

"Yes, but I also know about your stellar career with the FBI and about the unfortunate incident in Houston that got you fired."

Jack kept his expression fixed but felt his pulse quicken. How had she found out about Houston?

"Yes. I know all about the shooting at the diner after you were told to stand down but didn't. Six dead, including the gunman." Jack remained silent, and she continued. "And I know what happened to your grandparents in Baton Rouge."

Jack felt his body tense. He didn't want to talk about Houston or his grandparents with anyone, especially not someone as calculating and cold as Alice Fremont. "You've done your homework," he finally replied.

There was a smug look on her face. "It's my job."

They held each other's stare for what seemed like an eternity.

Alice was the first to speak. "You see, Detective, I investigate for a living, too. It's not exactly like what you do, but it's similar. However, my investigations—hence my novels—have made me millions."

"Have you investigated the whereabouts of your two living ex-husbands?" Jack let the question sink in. "I heard that *all* of your divorces were contentious but that those two were particularly nasty. They both made threats against you, didn't they?"

He thought it would make her angry, but it didn't. She looked amused.

Her lips curled with the hint of a smile. "I see you've done your homework, too."

"It's my job."

Alice nodded. "Touché." She crossed the room to the bookshelves. "Do you read, Detective?"

"Read?" Jack was confused by the question.

"Yes, *read*. Scanning groups of alphabetic characters left to right." She had her back to him, searching the shelves.

"On occasion," Jack answered. Although he was not one to pass judgment too quickly, he was finding it extremely difficult to like Alice Fremont.

"Well, I don't care if it's Dante, Danielle Steel, or Dr. Seuss. Everyone should read." She ran a finger along several book spines, still searching. "Here it is," she said, pulling one from the shelf.

Jack watched as she crossed the room toward him. Her fingers were thin and bent at the knuckles, but they were wrapped firmly around the book.

"Take this," she said, thrusting it at him. "It's *Don Quixote* by Miguel de Cervantes." She said it with the accent of someone fluent in Spanish. "I think you'll find the main character interesting and…familiar."

Jack turned the book over and was glad to see that it was in English despite the Spanish title.

"Take it with you," Alice said. "Even if you decide not to accept the job, I'd like for you to have it." She pointed a finger at him. "But read it."

Alice Fremont was a complex woman. Jack still wasn't sure he liked her, but he thanked her.

As he followed her to the front door, he caught another whiff of the familiar smell cutting through the musty odor of the old house. Then something triggered his memory, and he remembered what it was. He realized that, wherever Alice went, she trailed the rich scent of brandy.

He scanned the walls as he made his way across the enormous hall for a second time. On his way in, he hadn't noticed the large oil painting that hung high over the front door. It was of an elk being taken down by a mountain lion. Its face was contorted in agony and looked toward the heavens, its massive antlers falling back on themselves, as if pleading to be released from its cruel predicament. It was haunting.

The painting was nearly the size of the front door, and probably worth a fortune. Jack didn't know much about art, but he thought it was savage and cruel.

She saw him staring up at it. "It takes a lot of art to cover these walls. But that is one of my favorites. Do you like it?"

Jack was silent, not sure how to answer the question without offending her. "I do," he finally lied.

She swung open the front door, flooding the room with sunlight. But to the north, a bank of dark clouds was building.

Alice followed him outside. "You call me tomorrow and give me your answer," she said. "I'll make it financially worth your while. But if you don't want the job, let me know. I'll have to find someone else."

Jack nodded.

She studied the sky. "But you get going now, Detective. There's a storm coming."

"I heard on the radio on the drive over that it's supposed to be a big one."

"It could be the worst this season. Trees will come down. We'll lose some of the wildlife, I'm afraid." A shadow had fallen over her face. "It's going to be a killing storm."

CHAPTER 4

HUGH SHEPPARD SAT alone in the cold living room of the mansion he shared with his even colder wife, Eva. It was almost four o'clock, and he'd been home for nearly an hour. She was still nowhere to be found. Earlier, when he had texted asking where she was, she'd replied simply, *I will be home soon.*

The white leather sofa was stiff and creaked in complaint every time Hugh shifted his substantial weight, trying to get comfortable. Frustrated, he moved to a velvet side chair, repositioning his martini on the glass table in front of him.

Hugh surveyed the vast white room, regretting having given his Slovenia-born wife carte blanche on decorating the house. Together with her architect and design team, Eva had overseen the construction of what Hugh secretly referred to as his ten-thousand-square-foot igloo.

He looked past the colorless walls and out the floor-to-ceiling glass to the snowy peaks of San Sophia Ridge. Everything inside and out was white.

He checked his phone for the umpteenth time in the last hour. No text. Damned woman.

It hadn't been a good day. A trip to California to raise funds for his latest real estate venture had been unsuccessful. The potential investors he'd pitched the project to simply didn't have his vision. They were incapable of seeing the potential of the suburb he would carve out of the desert. It was only a three-hour drive from Los Angeles, and the demand for housing was there—Hugh was sure of it.

He could already see it, streets laid out in a loose grid, houses painted in various pastel shades, reflecting the colors of the surrounding desert. There would be shopping centers, schools, parks—and *snakes*. He couldn't believe he'd said it. But Eva had insisted the subdivision would be infested with them. He should have never shown her the location map. The blasted woman had infiltrated his thoughts at the most inopportune time. He hadn't meant to say it in his presentation, but there it was: "schools, parks...and snakes." Damned woman.

If he could only find the investors, Hugh was sure *this* development would make back the millions he'd lost on the previous ones. As he'd pointed out earlier that day, when the issue was raised, those failures were never Hugh's fault. The planners and architects had gone far over their original budgets. There were delays in permitting. Hugh had insisted the previous bankruptcies were due to circumstances beyond his control.

He twisted one way and then the other, trying unsuccessfully to get comfortable in the chair. He gave up, stuck out his bare feet, plopping them down on the glass table next to his drink. He hated the house.

Where was the blasted woman? He was hungry.

Hugh pulled his drink from the table and took a sip, then rested the glass on his belly.

"I am home, darling." Eva practically sang it in her Slavic accent as she waltzed into the room. She had a bag on each arm, her long blond hair dancing on her shoulders as she sauntered over and planted a kiss on each of his cheeks. "Did you miss me?"

Hugh's mood lightened a bit. For as much as she exasperated him, he was still in awe of her—all six feet, drop-dead-gorgeous inches of her.

"Of course I missed you," he grumbled. "Where were you this time?"

She beamed, holding the two bags aloft. "Shopping."

"I should have known." Hugh emptied the last of the drink, and it reminded him that Eva was quickly draining what was left of his inheritance. He needed to find investors for the next development, and fast.

Eva set the bags on the floor and slipped off her

fur coat, laying it over the arm of the sofa. "How is your mother today?"

"I haven't talked to her."

"Since when?"

"Since we had dinner with her last Sunday."

"Hugh! She lives in that enormous house all alone. You should check on her."

"She's fine." Hugh waved off her concern with his empty glass. It was early, but the alcohol had him woozy. "She's got that Indian woman and her husband. They'd let us know if anything was wrong."

Eva stared down at him, her hands on her hips, and he knew he was in trouble.

"First of all, they are not Indian, Hugh. They are—"

"Native American," he finished for her, rolling his eyes. "Forgive me for not being PC."

"Second, she is your *mother*. Call her." Eva sat down and pulled a cashmere sweater from one of the bags. She laid it across the arm of the couch and reached into the bag again. "How was your trip? Did you get the money from the investors?"

"No." The question made his bad mood worse.

"*That* is why you have not called your mother. You still need the money. You are angry with her for not investing again."

Hugh stood up and crossed the room to the bar, weaving slightly. Eva's stilted, foreign accent was beginning to grate on him. There had been a time he'd found it endearing. Not any more. "I have every right to be upset," he said, reaching for the gin.

"Do you?"

"Yes, I do." His voice was raised. He poured gin and vermouth into the shaker. "She could finance the entire development on her own, yet she won't lend me a blasted penny? And I'm her son!" He shook the cocktail shaker furiously.

"And she is your mother, not your banker."

Hugh poured the martini into the glass and started back across the room.

"She put money into the last development, Hugh. You lost it all. Remember?"

"Of course I remember." He took a drink, then wiped his mouth with the back of his hand. It wasn't his fault, but it was a failure his mother reminded him of often, another reason he didn't want to call her. No one suffers the wrath of Alice Fremont willingly. Except for maybe his half brother, Lars.

Hugh took a sip of martini and scoffed at the thought of his younger brother—his mother's favorite. If only Hugh had been born the son of Billy Fremont, Alice's fourth husband, the only one of the four she hadn't grown to despise.

Billy Fremont had been a ne'er-do-well like his son, but for some reason Alice had loved him. He died in a motorcycle accident when Lars was only seven. Hugh had been twenty-six.

Hugh's father had been Alice's *first* husband. And, by all accounts, should have been her favorite but wasn't. Marrying Warren Sheppard had, for the first time in her life, made Alice a wealthy woman. But the two barely spoke by the time Warren died of cancer only eight years into the marriage.

When Warren died, half of his fortune went to Alice and the other half into a trust fund for Hugh. At the age of thirty, Hugh was given access to it, and the balance had dwindled steadily in the twenty years since.

The way Hugh saw it, the inheritance his mother received from Warren was rightfully his. And now, as a multimillionaire author, she didn't need Warren Sheppard's money anyway. The least she could do was invest some of it into his new project, but she had refused.

"Well, that is it," Eva said, stuffing her purchases back into the bags. "I am going upstairs to put all of this away. Then I am going to change and go to town for yoga."

"Yoga? You went a few nights ago."

"Hugh, you know I have to stay in shape to ski."

Eva's obsession with fitness perturbed him. She had been an alternate on the Slovenia Olympic ski team in 2006 and was still in top physical condition.

For the life of him, he didn't understand why she obsessed over it so much.

Thinking about exercise reminded him he was hungry. "What about dinner?"

"I picked you up soup and salad from Altezza. It is in the kitchen on the counter."

Soup and salad? He would have preferred a burger or a pizza instead.

He glanced through the windows at the peaks to the north, where dark clouds were building. "They're forecasting a storm tonight," he said, trying to get her to change her mind.

"I will be back in a few hours." She picked up her bags, kissed him on both cheeks again, and left, leaving her fur coat draped across the sofa.

Hugh eyed the full-length fox coat, wondering how much he could get for it at a pawnshop in LA. He could take it without Eva knowing, blame it on the housekeeper.

He leaned back into the stiff chair, throwing his feet onto the glass table again and letting his thoughts turn back to his mother. He was running out of options. He needed to find the money. He would work on Alice, wear her down. As she had in the past, she would eventually give him what he wanted—he would make her.

He leaned forward, snatched the martini glass

from the coffee table, and swirled the liquid, spilling some.

Eva was right; he should call her. But not tonight, Hugh decided. The day had been bad enough.

CHAPTER 5

SAM BONNET HAD lived all seventeen years of his life in Telluride. He didn't care much for the tourists. They crowded the streets and, more importantly, crowded the ski slopes. But he had always heard "the tourists pay the bills," so he tolerated them. Working part-time at Waggoner Mercantile, he had heard Opal Waggoner say it many times.

"The customer is always right, Sam," she would insist. "And in this town, ninety percent of my customers are tourists." Sam wondered why Opal's sister, Ivy, never protested when Opal called them *her* customers or referred to the shop as *her* store. As far as Sam knew, Ivy owned half of it.

But that's pretty much how it went around Waggoner Mercantile—Miss Opal did most of the talking. Every day when Sam arrived at work, she would tell him to "look alive and be courteous," which Sam thought was ironic since Opal Waggoner barely looked alive and was almost never courteous. She was the wrinkliest old woman he had ever met and one of the grumpiest.

Miss Ivy, on the other hand, was funny—and nice. She wasn't attractive by any means, but she had a kind face and smiled a lot. Ivy was the friendlier of the two sisters—the one everybody liked. She took care of the bookkeeping and inventory, which meant that Sam worked more closely with her than with Opal, and he was grateful for it.

When Sam got to work that afternoon, he was surprised to find the store full of customers. By mid-January, the tourist crowd usually would start to thin before picking back up closer to spring break in March. For some reason, they seemed to be hanging around this season.

Opal was helping a customer try on a pair of turquoise earrings. She looked up when he came in. "Sam, go tell Ivy we need to restock the small wool blankets. I've sold three already today."

"Yes, ma'am."

"And grab a medium-sized painting to put in the place of the one I sold earlier." She nodded toward an empty spot on the wall where a painting of a herd of buffalo running through snow had hung. Sam would miss the painting. It was one of his favorites.

Except for the void where the missing artwork had hung, the store was packed with goods floor-to-ceiling. Colorful wool blankets and rugs were stacked on shelves that reached from the plank wood floor up to the pressed-tin ceiling, the top rugs accessible only by an old rolling ladder. It was Sam's job to go up and down it, and he always held his breath the old thing wouldn't fall apart when he did.

Larger rugs hung from a metal rack where customers looked through them like the pages of a magazine. Glass cases held turquoise and coral jewelry—necklaces, bracelets, bolo ties, and earrings. Tables of various sizes set throughout the store displayed everything from antique pottery and baskets to old books. Every square inch of the store displayed something the Waggoner sisters would sell.

Aside from an assortment of scented candles arranged near the cash register, the place smelled of wool and wood polish. Sam had worked for the sisters for nearly a year and hated to think about how many hours he'd spent dusting and polishing, preferring to spend his time working with Miss Ivy in the back.

But for the most part, he enjoyed working there. The shop occupied part of a building that dated back to 1889 and had once been a hardware store supplying miners with the tools of their trade. Sam found the building's history interesting.

Another thing he liked was the store's location near the corner of Oak Street and Colorado Avenue—often referred to as Main Street—across from the historic county courthouse in the center of town. But mostly he liked that it was a straight shot up Oak

Street from the gondola that connected Telluride to Mountain Village. On days when Sam didn't have school, he'd spend as long as he could on the mountain snowboarding before taking the gondola back to town and rushing to work. He knew how to time it just right, arriving a minute or two early.

"Hop to it, Sam," Opal instructed. "Get the lead out."

Sam slipped through the back door into the storeroom.

Miss Ivy was at her desk in the corner, hunched over the ledger book she used for accounting. The sisters didn't own a computer.

She heard him come in and turned in her chair. "Good afternoon, Sam."

"Good afternoon, Miss Ivy," Sam said with a nod. "Miss Opal asked for—"

"I heard. She's got the voice of a foghorn, don't you think?"

Sam bit his lip. He wasn't about to reply.

Ivy pointed toward a maze of wire shelving. "Be a dear and pick a few blankets out for me and take them out to her." She twisted in her chair and pointed to a far wall. "Then take her a painting the size she needs. You can pick it. Thank you, Sam."

Three hours later, when the last customers had left, Opal locked the shop's front door and turned the sign in the window from OPEN to CLOSED.

Sam was wiping fingerprints from a glass jewelry case. It had been a busy afternoon, and it was his job to straighten things and clean up at the end of the day.

Ivy walked in from the back room. "Opal, Alice Fremont called. She asked us to bring two necklaces she was considering when she was in here last. Do you remember which ones they were?"

Sam kept cleaning but watched the sisters out of the corner of his eye. If they were going to make a trip to Mrs. Fremont's estate, he would be the one to drive them out there.

Opal leaned on her cane and scowled. "Of course I remember which ones they were. But I'm tired of that woman insisting we bring things to her like we're hired help. Then, when she doesn't like it or changes her mind, we have to go trudging back out to the boondocks to pick it up."

"Alice is our best customer," Ivy said. "We'd be lucky to have more like her."

Opal ignored the remark but struck the floor with her cane, causing Sam to jump. "Well, I'm not about to go out there tonight when there's a whopper of a storm coming. Sam, you can drive us out there tomorrow. Alice Fremont can just wait until then." She hit the floor with her cane once again, as if making her point.

Opal brooded for a moment, then turned to her sister. "Ivy, I have an idea."

"Uh-oh."

"If we have to go all the way out there, then we might as well take advantage of it."

Ivy sighed. "I don't like the sound of this."

"You don't have to. That's why I do all the thinking." Ivy rolled her eyes, but Opal kept talking. "When we're inside the house, I'll distract Alice and you hunt for that book she's working on."

Ivy shook her head. "Uh-uh. No way. You're going to get us arrested one of these days."

Opal ignored her. "It's a perfect plan."

"So said Nixon."

"We can finally get a look at that book of hers and see if we're in it. It's a brilliant idea if you ask me."

"Nobody asked you," Ivy replied.

Sam had heard the rumors about the book Mrs. Fremont was writing—probably everyone in town had. With a population of less than two thousand, Telluride was small enough that locals knew one another, and rumors spread fast—especially rumors of a famous author writing a book about some of them. It had everyone in town on edge, wondering who would be skewered in it. Sam had never read a book outside of school but decided he might read Mrs. Fremont's if it was really about people in Telluride.

There were a lot of residents he thought would be interesting characters for her to write about—celebrities and really rich people—but not Opal or Ivy Waggoner. He couldn't understand why they were so paranoid about it, talking about it practically every day.

"I'm not doing it," Ivy said.

"Then you distract her and *I'll* do it," Opal replied, rapping the floor with her cane again.

"Opal, you're going to finally drive me crazy. We're not going to snoop through Alice's house, and that's final."

"Yap, yap, yap. You sound just like old man Rucker's rat-faced terrier."

"Better to sound like one than look like one," Ivy muttered under her breath.

"What was that?"

"Nuh-thing." Ivy sang the word.

Sam turned away to keep from laughing. He slid his navy jacket from under the counter and pulled it on.

"Sam." It was Opal.

"Yes, ma'am?"

"I was besieged with customers earlier and couldn't say anything, but before you go, get that darned thing you brought out earlier off the wall and replace it with something else."

Sam glanced at the watercolor of an owl—he liked

it. And it was almost exactly the size of the buffalo painting it replaced.

Ivy pulled up the glasses that hung from her neck and put them on. "What's wrong with it?"

"Ivy," Opal said, leaning on her cane. "That's one of the two you took on consignment from Celeste Bailey that she likely bought from Quinn Gallery. How could you forget?"

Sam watched as Ivy remembered, the strain showing on her face.

"But we don't know for sure that she bought it from Quinn Gallery," Ivy said quietly.

It had happened one afternoon while Opal was down the street at the bank. Celeste Bailey had brought in two watercolors—a bear and the owl. Ivy had agreed to take them on consignment. She and Sam both liked the pieces.

Later, when she was back from the bank, Opal had blown a gasket, saying she didn't want anything that could have been in "that man's gallery" hanging in her store. Sam didn't know why, but she had gone so far as to call Gordon Quinn a crook.

Ivy took off her glasses, letting them dangle again from the beaded lanyard around her neck. "Sam, you and I can choose another one tomorrow. It's been a busy day."

"Yes, ma'am."

"I'll see you in the morning, Sam." Ivy turned

and disappeared through the door to the back room, leaving him alone with Opal.

Sam sucked in a deep breath and held it, knowing from experience she wouldn't be finished with her tirade.

"I can't leave this place for a minute," Opal said. "That's the kind of thing that happens when I'm not around. You mark my words, young man. If there's one thing I know about, it's crooks. And one day that crook Gordon Quinn is going to get caught with his hand in a cookie jar, but it won't be mine." She pointed a finger at him when she said it.

"Yes, ma'am," Sam said, shrugging on his coat.

"You go on home now. Tomorrow you can drive us out to Alice Fremont's," Opal said, shaking her head and turning away.

Sam was looking forward to the trip, but he didn't tell her that.

"Yes, Miss Opal. Good night." He pulled up his coat's hood and turned to leave. She never saw him smile.

CHAPTER 6

JACK AND CROCKETT got back to the campground just ahead of the storm. The two sat on the open tailgate of the truck, sharing the contents of a Styrofoam container from a Mexican restaurant in Delores.

It was cold out but beautiful. The sun was somewhere behind the clouds to the west, quickly making its way toward the horizon. As he ate, Jack watched a bank of heavier clouds to the north roll his way. It wouldn't be much longer before the storm hit.

He rolled a flour tortilla and gave Crockett half, his thoughts drifting back to Alice Fremont. She was looking for a bodyguard—not a detective—and Jack wasn't a bodyguard. Although he could use the money, he decided to call her in the morning and decline the offer.

He told himself he wouldn't want to work for someone like her anyway. Alice seemed to be the type of person who was perpetually angry, the type who lived to piss people off.

And then there were her books—scathing commentaries about some of the most powerful people in the country. He wasn't surprised that she had received threats and had even been physically assaulted on at least two occasions.

Finished eating, Jack wiped his mouth with a napkin and stuck all the trash into the bag. Crockett leaped from the tailgate to chase a snow hare that had emerged from behind a tree. Jack sat a moment longer, watching the storm as it sped toward them.

He wondered how Alice had found out about Houston. But she had mentioned that, like Jack, she was an investigator. She must have had an inside source. He had worked hard to put the memories behind him. Alice had brought them up like she was pulling a trump card, and it made him angry. Jack wondered how much of the story she really knew.

His mind drifted back to the diner off Interstate 10, east of Houston. He remembered every detail. It was a brutally hot April day, and he'd pulled off the highway for a bite to eat. As he had gotten out of the truck, he heard gunshots ring out from inside the restaurant. An older couple crossing the parking lot heard them, too, and ran back toward their car. Jack ran toward the diner.

Jack screwed his eyes shut, trying to push the memory away. But it was there. Like the eyes of the elk in the painting that hung above Alice's door, the eyes of the shooter that day still haunted him.

When Jack had called in the shooting and identified

himself as an FBI agent, he'd been told to stand down. He hadn't. Six people lost their lives that day, including the gunman. But if he hadn't intervened, there would have been more.

The turn of events that followed had gotten Jack fired, but he would never regret what he'd done.

Following the shooting, Jack spent a year and a half fighting his own storm. But he'd gotten through it. The job in Aspen had helped. He'd always suspected his boss at the FBI had something to do with getting it for him, but Jack had never asked.

The Aspen gig was what had brought him to Colorado, and he was grateful for it. He had grown to love the mountains. But the mountains tonight scared him.

The forest around the campground grew dark as the storm raced closer. A minute later it hit like a freight train. Jack's face and ears grew numb from the wind and cold.

"Let's go, Crockett," he hollered as he hopped from the tailgate and shut it.

He unlocked the trailer door and let the dog inside, then stood, taking one last look to the north. His eyes were slitted against the freezing wind that now howled like an injured animal, rocking the trailer back and forth. The snow hadn't started, but the clouds were boiling overhead. He heard an aspen snap and turned in time to see it fall.

Jack pulled the trailer door shut and latched it. They were in for a wild ride. The storm was going to be a bad one. Alice Fremont had called it something.

Then he remembered.

A killing storm.

CHAPTER 7

Sunday, January 9

HUGH SHEPPARD HAD managed to cobble together only a few hours of sleep, tossing and turning as the storm raged outside the bedroom window. At dawn, he had given up and gotten out of bed.

Dressed in a T-shirt and boxer shorts, he stood in the bathroom in front of the full-length mirror, his bare feet cold on the white marble. He pivoted sideways and studied his paunch in profile, then sucked in his gut. After only a few seconds, he exhaled. It was no use. He was a middle-aged, fat, bald man, and that was that. He was neither handsome nor ugly, just plain. Plain old Hugh, the eldest son of one of the world's most successful authors.

He switched off the light and plodded back through the bedroom. Eva was still sleeping, and as far as Hugh could tell, she had slept through the storm like a baby. Then again, she almost always did. Maybe there was something to evening yoga classes after all.

He shut the bedroom door quietly and made his

way downstairs to the kitchen. By the time he settled into a chair with his coffee, it was just after seven o'clock. He glanced through the window and saw stars still visible in the pale pink sky. The storm had moved out overnight, taking with it the clouds and wind.

He blew over the hot coffee and went to take a sip but stopped short. He pulled the cup away and looked at it—white porcelain. His eyes swept the room. White—the walls and floors, the cabinets and quartzite countertops. Even outside, the snowdrift from the storm had settled nearly two feet above the bottom of the window. White everywhere. He hated it.

In LA the day before, the temperature had been in the seventies. He should have stayed. He thought of their home in Brentwood, a beautiful Spanish Colonial Hugh had purchased from the estate of a Hollywood movie producer, one of his father's old colleagues.

The house had cost him a large chunk of his inheritance, but it had been worth it. There was nothing more exhilarating than conducting business in his swim trunks, lounging in the sun next to the sparkling pool. It made Hugh feel like Don Corleone or Jay Gatsby, the lord of his own kingdom.

But the Brentwood house was getting more expensive to maintain. Utility costs had gone up and property taxes had skyrocketed. Hugh knew that if he wanted to keep the house, he'd have to get his hands on more money soon.

Several days earlier, he'd made the mistake of suggesting to Eva that they sell the house in Mountain Village. Since they'd completed construction on it only two years earlier, the real estate market had gone nuts. He was sure he could flip it and make millions. The money would go a long way in solving his financial problems. But Eva had balked at the idea, telling Hugh that she would never consent to selling *her* home.

As an avid skier, Eva insisted on spending entire seasons in the mountains. Hugh had lost count of how many years, from November to March, he'd spent stuck in the godforsaken snow. He was sick of it.

Hugh sat slouched in the white velvet chair. He hated the chair and hated his life.

He took a sip, then pulled the cup away, studying it again. Then he pushed himself out of the chair, padded across the room to the kitchen, and dug around in a cabinet until he found what he was looking for—a chipped brown mug with the town logo emblazoned on it. The mug was old and, according to Eva, *tacky*. But it was his.

He poured the coffee from the porcelain cup into the mug, then stuck the white one in the dishwasher.

"That's better," he mumbled to himself. It was a minor victory, but a victory nonetheless.

He recrossed the room and plopped down again into the chair. The sun was just cresting the mountains to the east. There wasn't a cloud in sight.

"Thank God," he said aloud, glad there would be no more snow.

"What was that, sweetheart?"

Eva swept into the kitchen, an ice goddess with her platinum-blond hair and wearing a white cashmere robe. Even first thing in the morning without makeup, Hugh thought she was stunning.

"Uh…nothing," he answered. "Just talking to myself about the storm last night."

She poured herself coffee, crossed over the room and planted a kiss on the top of his head, then dropped onto the sofa. She pulled up her feet, tucking them underneath her, and took a sip of coffee.

"Did you check on your mother this morning?"

"I tried once," Hugh lied. "She didn't answer."

"It is probably too early. You should try again later." Eva glanced through the window and her face lit up. "Look at all the fresh snow, Hugh." She untucked her feet and walked to the window. "It is beautiful. I must have slept through the storm." She stood staring out the window as she drank her coffee.

Hugh watched her. Her tall, slender figure was a painful reminder of what he'd seen in the mirror earlier that morning. Eva still looked gorgeous. But why shouldn't she? She was ten years younger.

"How about skiing with me today?" she asked, turning around and catching him watching her. "The powder will be fantastic."

There wasn't a chance Hugh was going out into that wintery hell. "I'd love to," he lied, "but I have work I need to get done today."

"Oh, poo," Eva said, turning back to the window. "All you do is work."

"That reminds me. There was a file on the desk in the study. I couldn't find it this morning. Did you happen to see it?"

She waved a hand, her back still to him. "I am sure the housekeeper put it somewhere while she was cleaning. It will turn up."

"But I need it *today*." The urgency in his voice got her attention, and she turned around.

"Why is it so important?"

Hugh exhaled, frustrated. "They're financial statements, Eva. I need to work on them."

He would have to pitch the subdivision project to another investor group, but before he did, he wanted to tweak the statements. He needed to beef up the numbers, find a way to make his precarious financial situation appear stronger.

She once again waved aside his concern. "They will turn up," she said. "Or just print them again."

Eva was beautiful—and smart—but she knew nothing about business. Their finances were precariously thin, and she was either in denial or didn't care. Hugh knew she *would* care as soon as he was no longer able to pay her credit card bills.

"I have an idea," Hugh said. "The next time we visit Mother, I'll distract her and you look for her stashes of money. She's bragged about hoarding cash for years, hiding it in secret spots around the house, not trusting banks. There's no telling how much she has tucked away in that old place."

Eva was staring at him, a look of disgust on her face. "Hugh?"

"Oh, she won't miss it. Besides, if she'd just lend me some, we wouldn't have to. It's my money anyway—my *inheritance*."

"Not all of it."

"A lot of it is," he protested. "She doesn't need it anyway. There's no telling how big her advance is for her next book. She doesn't need the money, Eva, but we do." His voice had risen and surprised both of them.

Eva set the cup down on the coffee table. "I am not going to steal from your mother, Hugh."

"It's not stealing when it's my money."

"This conversation is ridiculous."

"It's not," he insisted. "Just see what you can find.

As paranoid as she is, I bet she's got a hundred thousand or more stashed around in places."

"Even if she does, it will not be enough to finance your subdivision. So what difference will it make?"

He leveled a cool look at her. "A hundred grand will pay a couple of your credit card bills." He knew he was skating on thin ice, but he wanted to get her attention. That had done it.

She glared at him. "Now you are really being ridiculous."

He slammed a fist on the arm of the sofa. "Dammit, Eva. Business is bad. The markets are down and our expenses are up. Do you think I can just pluck money off a tree?"

Her eyes blazed before slowly softening. She came around the coffee table and sat down on his lap, wrapping an arm around him.

"I know you will figure it out, sweetheart. You are a very smart man. You always figure it out."

Hugh wasn't sure if he should be flattered or infuriated. He had brought the subject up several times before, but Eva still didn't get it. Their accounts were running dry, yet she continued to spend money like there was an endless supply. If he didn't find money soon, he'd be forced to take even more drastic measures than he already had.

CHAPTER 8

SALLY EAGLE HAD worked for Alice Fremont for more than twenty-three years, ever since Alice bought Castle in the Clouds, as the locals had always referred to the estate.

Sally had been almost thirty when she was offered the position of housekeeper, a step up from the job flipping burgers at Bubba's Snack Shack in Norwood, where she'd worked since she was a teenager.

Sally's father had been employed by the previous owners of the estate. Sally had grown up playing on the expansive front lawn, and later, when she was older, in the mountains behind the house. The estate had been a wonderful place to spend a childhood.

The previous owners, Alfred and Jean Roderick, had been a kind, elderly couple. Growing up, Sally had always heard they were from somewhere back East. For years, she thought that meant Denver. The state capital was as far east as a poor girl growing up on the western slope could imagine—clear on the opposite side of the Rockies. Only later did she learn they were from New York City, which might as well have been the moon.

But Sally had liked the old couple. Whenever they traveled, Mrs. Roderick brought back chocolates for her. Sally had been heart-struck when the old woman died. Her husband lived several years longer, and Sally's father had worked for him until the end.

Following Mr. Roderick's death, the mansion sat vacant for years. Then one day Sally's father got a call from the man who had been the estate manager. Castle in the Clouds had a new owner—a woman, and she needed help cleaning and refurbishing the house and grounds.

By then Sally's father had grown old and declined the offer to return to work but suggested that his daughter and her husband could help. Sally and Johnny Eagle had worked for Alice Fremont ever since.

It was a good job. Sally took care of the house, cleaning and cooking for Mrs. Fremont when she was in residence. But because of its size, cleaning was a full-time job even when Alice was away. In the dry mountain air, even when the house sat vacant for months, there was always something that needed dusting. Sally was relieved when Mrs. Fremont decided early on to close off the third floor, complaining about having to heat the empty rooms. If she hadn't, the job would have been impossible for only one housekeeper.

Johnny Eagle worked outside. In the summer, he would care for the huge lawn and trim trees, clearing out the deadwood from the surrounding forests to help protect the house in the event of a wildfire. During the winter, Johnny kept the roads and patios cleared of snow. He also drove Alice to town every Sunday for church.

Mrs. Fremont wasn't easy to work for, but she was fair. From the beginning, Sally and Johnny were instructed to show up no earlier than nine. Alice regularly read or wrote her books late into the night. She slept in most mornings and didn't want to be disturbed by someone inside the house or running machinery outside.

When Mrs. Fremont wasn't writing one of her own books, she read. Sally was sure the estate's library held more books than the public library in Norwood.

It was just before nine o'clock Sunday morning when Johnny pulled through the standing log gate. The storm the night before had covered the road to the house with a couple of feet of fresh snow. No one had been in or out of the estate since. Sally tensed as Johnny drove the truck slowly, careful to keep it in the center of the unseen gravel road. A slip too far one way or the other and they would have to trek the rest of the way on foot.

Johnny would have just over an hour to get the driveway cleared before they would take Mrs. Fremont to town for church.

When she was in residence, their schedule was the same every Sunday. Johnny would park Mrs. Fremont's Suburban at the curb in front of the church, help her up the steps and inside. Next, he'd drop Sally at Clark's Market to do the weekly shopping for the estate.

After church, Mrs. Fremont would walk the few blocks to Pandora Café for lunch. Sally and Johnny would go to Cornerhouse Grille for a burger. After picking up Mrs. Fremont from the café, it was back out to the estate, where Sally and Johnny would unpack all the groceries, then be finished for the day. It was the same every Sunday.

Sally checked her purse for her list. She had written down the cleaning supplies she needed but had to go over the week's menu with Mrs. Fremont before she would know what food to buy.

After a few minutes, the house finally loomed in the distance, and Sally breathed a sigh of relief. Johnny drove around to the back of the house and stopped at a small covered porch off the hallway that led to the kitchen.

Sally stepped out of the truck. "I will have coffee ready inside when you are finished with the snow."

She watched as he drove slowly in the direction of the barn, hidden from the house by a clump of trees.

Sally took the key from her purse and slipped it into the dead bolt but was surprised to find it already unlocked. The evening before, with the approaching storm, Johnny had been in a rush to get home after work. Sally wondered if she had forgotten to lock it. A rush of warm air hit her as she opened the door and stepped inside.

In the kitchen, she flipped on the lights and glanced around. Everything seemed as she had left it the evening before. She scanned the room a moment longer. She'd seen pictures of much fancier kitchens in the large homes in Telluride and Mountain Village, where her friends worked. She'd marveled at the acres of shiny new countertops, matching appliances, and soaring ceilings. The kitchen at the Castle in the Clouds was nothing like that.

The kitchen Sally worked in was built during the Gilded Age, a time when kitchens were the domain of the staff. Owners rarely made an appearance in them. And although a hundred and twenty years had passed since the end of the era, Alice Fremont preferred to live much the same way. Sally could count on one hand the number of times Mrs. Fremont came into the kitchen while Sally was there.

It was a large room, but industrial, with white walls and cabinets. Mixing bowls and serving pieces of various sizes sat on open shelves above the counters. In the center of the room was a long table where staff once gathered for meals.

Sally peeled off her parka and hung it in a closet. Then she changed out of her snow boots into rubber-soled shoes that allowed her to move through the house without being heard. Mrs. Fremont insisted on silence when she was writing or reading.

Next Sally made coffee, poured it into the antique porcelain service, and set the pieces on a silver tray. It was the same routine every morning. Exactly the way Mrs. Fremont wanted it.

Sally carried the tray through a maze of corridors to the entrance hall, then took the nearest set of stairs to the second floor, holding the tray carefully.

Upstairs, she set the tray down on a table outside Alice's suite. She checked the time on her watch. Nine fifteen. She knocked lightly on the door. Mrs. Fremont would be awake by now, dressing for church.

Sally listened for a reply but heard nothing. She knocked again, waiting to be instructed to enter. But there was still no reply. She turned the knob and pushed the door open gently.

"Good morning, Mrs. Fremont," she called softly. "I have coffee."

Sally stood at the threshold and listened. But there was only silence.

"Ms. Fremont?" Sally nudged the door open further.

Alice Fremont was as predictable as the mantel clocks scattered throughout the house that Sally wound on the first day of every month. Unless she required Sally's assistance, she would be already dressed and waiting every morning when Sally brought her coffee up at nine fifteen. It was the same every morning for twenty-three years.

Sally stood in the doorway, peering past the sitting room and into the bedroom, growing increasingly nervous with each passing second. She wasn't sure what to do. This had never happened before.

"Mrs. Fremont?" she called again, her voice quivering. She waited a moment longer, then stepped inside.

The sitting room looked exactly as she had left it the evening before. Two wing-back chairs, centered on the fireplace, cashmere throws folded perfectly and draped over the backs of each, identical tea tables set to the sides. On either side of the marble mantel, bookshelves were set against the wall. Nothing on them looked out of place. Across the room, the desk where Alice wrote her books was cleared of everything except the typewriter and a blue and white Chinese lamp. A large oil painting hung above it. Two smaller paintings sat on the floor, propped against the wall. The velvet desk chair was still tucked in the knee space as if it hadn't been used.

Sally took several steps into the room, then stopped.

"Mrs. Fremont?"

Silence. She took several more.

"Mrs. Fremont?" Her voice was now barely a whisper.

Sally took one last hesitant step and peered around the corner into the bedroom, but no one was there. She checked the bathroom and the closet, then stood in the center of the bedroom, confused. Where was Alice Fremont?

CHAPTER 9

BUCKLEY BAILEY TOSSED his cell phone onto the countertop, ignoring the clattering sound it made in the spacious bathroom he shared with his wife, Celeste.

She sat perched on the suede bench, applying mascara. "Darling, you're going to break it."

Buckley ignored her. He had bigger problems than breaking a damned iPhone. Time and money were valuable commodities in politics, and he was running out of both.

Buckley Bailey was a larger-than-life former governor, but he wanted to be president. A swashbuckling Texan with an ego the size of his ten-gallon hat, he lost no opportunity to regale anyone within earshot on his sizable net worth. What he regularly failed to mention was that the bulk of his wealth came from marrying Celeste.

People meeting the couple for the first time were usually surprised. For as flamboyant and arrogant as Buckley was, Celeste was surprisingly modest and soft-spoken. But for reasons unknown to anyone outside the marriage, their union seemed to work.

Buckley had been a three-term governor of Texas, and although many people thought he was a buffoon, few were foolish enough to underestimate him. He was a shrewd career politician with a penchant for the perks of the office. Buckley was a favorite among his constituents, but many thought that while he was governor he'd gotten away with everything but murder. Then one day it had all caught up with him.

Near the end of his third term, the *Dallas Morning News* ran a scathing exposé that uncovered years of questionable activity: dubious campaign donations, rumors of bribes and cash for political access, free rides on corporate jets. The list of accusations was nearly endless. The opposing political party had tried in vain to have Governor Bailey impeached. Their efforts failed, but it had cost him reelection.

At the time Buckley had assured his supporters he would return to office. On the steps of the Governor's mansion his last day in office, he'd flashed a two-finger salute reminiscent of Nixon that was caught by a local photographer. The next day, the photograph emblazoned the front pages of newspapers across the nation.

After one failed attempt to regain his gubernatorial seat and an unsuccessful run for the US Senate, his political ambitions had only been inflamed. Soon after the senatorial defeat, he'd formed the Buckley

Bailey for President exploratory committee and began raising campaign funds.

Buckley paced back and forth across the bathroom, the rubber soles of his slippers shuffling on the limestone floor.

He threw up his hands. "I phoned Alice twice this morning. The blasted woman isn't answering my calls."

"Maybe she's in California, darling."

Celeste Bailey was a petite woman with delicate features, always meticulously groomed. She had regularly appeared on the Texas Best Dressed list for more than a decade, until finally awarded an honorary lifetime spot several years earlier to give other women a chance. Celeste had been a popular first lady of Texas, overseeing the renovation of many of the state's historical landmarks.

"She's here," Buckley said, stabbing a finger at the floor. "I called yesterday. That housekeeper of hers answered the phone and put me on hold, then told me Alice said she was busy and would call back later, but she didn't."

Celeste was brushing her pixie-cut dark hair. "Maybe she went into town this morning."

"She never leaves that godforsaken haunted house of hers." Buckley shook his head. "No, she saw it was me calling and just didn't answer her phone."

"It's Sunday, Buckley. She went to church."

He stopped pacing. "Of course she did. How could I forget?" He leaned over and gave his wife a giant kiss. Then he thought about it for a moment longer and shook his head. "But I called too early. She wouldn't have left for church yet." He started pacing again. "She's avoiding me."

"Darling, I'm sure that's not true, but would you blame her if she *was* hesitant about donating to yet another campaign? Alice has underwritten every one of yours in the last thirty years. Including the last two that you lost. Remember?"

"Of course I remember." Buckley ran a hand through his mane of salt-and-pepper hair. "But this campaign is a big one, Celeste. The biggest!" He thrust a finger at the ceiling when he said it.

Buckley blamed his failed political races on bad luck and negative media coverage, but now he had set his sights even higher. Before that pesky reporter with the *Dallas Morning News* had published her spurious article, he'd been a popular governor. He was convinced he'd be an even more popular president, maybe the most popular ever. But first he needed campaign money. He paced the floor again.

"Calm down, darling," Celeste said, putting on an earring. "I'm sure Alice will call you back."

Buckley wasn't so sure. "She better." He debated how much more to tell her, then cleared his throat. "I would hate to have to resort to drastic measures."

Celeste dropped her hands to her lap and lowered a cool gaze at him in the mirror. "Buckley, we've talked about this. You're not foolish enough to threaten Alice Fremont, are you?"

He shrugged.

Celeste had finished her hair and stood up. "I've told you before—don't be a fool," she said, walking out of the room.

Buckley turned to the mirror, put a hand on either side of the sink and leaned in, studying his face as he thought about what to do next.

The things he knew about Warren Sheppard could destroy Hugh. The Sheppard name would be ruined. By the time Warren died, he and Alice had grown to hate each other. But Buckley knew Alice would do anything to keep her son from being humiliated.

Buckley had always considered the information on Warren Sheppard his insurance policy. He had never expected to have to use it. But if he needed to, he would.

Buckley and Alice had been acquaintances for years, but he wasn't sure he liked her and couldn't think of anyone who really did. More than once, she had turned on friends, pilfering their lives for story lines for one of her books. No one, it seemed, was off-limits.

The more Buckley thought about it, the angrier he got. Alice Fremont was a horse-faced battle-ax who tried his nerves, and he had spent decades having to suck up to her. But now he couldn't get Alice on the phone, and he worried that the plans he'd set in motion weeks earlier had gone terribly wrong.

CHAPTER 10

SAM BONNET DROVE slowly with two hands on the wheel, careful to keep the Subaru wagon from sliding off the highway. The road had been cleared of the snow from the storm the night before, but the occasional ice patch was hard to see in the midmorning sun. Every few minutes the car would slip to one side or the other before he could right it, pulling it back to the center.

Just past the turnoff to the old Ames Power Station, there was a bend in the road still shaded from the morning sun. He hit another ice patch, and the car slipped toward the opposite lane.

"Slow down, Sam," Opal Waggoner hollered from the back seat, rapping her cane on the floorboard. "You're going to kill us."

Sam checked the speedometer. He was going 25, the speed limit was 60. He glanced at Ivy Waggoner sitting in the passenger seat in time to see her roll her eyes. He turned his attention back to the road, suppressing a smile.

The sisters weren't always easy to work for, but

they were entertaining. And Sam knew it could be a lot worse. He could be stuck in a job schlepping food to tourists like most of his friends.

"Darn storm," Opal said from the back seat. "If there's one thing I know, it's you shouldn't be out driving in conditions like this."

Sam could hear her impatiently opening and closing the box he knew was sitting on her lap. He glanced in the rearview mirror and saw her shaking her head, looking out the side window.

Since starting work for the sisters a year earlier, he'd made several trips out to Alice Fremont's estate. He would drive Opal and Ivy from town to the massive old home hidden in the forest past Trout Lake. Sam would sit in the car and wait while the sisters brought whatever it was Mrs. Fremont wanted to see that day inside. Sometimes it was art or blankets. But mostly, like today, it was jewelry. He'd learned early on that Ms. Fremont was their best customer.

Every trip out was the same. Opal would spend the drive complaining about having to make a house call. "She's got more time than we do," Opal would say to Ivy. "She should do us the courtesy of coming into the store instead of ordering us out to the boondocks like her hired help." Ivy would ignore her sister, preferring to spend the drive admiring the mountain views and pointing out any wildlife she saw.

Sam had never told them, but he liked the trips to

Mrs. Fremont's. It was a welcome break from dusting, unpacking inventory, and restocking shelves. He liked any excuse that got him out of town.

Before Sam started work the year before, he would spend summer vacations camping in the mountains. The camping trips had come to an abrupt end when his father died, leaving his mother in need of help to make ends meet.

Now, aside from hitting the slopes in winter to snowboard when he could, Sam was lucky if he got out of town once a year. So, unbeknownst to the Waggoner sisters, he welcomed their excursions to Trout Lake.

Opal leaned forward. "Ivy, did you find out anything else about Alice's book?"

"No. Nothing."

"Well, what about on the internet? Did you have Judith check on her computer like I told you?"

Sam knew Opal was referring to Judith Hadley at Pandora Café. Everyone in town knew Judith.

"We checked," Ivy replied.

"Well?"

"Nothing."

Opal dropped back into the seat. "Well, let's hope that gossip doesn't know what she's talking about."

"I think Judith's nice."

Opal ignored her sister's remark. "If there's one thing I know, it's that if Alice's book really *is* about people in Telluride this time and not her fancy-pants friends in California or New York, there's going to be some mighty unhappy folks around town."

Out of the corner of his eye, Sam saw Ivy nodding in agreement.

Opal was still talking. "You'd think she'd have plenty of stories about her highfalutin friends elsewhere to keep filling her trashy books. Heaven only knows why she thinks she needs to come pick on us way out here. Why, the only person in Telluride I can think of worth mentioning in a trash novel is that shyster Gordon Quinn."

Sam glanced in the rearview mirror in time to see Opal stab the air with her bony finger when she said the name.

"Now, that would make a good book," she said. "And let's hope it's a murder mystery." Opal laughed at her own joke. Phlegm caught in her throat, and she coughed.

Sam stole a sideways glance at Ivy in time to see her roll her eyes again.

Before he worked for the Waggoner sisters, he'd never heard of Alice Fremont—or her books. But he'd learned enough from listening to know that the novels she wrote made lots of people angry. But they made Mrs. Fremont a very rich woman. Sam had often wondered if she had a secret vault full of money hidden somewhere in that creepy old house of hers.

He turned slowly off the highway onto Trout Lake Road, careful not to fishtail the back end of the wagon, and was relieved to see the road around the lake had already been traveled multiple times that morning. Most of the fresh snow from the night before had been pushed out of the way.

They bounced over gravel and chunks of ice as they made their way around the lake, prompting more complaints from Opal about having to make the trip. Ivy pointed to some unseen fox in the distance.

As they approached the tower of logs that marked the entrance to Mrs. Fremont's estate, Sam was distressed to find the road to the house hadn't been cleared. He slowed at the open gate, studying the two ruts through the fresh snow. Sometime after the storm, a single vehicle had passed in or out. Sam was glad it had been something larger than the Subaru.

Opal leaned forward in her seat. "Isn't that just fine and dandy. Order us all the way out here and not even have the road safe to drive on."

"I think we can make it, Miss Opal," Sam said. "The Subaru has four-wheel drive."

"Step on it, then," she said. "If there's one thing I know about, it's driving in the snow. You can't go too slow or you'll get stuck."

Sam was pretty sure that was how you were

supposed to drive in mud, not snow. He glanced at Ivy, who looked at him and quietly shook her head. Sam gave her a single nod, hoping Opal wouldn't notice, then eased through the entrance and toward the house, careful to keep the car in the ruts that were already there.

After they cleared the last of the trees and the manor house came into view, Sam noticed someone in a snowplow clearing their final approach. The driver moved the tractor off the road and watched with humorless dark eyes as they passed. Sam had seen the man here before. He never spoke, but just stared at them. He gave Sam the creeps.

He watched in the rearview mirror as the man pulled the tractor back onto the driveway and continued in the direction of the lake. At least the road would be cleared before they headed back to town. He stopped the car close to a cleared path that led to the front door.

Behind him, Opal huffed. "At least the woman had the decency to clear the walk for us," she said, swinging the car door open.

Sam rushed around and helped both sisters out. As he typically did if there wasn't anything heavy to carry inside, he stayed in the car and kept it warm.

He watched as the sisters shuffled up the sidewalk to the front door. They stood for a while. After a couple of minutes, he saw them talking to someone inside. Opal appeared hesitant, but she handed over the box with the necklaces. They shuffled back, and Sam helped them into the car.

"Well, I've never been so insulted in all my life," Opal said, settling onto the back seat and jerking her cane into the wagon.

Sam got in and turned the car toward Trout Lake.

Opal let out an exaggerated huff. "Summoned us out here like she was the queen of England instead of some two-bit trash novelist. The nerve of some people."

"Alice is our best customer." Ivy's usually calm tone sounded strained. "We should have brought them out last night like she asked."

"You should have *never* agreed to leave those necklaces for her. Who knows if that housekeeper of hers is honest. She was jumpy as all get-out. She's probably going to take them home for herself. I guarantee you *she* knows what all that silver and turquoise is worth."

Sam peeked in the mirror. Opal's face was flushed despite the cold. It made him nervous when she was angry.

"And you mark my words," Opal continued. "If that housekeeper *doesn't* steal them, Alice Fremont will demand we come all the way back out here to pick them up when she decides she doesn't want them. Waste even more of our time. Step on it, Sam. We need to get back and open the store."

Sam tightened his grip on the wheel, afraid to drive any faster. He didn't know what to say.

Ivy turned her head. "You're doing fine, Sam."

"For the life of me, I'll never understand how that woman can treat people the way she does and get away with it. Worse than disrespectful—downright slanderous, if you ask me."

"Nobody asked you," Ivy grumbled under her breath.

Opal harrumphed.

They sat in silence as Sam drove through the log entrance and around Trout Lake.

"Have you read any of her books, Ivy?"

Ivy sighed, not answering the question.

"Well, have you?" Opal asked again, impatient.

"No," Ivy finally said.

Sam was fairly certain he'd seen one of Mrs. Fremont's books stuck in the bottom drawer of Ivy's desk at one time or another, but he kept quiet.

"Well, I have," Opal continued. "And they're trash. Trash, I tell you. They're supposed to be fiction, but anyone with half a brain can tell who she's talking about. I can't imagine why someone hasn't already put the world out of its misery and murdered the damn woman. And if there's one thing I know—"

"It's how to blow hot air," Ivy finished for her. "Shut up, Opal. You're steaming the windows."

CHAPTER 11

WHEN LARS FREMONT knocked on the massive wood door, the house sounded hollow. But he knew it wasn't. It would be filled with heavy dark furniture, the windows cloaked in weighty fabrics that blocked out any semblance of the sun, and thick carpets with dizzying patterns would be laid over the floors. He'd been there too many times to count, dragged out to the mountains summer after summer.

He didn't mind Colorado so much, but he loathed the old house. It was full of spooky antiques and artwork. What he hated most were the animal heads that littered the walls. As a child, he'd been convinced their glassy black eyes followed him wherever he went.

Entire summers were spent alone on the estate. Well, not exactly alone. His mother had been there. But she was always preoccupied, either in the downstairs parlor reading or in her bedroom suite working on her latest novel. There had been the housekeeper and her husband, but they were quiet, neither speaking unless they were spoken to first. Lars had never trusted them.

For more years than he could count, he'd spent summer days building forts in the forest or playing on the antique ski lift that had once pulled the house's earliest occupants up the private slope behind the house. The lift had rusted, and the slope had grown over long ago, making it an even more intriguing place to play.

But they had been long, lonely summers. Lars remembered dreaming of kickball games or riding bikes with his friends back in California. He rarely visited his mother in Colorado anymore, regularly making excuses of why he couldn't come when he was invited.

And being in Telluride increased the risk of running into his half brother, Hugh. Hugh was nineteen years older than him and a pompous ass. He'd rarely come around when Lars was a child. When he did, it was usually to suck up to his mother, trying to mooch money from her for some harebrained scheme of his.

"Hugh has a lot of his father in him," Lars had heard his mother say on several occasions. She'd never elaborated, but Lars knew it wasn't a compliment. Hugh's father had been Alice's first husband, and he'd heard that they couldn't stand each other in the end.

No one came to the door, and Lars knocked again,

harder. He waited a moment, then dug his cell phone from the pocket of his coat. He pulled off a glove with his teeth and touched the phone's screen. No missed calls or messages. He called the home phone, but after several rings, he hung up. If only she'd get a cell phone. But his mother was stuck in the Dark Ages, suspicious of technology.

"Where is she?" he wondered aloud.

He dropped the phone back into his pocket, then blew on his hand, warming it, his breath fogging the air. He pulled the glove back on.

He couldn't imagine where she was. He'd called her the morning before from California to let her know he was coming for a visit. She had sounded surprised, maybe a bit suspicious, but happy.

Lars glanced around at the growing darkness. It was late afternoon on Sunday. The housekeeper and her husband would be long gone. He needed to find a way in or he'd have to drive to town and look for a hotel room. Or worse, he'd have to call Hugh.

On several occasions, his mother had given Lars a key, but each time he'd thrown it away, hoping the latest trip would be his last. Standing now in the waning daylight and cold, he wished he'd kept one.

Then he remembered the hidden key.

"It'll be a miracle," he mumbled, trudging around the side of the house through the snow.

The metal box he remembered as a child was still

bolted to the wall next to the back service door. It was black and had rusted over time, but Lars could still make out the molded gargoyles mounted to the bottom, making it appear as if they were holding the box aloft.

He opened the lid, cleared out several handfuls of dirt and pine needles that had settled at the bottom, and dug around until he found the hidden finger pull. With a quick tug, the false bottom sprang open, and Lars peered inside.

"You've got to be kidding," he said, taking out the key and letting the lid slam shut. He couldn't believe the key was still there after all these years.

Inside, the house was dark. He turned on lights as he made his way toward the front, the wood floors creaking with each step.

"Mother?" he called up a set of stairs, his voice echoing through the entry hall.

There was no answer. Except for the ticking of a clock somewhere, the house was quiet. Lars flipped the switch that lit two bronze chandeliers, shrugged off his coat and laid it across the banister.

"Mother?" he called again, making his way up the stairs.

The second floor was dark. He turned on a lamp and went directly to his mother's suite but found it empty.

Where was she? Maybe an unexpected trip to New

York, he thought. Probably something to do with her books. But she knew he was coming.

He stepped outside the sitting room and looked both ways down the wide hall, wondering what to do next. He hated the thought of staying in the old house alone. He wanted to go back to California but knew that wasn't an option.

He needed to talk to his mother, convince her to once again advance him money from his trust fund. She had done it under protest twice before but swore she wouldn't do it again. Lars knew that if he spent a few days schmoozing her, he could get her to change her mind. He would stay just long enough to get the money, then split.

His music producing career hadn't taken off as fast as he'd expected, but there were plans in the works that would turn his luck around in no time if he could just get the money.

Lars went back downstairs and pulled his phone from the coat still lying over the banister. He called the home phone again, hearing it ring in the kitchen. When the answering machine picked up, he left Alice a message.

"Mother, I've arrived at the house in Colorado and was disappointed to find you weren't here. I'll be here when you get back. If you get a chance, call and let me know when that'll be. Can't wait to see you."

There, that should do it, Lars thought, clicking off his

phone. If she called in to check messages, she would know he was there and was concerned about her. If she didn't call, he could have her listen to it when she got home. Either way, his bases were covered.

His stomach growled, reminding him he hadn't eaten in hours. He started for the kitchen and the large walk-in pantry.

He would eat first, then search for the secret hoards of cash he knew his mother hid around the house, sure she wouldn't miss any of it until after he was gone.

He would start his search on the first floor and work his way to the attic.

There's no telling what I'll find in this dilapidated old place, he thought.

CHAPTER 12

Monday, January 10

THE NEXT MORNING, Sally Eagle arrived at Castle in the Clouds and found the back door unlocked. Mrs. Fremont must have come home, she thought, relieved. Then something troubled her.

Alice had always insisted that all outside doors be kept locked, day and night. Long ago, she had told Sally that it was a precaution to keep out bears. Although it wasn't unusual for bears to make their way into mountain homes occasionally—it had happened to Sally's sister in Norwood several years earlier—Sally knew that bears weren't the real reason for Alice's concern.

Decades earlier, during their employment interview, Mrs. Fremont had pulled Johnny aside. She had told him to keep their conversation confidential, but over time Sally was able to pull enough information out of him to figure out what was said.

Alice had asked Johnny if he could shoot a man if she needed him to—if one was crazy enough to follow her to Colorado and pose a threat. Sally had always assumed Johnny assured her he could. Both Johnny and Sally had been hired later that same day.

From the beginning, Alice instructed Johnny to always have a firearm within reach. And for all these years, as far as Sally knew, he had.

Sally had later read on the internet about the attacks against Mrs. Fremont and understood why. She suspected that was why Alice insisted on always keeping the doors locked.

Sally stepped into the kitchen and shrugged off her coat, then changed out of her boots and into shoes. She made coffee and carried the tray through the maze of hallways to the entrance hall but stopped at the base of the stairs.

There was a man's coat draped over the banister. It hadn't been there the evening before. Sally stared at it, wondering who it belonged to, then remembered the unlocked back door. Her heart beat faster. As she slowly climbed the stairs, she listened for any sounds in the house, but there were none.

She found the door to the master suite open, but the rooms were empty, and the bed was still made. Alice hadn't slept in it for two nights.

She set the coffee down and searched the second floor, discovering one of the guest rooms had been slept in. She snooped through a duffel bag lying next to the unmade bed and realized it belonged to Lars, Mrs. Fremont's youngest son. The coat would be his, too. She was relieved it didn't belong to a stranger. But where was Lars?

Sally climbed the stairs to the third floor, then into both of the towers that loomed at opposite ends of the house. From a tower window, she could see Johnny in the distance, shoveling snow that had fallen from the roof of the barn. She felt for the phone in her pocket and wanted to call him, tell him something was wrong—Alice was still missing. But she didn't.

As he had the day before, Johnny would tell her she was being nosy and to mind her own business. He would remind her of the time Alice had caught her looking through one of the books she was working on. Sally swore she was only straightening the pages on the desk, but Alice had accused her of spying and fired them both on the spot.

The termination had lasted only a week. It was never said, but Sally assumed Alice's son Hugh had stepped in and talked her into rehiring them. He was there to apologize the day Sally and Johnny returned to work.

But now it had been two days, and Mrs. Fremont was still missing. There was no letter or call to explain where she'd gone. In all the time Sally had worked for her, she had never disappeared before.

Lars's unannounced visit seemed suspicious. Alice

would never have missed being home to welcome her favorite son to Colorado.

Sally was positive something was gravely wrong.

CHAPTER 13

IT WAS MIDMORNING and Jack sat on the tailgate of the truck, rubbing a sore shoulder. He'd spent more than an hour digging the truck and the Airstream out of the snow, feeling every day of his forty-three years.

He had spent the day before cutting and moving several trees that had fallen across the road that led to the highway. The only other inhabitants of the campground—the middle-aged hippies—had spent the day watching and smoking weed but not offering to help.

Jack wiped sweat from his forehead with his shirt-sleeve and glanced toward the sun. The sky had been cloudless since the storm, but he knew it was only a matter of time before they rolled in again. He was determined to head south to Santa Fe before the next blizzard hit.

It was mid-January in the Rockies, and it didn't matter what the meteorologists forecasted; he'd been in the mountains long enough to know the weather could change on a dime.

He needed to secure things inside the trailer, then hook it up to the truck.

As he hopped off the tailgate, the phone in his pocket vibrated. He glanced at the caller ID but didn't recognize the number. He hesitated to answer the call. He had things to do before he could get on the road.

"Ah, hell," he said aloud, then answered the call. "Yep?"

The caller hesitated. "Is…is this Mr. Jack Martin?"

It was a woman. She spoke in a quiet voice with an accent Jack didn't recognize.

"It is."

She cleared her throat. "Mr. Jack Martin, I work for Mrs. Fremont."

"Who?"

"Mrs. Fremont." She sounded nervous.

"Alice?"

"Yes."

Jack recognized the housekeeper's halting voice. "Your name is Sally, isn't it?"

She hesitated before she answered. "Yes." There was another pause.

"What can I do for you, Sally?" Jack was growing impatient.

She told him that Alice had been missing for two days, that she never left unexpectedly without explanation. Sally said that she knew Alice had called Jack to protect her and that now she was gone.

Jack told her there would be some logical explanation, that she'd show back up. But the more Jack tried to reassure her, the more Alice's housekeeper pushed back. She said she'd found the back door unlocked Sunday morning when they'd come to take Alice to church but that she was almost certain she'd locked it when she left the evening before. And there was no reason for Alice to open the door. Jack could tell that Sally believed something was terribly wrong.

He thought about it, remembering the hint of fear in Alice's voice that she had tried to cover up. He thought of the past threats and attacks he'd read about online.

He'd meant to call her the day before, decline the offer. But after the storm, he'd been preoccupied moving trees and cleaning up and forgot.

When Jack left her house on Saturday, Alice had asked him to get back with her the next day. She wasn't a patient woman. And now that he thought about it, Jack was surprised she hadn't called for an answer. Could something really be wrong? Jack worried he might have been too quick to dismiss Alice Fremont as a paranoid crackpot.

He hung up the phone and wondered what to do next. After chasing a rabbit through the snow,

Crockett was now panting at his feet, his tongue lolling.

Jack took the steps into the trailer in a single leap, then grabbed his jacket and keys. "Change of plans again, Crockett," he said, locking the door. "Let's go."

On the way to Telluride, Jack saw the devastating effects of the storm two nights before. The highway had been plowed, but large berms of snow lined both sides of the road, and fallen trees lay in freshly cut sections on the shoulder. The sparse traffic moved at a crawl.

At the manor house, the front door swung open just as Jack reached it. It was the second time it had happened. He wondered if Alice Fremont's housekeeper spent her days watching for visitors.

"Thank you for coming, Mr. Jack Martin," she said, and stood aside for him to enter.

Jack stepped inside and let his eyes adjust to the darkness. He never understood people who insisted on living in the dark, shades drawn tight, only a lamp here or there turned on. He resisted the urge to throw open the heavy velvet curtains that covered every window.

The housekeeper stood watching him, waiting for him to speak.

"Alice isn't back?"

The woman shook her head.

"And you still don't know where she is?"

"No."

"Did you try her son?"

"I called him, but he did not answer."

"And she didn't leave a note anywhere? No explanation?"

She shook her head again. The woman was practically mute. This wasn't going to be easy.

Jack glanced at the windows flanking both sides of the front door. Alice had heard someone trying to get in through them. He thought of Sally finding the unlocked back door, and his concern for Alice grew.

"I need to see the rest of the house," he said. "Can you show it to me?"

They started with the assortment of rooms that opened off the entry hall, the sitting room where Jack had met Alice on Saturday—Sally called the room the "parlor."

Next, he saw the dining room. Like the entrance hall, its ceiling soared high above. A long banquet table was set in the center with dozens of chairs pushed in around it; several more were placed along the walls. Overhead, bright flags hung down two sides of the room. Jack squinted, peering up at them. They weren't state flags but looked like crests or coats of arms. It reminded him of a medieval castle, something out of an old movie.

He toured the billiard room and the smoking room, both dark with heavy furniture.

Sally showed him the kitchen, multiple pantries, and the laundry area. There were two more sets of stairs, none as grand as the staircases in the front hall but obviously meant for servants. One narrow set of stairs led down to a subterranean wine cellar, its walls and ceilings made of rock.

The back rooms were connected by a spiderweb of corridors and narrow hallways. Jack had never seen anything like it.

Back in the entrance hall, on the far side of the room, Sally slid open one last set of doors. "Mrs. Fremont calls this room the conservatory."

A conservatory? Jack had heard of them but had never seen one and wasn't sure he even knew what one was. The room was lighter in color than the others, the walls covered in a cream fabric that had been painted floor-to-ceiling with grapevines. It was filled with elaborately carved furniture and knickknacks. A gold harp sat propped in one corner. The sight of it all made Jack nauseous.

A conservatory and a billiard room? The strange old house was beginning to resemble the board game Clue.

Sally pulled the doors shut, and they went upstairs.

The second floor was a maze of fancy bedrooms and sitting rooms that Sally called "suites."

One of the bedrooms had been slept in. It smelled

of dirty clothes and marijuana. She told him the things belonged to Alice's youngest son, Lars.

Jack wanted to talk to him.

Just inside the master suite, Sally hesitated. Jack could tell she wanted to say something.

"What is it?"

She pointed to a desk pushed against a wall. "Mrs. Fremont works here."

Jack looked at the desk. It was small and fussy, elaborately carved legs ending in tiny ball and claw feet. The only things set on top were a lamp and a typewriter that looked as old as the house.

"When she is working," Sally said, still pointing, "she always leaves her papers there."

"Her papers?" Jack asked. "You mean her book?"

Sally nodded.

"The one she was working on?"

She nodded again. "But they are gone."

Alice and her manuscript were *both* missing. It would explain everything. She had probably gone to see her publisher, or her agent if she had one.

"She must have taken it with her," Jack said.

"But there is something else. Mrs. Fremont always takes the Olympia with her when she goes."

"The Olympia?" What was she talking about?

Sally pointed at the old black typewriter. Above the keys was a small metal plaque with the word "Olympia" spelled out in script.

"The Olympia," Sally repeated.

"Alice travels with her typewriter?"

Sally nodded, and Jack's concern for Alice grew.

They finished touring the second floor, then climbed the stairs to the third. More bedrooms, but smaller. Gone were the fancy velvet and silk wall coverings he'd seen on the floor below. The walls on the third floor were painted a mint green that peeled at the baseboards. Staff quarters, he thought. In its heyday, the estate had probably employed dozens of full-time workers.

They stepped into one of the bedrooms. Two rusting cot frames without mattresses were shoved into the far corners. A small metal table sat between them, a thin layer of dust covering everything. It seemed the third floor hadn't been inhabited in decades.

Alice had said she lived in the house alone, but with all the bedrooms—twelve on the second floor and probably more on the third—it was hard for Jack to believe.

"Alice lives here alone?" he asked.

Sally nodded.

He thought of the unlocked back door. "Besides you and Alice, who has a key to the house?" Alice had already told him, but Jack wanted to hear what Sally would say.

She thought about it. "Her sons. And maybe Mrs. Eva."

"Mrs. Eva?"

"Her daughter-in-law." Sally mentioned Lars again, then gave Jack the name of Alice's oldest son, Hugh Sheppard, who had a home nearby in Mountain Village.

Jack pulled a small notebook from his pocket and scribbled the name in it. "Anyone else have a key?"

Sally thought about it, then shook her head.

"What about visitors?" he asked. "Does anyone come out regularly? Friends, family, someone she would have let in?"

She took her time answering. "Hugh and Mrs. Eva come to dinner sometimes."

He wrote down the name of Hugh's wife. "Anyone else?"

"Mr. Bailey."

"He's a friend?"

She nodded, and Jack wrote *Bailey* in his notebook.

"Do you know his first name?"

She shook her head.

It didn't matter. Jack would ask Alice's son Hugh Sheppard when he talked to him.

Sally and Jack climbed both of the towers he'd seen from the outside. The rooms at the top were empty but offered gorgeous views of the surrounding mountains.

The house was mind-boggling, with all the rooms

and passageways. They had searched every inch of it. There was no sign of Alice Fremont.

CHAPTER 14

JOHNNY EAGLE HAD spent the morning shoveling snow. It was how he spent most winter mornings. The roads that crisscrossed the property, the sidewalks, the large patio on the east side of the house. There was always somewhere that needed to be cleared of snow.

The day before, he had shoveled the drifts that had blown against the barn's large rolling doors during the storm. He needed to get the snowplow out to clear the driveway.

Today he would clear around the perimeter of the barn. When he got to work that morning, he'd found a snow berm encircling the building. The snow that had accumulated on the metal roof during the storm had started to slide off with the sun and warmer temperatures.

Johnny was just finished and about to put the shovel away when he noticed a truck driving toward him. He watched as it came closer. He didn't recognize the driver but was surprised to see Sally sitting in the passenger seat.

The truck came to a stop, and the driver got out, followed by a brown dog.

Sally came around the front of the truck. "Johnny, this is Mr. Jack Martin, the man I told you about who came to see Mrs. Fremont."

Johnny eyed the man suspiciously, wondering why he'd come back and what he wanted from them. He gave the man a single nod but remained silent.

Sally spoke again. "He wants to know if Mrs. Fremont's car is in the barn."

Johnny looked at the man. He was tall, with dark hair and a face that revealed no emotion. Why would he care about the car? But it wasn't Johnny's business. Without saying a word, he rolled open one of the large doors and gestured toward the Suburban parked inside.

The man stepped forward and looked in. "Was it here yesterday?"

Johnny nodded once.

"Does Alice ever get picked up by a commercial driver or a friend, maybe?"

Sally shook her head.

"I drive Mrs. Fremont," Johnny said.

The man named Jack Martin stood thinking. "I'm going to have a look around," he said.

Johnny watched as the man disappeared inside.

The brown dog had been sniffing at the snow around the barn and came loping back. He stopped at Johnny's feet, looked up at him, and cocked its head to one side. Johnny stared back at the dog and determined he was a good animal. He squatted next to him and scratched behind his ears.

"Ahnah ne gut?" What's your name? Johnny asked in Ute.

He was still scratching the dog several minutes later but stood up when the man came out.

"Mr. Eagle, did you notice anything unusual yesterday morning when you got to work? Anything out of place or that looked disturbed? Here in the barn or elsewhere on the property?"

Johnny shook his head. "The barn was locked, as it should be."

The man thought about it a moment, then nodded. "Okay, thank you for your time." He turned to Sally. "I'm done here for now. Let me think about everything. I'll give you a call later today. I have your number."

"Thank you," Sally said quietly.

"Can I give you a ride back to the house?"

"I will take her," Johnny answered, jerking his chin toward his truck parked to the side of the barn. He wanted to talk to Sally, find out who the man was and why he had come. They weren't used to strangers at Castle in the Clouds. But there had now been two in two days. A suspicious truck had pulled onto the property and turned around the day before. It made Johnny nervous.

Sally looked at the man. "You will help find Mrs. Fremont?"

He didn't answer right away. "I'll be in touch."

Johnny watched as Jack Martin and his dog drove away.

"Did you call him?" Johnny asked after the truck had disappeared through the trees.

Sally had a nervous look on her face and hesitated before she answered. "Mrs. Fremont was not here again," she finally said. "He is the one she asked to come…to *help* her."

Johnny held his temper, but Sally saw that he was angry and dropped her gaze.

"I told you to leave this alone," Johnny said, his jaw tense as he spoke. "It is not your business to interfere."

"But Mrs. Fremont could be in danger."

Johnny narrowed his eyes. "You are innocent of the world, *pe wun*. There are things you do not know." He turned away from her. He would let her walk back to the house alone.

CHAPTER 15

JACK HAD NEVER heard of Mountain Village, so before he left Trout Lake, he'd googled it. He learned that it was a relatively young community, developed to complement the ski resort. It sat perched high above the valley floor and Telluride, the two towns connected by a gondola.

Jack turned off Highway 145 onto Mountain Village Boulevard and wound his way through the snowy landscape, catching glimpses of houses through the trees, clusters of million-dollar homes scattered across the mountain and hugging the lower ski slopes.

As he approached a bridge, Jack saw skiers slide underneath, emerging on the other side. He drove farther and crossed under a lift hauling other skiers back up the mountain. The town was alive with activity.

He followed the GPS directions, turned onto a street named San Joaquin, and headed up the mountain. The road was iced over in places, and he drove slowly. When his GPS indicated he'd reached his destination, he double-checked the address he'd written in his notebook. The street numbers matched.

Jack took the long sloping driveway up toward the house, a modern behemoth that looked out of place in the rugged Rockies. Two stories of gray brick and glass that loomed over its winter surroundings—and looked as cold.

Jack parked the truck in front, left it running with the heater on, and got out. The afternoon sun had drifted toward the horizon, chilling the breeze.

"Stay here," he told Crockett as he shut the door.

He rang the doorbell and waited. A few seconds later there was a whirring sound above him, and he looked up. A security camera perched near a corner of the door slowly turned in his direction.

A man's voice came through a speaker mounted next to the door. "Yes, what do you want?"

"I'm here to see Hugh Sheppard."

"You have to push the button." The man sounded annoyed. "I can't hear you."

Jack leaned over, found the square button and pushed it. "I'm here to see Hugh Sheppard."

"Who are you?"

"My name is Jack Martin. I'm a detect—"

"What is this regarding?"

Now Jack was the one getting irritated. And he felt stupid talking into the box. He stuck a hand on a hip and pushed the button again.

"I'm here to talk to Hugh Sheppard about his mother."

There was silence. "What about her?"

"She's missing." To hell with being subtle, Jack thought. The guy was a jerk.

There was silence again. Jack heard someone unlock the front door. It swung open, revealing a squat little man with an expanded waistline. He wore a polyester tracksuit, the bottom of his jacket not quite meeting the top of his pants, a sliver of pasty skin exposed between the two. He held the door in one hand, a martini in the other. And, despite the freezing temperature outside, was barefoot.

Jack recognized the family resemblance immediately. The man had Alice Fremont's long face and dark, beady eyes. He was taller than his mother, but not much, and was exponentially wider. And by the look on his face, he wasn't happy to have received a visitor.

"What's this about my mother being missing?" he asked, not bothering with greetings. He spoke in the drawn-out tones of a snob that Jack couldn't stand in a woman but hated even worse in a man.

"Are you Hugh Sheppard?"

"Speaking. Now, what's this about my mother?"

"I met with Alice on Saturday. She offered me a job. She wanted me to move into the house for a few months and provide security." The man's eyes widened. Jack had his full attention and continued. "She was concerned about her safety. Has she mentioned anything to you about feeling threatened?"

"No."

"Her housekeeper called me this morning and said that Alice hadn't been at the house the last two days."

"Sally called you?"

"She did."

"But why?"

"I told you. She thinks your mother is missing. No note, no message. Nothing."

Hugh Sheppard rubbed his chin with a chubby hand, still holding the martini in the other. "Sally left me a message this morning, but I haven't had time to listen to it. That must be why she called you." He thought about it. "I'll drive out tomorrow. I'm sure everything is fine. She probably had some unexpected trip to New York come up. She's an author, you know?"

"She told me. Does she usually leave town without telling you?"

Hugh stood silent, and Jack knew by the look on his face that she didn't.

"When was the last time you spoke to her?" Jack asked.

"I don't see how that's any of your business, but I saw her last weekend—Sunday night."

"She didn't mention leaving town?"

Hugh shook his head.

"So as far as you know, no one has seen her or been in touch with her in the last two days?"

Hugh took a moment, thinking about the question. "Not that I know of," he finally said, not seeming to care in the slightest. "I'll give you the name and number of her agent. Mother keeps him abreast of her comings and goings more than she does her own family. Stay here."

Hugh closed the door on Jack and was gone for several minutes. Jack suspected it was longer than what was necessary, Hugh Sheppard wanting to leave his unwelcome visitor standing in the cold. The sun was creeping closer to the horizon.

When Hugh finally returned, he handed Jack a small piece of paper. "Douglas Townsend. I put his office number on there. He's in San Francisco. Now, if that's all."

Jack read the name, then stuck the paper in his pocket. "Your mother didn't tell you that someone tried to break into her house several nights ago?"

Hugh Sheppard was startled. The question had obviously caught him off guard. "She did not."

Jack waited for him to voice some sort of concern, but he didn't.

"What about your wife?" Jack asked.

"What about her?"

"Sally mentioned she also comes to visit your mother."

"Eva helps me monitor her. My mother can be a very imperious woman. We both provide damage control when needed."

"Is she here? I'd like to speak with her."

"She's not. She's skiing."

Jack looked at his watch and saw that it was almost three o'clock. "Maybe I'll wait," he said. "The lifts will be closing soon, won't they?"

Hugh shifted his weight from one bare foot to the other, a nervous response. But why? Did he not want Jack to talk to her?

"I suppose they will," Hugh finally answered. When Jack waited for him to elaborate, he added, "But Eva will probably go to one of her yoga classes afterward, not that that's any of your business, either."

Jack ignored the comment. "I want to ask her about the last time she spoke with Alice."

Hugh drew in an exaggerated breath, the smug look back on his face. "I will ask my wife that *myself* when she gets home. I assure you, my mother is fine, and you're wasting your time. Now, if that's all, Mr...." His voice trailed off.

"Martin. Jack Martin."

"If that's all, Mr. Martin. I'm a very busy man."

Jack doubted it. "One more thing. Sally mentioned the name of someone who visits Alice regularly by the last name of Bailey. Would you happen to know his first name?"

"Of course I would," Hugh said, acting like Jack was an idiot for having to ask. "Buckley Bailey. *Governor* Buckley Bailey."

It was Jack's turn to be surprised. The former governor of Texas regularly visited Alice Fremont? Living in Texas, Jack knew all about Buckley Bailey— his exploits and scandals. But friends with Alice Fremont? It was an odd friendship he would look into further.

Jack took his notebook from his pocket, wrote his name and cell phone number on a page and tore it out. "Here's where you can reach me. Call me if you think of anything, or if you hear from Alice," he said, handing it to Hugh.

"Is that *finally* everything?" he asked, snatching it from him.

Jack stared at him for a moment. For someone whose mother had been missing for two days, he didn't seem at all concerned. Or was it an act? Did he know where Alice was?

Jack wondered what it was that Hugh Sheppard knew but wasn't telling.

CHAPTER 16

ALICE FREMONT WAS nowhere to be found, and Buckley Bailey wasn't sure if he should be angry or afraid. He'd driven all the way out to her house, but she wasn't there. Something about the way the housekeeper had acted when she said that Alice wasn't at home and didn't know when she would return made him suspicious. Buckley was sure she was lying.

He jerked the car off the road onto the driveway in Mountain Village. He was a very important and powerful man, not one to be ignored. And if Alice was avoiding him, he would make her regret it. She was going to contribute to his presidential campaign whether she wanted to or not.

He held the trump card, and if necessary, he would threaten to leak information on Alice's first husband that would ruin her son's life. Buckley knew she would never let that happen. She *would* contribute.

He pulled the black Escalade into the garage and got out.

Buckley couldn't bring himself to seriously consider the alternative, that the infuriating woman wasn't avoiding him but was actually missing. He ran a finger around his shirt collar. Thinking about it made him sick to his stomach, so he decided not to.

Inside the house, he hollered for his wife. "Celeste." Where was she? "Celeste!"

He heard the tap of delicate footfalls on the second-floor landing and looked up.

"I'm here, darling."

Buckley watched in admiration as she descended the stairs. Celeste moved with an easy elegance achieved through generations of wealth and privilege. She faced life with a grace and composure that, after all these years, still baffled him. Buckley admired her for it but was also jealous as hell.

He'd grown up in the Texas Panhandle, the son of a sharecropper, fed hand to mouth by his poor worn-out mother who looked sixty by the time she was forty. Buckley grew up without any of the advantages of family money or connections. All of his successes, he'd earned. Years earlier, through grit and determination, he had clawed his way out of poverty and the Panhandle, leaving his impoverished upbringing in his rearview mirror.

Buckley knew he should be proud of his past and how far he'd come, but he secretly wished he'd been born to money. He envied Celeste's ability to move effortlessly among the wealthy. He admired her for it—loved her for it—but it also infuriated the hell out of him.

Unlike Celeste, Buckley knew he'd never have the respect of the old-money crowd. They considered him an upstart, an interloper. Maybe he was, but it hadn't held him back. And Buckley was going to make sure he had the last laugh. He was going to be president of the United States. And if the insufferable snobs still didn't offer their respect, he would be able to demand it.

"Darling, you look dreadful," Celeste said, laying a hand on his arm. "Let me get you something to drink."

Buckley felt his body relax. There was something magical about Celeste. Just being in her presence made him feel better.

"Make it a whiskey," he said, shrugging off his coat and following her into the living room.

"Already? It's still early."

"I need it. Alice wasn't home, or at least that's what that Indian housekeeper of hers told me."

"She's not Indian, Buckley. She's Native American," Celeste said, filling a crystal glass with ice.

Buckley waved a hand dismissively. "I don't care what she is. She's not telling me the truth."

"I take it Alice wasn't home." She held out the glass. "Darling, I told you to call before you drove all the way out there."

Buckley took the whiskey from her. "Thank you." He plopped down onto the sofa and stuck his long legs out, setting his feet on the coffee table, not bothering to take off his boots.

"She's there," he said, then took another drink. "She's just avoiding me. And that can only mean one thing: the rumors about her next book are true. And who does she know in Telluride that would make a more interesting character in a book than *me*?" Buckley took a long drink and wiped his mouth with the back of his large hand.

"Even if she is writing a book about Telluride, you're her friend—"

"I was *Warren's* friend first, not Alice's. And besides, that doesn't matter; she's thrown plenty of friends under the bus in her books. That woman has no scruples." Buckley snuck a sideways glance at his wife and caught her watching him. He cleared his throat. "I'm sure Warren told her things…things from my past."

"That's ancient history, darling. That was years ago. Besides, Warren got the bribery charges dismissed."

"If she puts anything remotely similar in her book, I'm sunk."

Two decades earlier, the bribery scandal had nearly ruined Buckley's fledgling political career. He was a state senator at the time but ran for governor the following year. He never told Celeste how much it had cost him in cash and political favors to have Warren Sheppard fix the case.

Warren had been married to Alice at the time, and Buckley was now convinced she knew what had happened and was going to put the story in her book. If it was anything like her previous novels, the characters would be thinly veiled depictions of people that Alice knew. If there was a crooked politician in it, Buckley's presidential bid would be lost before it ever got started. He would do whatever he needed to ensure that didn't happen.

But it was the plans he had already set in motion that made him nervous. Charlie Dungee's man was supposed to wait until Sunday, when Alice was away at church, to break into her house. Had he gone in early? Was Alice there when he did?

Buckley broke out in a cold sweat and threw back the rest of the whiskey.

CHAPTER 17

IT WAS LATE afternoon by the time Jack got back to the campground outside Durango. When he waved at the hippie couple, they either didn't see him or acted like they hadn't. That was it. Jack wished he were anywhere else.

He hated camping alone. It was like being back in Aspen when he had been stuck on a plot of land outside town. It wasn't so much the company that he wanted; it was activity. He needed the distraction. He missed the lively campground on the banks of Shadow Mountain Lake. Maybe he'd move back for the summer.

In the trailer, Jack pulled the map of New Mexico out of the cabinet, laid it on the table, and slid onto the bench facing the door. He found Santa Fe and traced the route from Durango with his finger.

But something nagged at him. Alice Fremont.

He tried to put her out of his mind. She wasn't his problem. Or was she?

As unlikeable as she had been and as horrible as the research he'd done made her seem, she had asked

Jack for his help. Now she was missing. The people who worked for her didn't know where she was, and her own son didn't seem to care.

Jack dug the piece of paper from his pocket and looked at it. Douglas Townsend. If Alice made an unexpected trip regarding her upcoming book, taking the manuscript with her, her agent would know about it.

He checked the time on his phone. It was an hour earlier in California. With any luck, Townsend would still be at the office.

Jack dialed the number.

The woman who answered was reluctant to put Jack through to her boss. But when he mentioned it was regarding Alice Fremont, she put him through immediately.

"I haven't been able to get ahold of her for days," Douglas Townsend said. "I'm supposed to be in Telluride tomorrow to pick up the completed manuscript."

"Will you still come?"

"Of course."

Jack wondered why a literary agent in California would fly to Colorado. "I don't know anything about the publishing business," he said, "but couldn't she just email it to you?"

Townsend chuckled. "My other clients do, but not Alice. Alice is old-school; she doesn't *have* email. She types on an old manual typewriter and insists on hand delivering the manuscripts if she's in San Francisco—which she's usually not. I typically have to fly to LA or Telluride to get them from her. Neither one of us trusts the mail. Besides, the trips are an excuse for us to meet face-to-face every year or so. It's good for business."

Jack thought it seemed like a colossal waste of time, but who was he to say. He told Townsend about his meeting with Alice and how no one had seen her since the housekeeper left later that day.

"When was the last time you talked to her?" Jack asked.

"Last week. I called her once yesterday and twice today, trying to confirm my trip, but I never could get ahold of her."

"When and where are you supposed to meet?"

"The restaurant at the New Sheridan Hotel at seven tomorrow."

"I talked to her son," Jack said. "He doesn't know where she is but thinks she could be on a trip related to the book."

"She's not. I would know about it. Alice keeps me informed of everything—her travel schedule, how far along she is in a manuscript—everything."

It wasn't what Jack wanted to hear. His concern for Alice was growing. "Will you still come to Telluride?"

"I'll be there tomorrow afternoon. Alice is

eccentric. I'm betting she shows up tomorrow night, as planned, with some outlandish explanation for where she's been. But I need that manuscript." The tone of his voice grew more insistent. "She sent portions of it to give us an idea of what the book was about and to help the publisher with marketing and pre-publicity. And I can tell you, from what I've read, it's going to be another blockbuster. The publisher agreed and has already offered her a sizable advance."

"And if she doesn't show tomorrow?"

There was silence on the other end of the line. "Then we've got problems."

The call ended, and Jack leaned back on the bench, thinking. When he'd met her, Alice Fremont had tried to cover it up, but he could tell she was scared. But scared of what? Or who? He thought about her books and the people in them, thought of the past threats and attacks. He wished he'd taken her concerns more seriously. But how was he to know she'd go missing?

Maybe she *would* show up at the restaurant with an explanation about where she's been. But the more Jack thought about it, the more his gut told him that wasn't going to happen.

Jack pushed the maps aside, then leaned over and spoke to the brown dog lying at his feet. "What do you think, Crockett? Want to go to Telluride?"

The dog looked up and cocked his head to one side.

"That settles it," Jack said. "Let's get out of here."

CHAPTER 18

Tuesday, January 11

THE NEXT MORNING, Jack and Crockett were on the road just after dawn. Two hours later, when the highway ended in a roundabout, he turned east, heading into the frozen box canyon toward Telluride. The sun had crested the mountains, making the snow along the road shimmer.

In town, he drove slowly, taking it all in. Buildings dating back to Telluride's mining days lined both sides of the street and looked like they'd been pulled off the snowy movie set of a Western. Main Street had been plowed, the snow pushed into a tall berm that ran down the center.

There wasn't a single traffic light, but Jack stopped at an intersection, letting a group of kids dressed in puffy jackets and helmets and carrying snowboards cross the road in front of him. There was a smattering of people on the sidewalks, many holding skis.

Jack found the campground on the eastern edge of town. The price per night was higher than he was used to paying, but he liked that the campground looked busy. He paid for a week in advance and was assigned campsite twenty. He maneuvered the gravel road, threading the trailer through the trees, and was pleasantly surprised to find that his spot backed up to a small river.

Jack parked the trailer and let Crockett out of the truck. The dog immediately headed for the river, loping through the snow. Jack unloaded a few things from the truck and noticed the book Alice Fremont had given him sitting on the floorboard. He grabbed it, tucking it under an arm as he turned for the trailer.

"Whatcha readin'?" It was a deep, gravelly voice.

Jack looked over.

An old man, shriveled from the sun, leaned on a cane that had been shaped from the branch of a tree. He had a long gray beard and was dressed in worn canvas pants and a tattered coat, neither of which looked like they'd been washed in years. His boots didn't match. He had to be pushing eighty, but his crystal-blue eyes were bright and alert.

Jack pulled the book from under his arm and looked at the cover. "*Don Quixote.*"

The old man looked at it and nodded. "That's a fine read."

Jack doubted the drifter had actually read it, but he seemed friendly enough.

"You camping here?" Jack asked.

"Right next to you." The old man lifted his cane

and pointed through a stand of bald aspens to an army surplus tent perched on the edge of the river. A rusted bicycle missing several spokes rested against one of the tent poles.

He stuck out a leathery hand, and Jack shook it. "Otto Finn's the name." His handshake was strong.

"Jack Martin. Nice to meet you."

"You look like you could use some coffee."

It was a statement, not a question. And although Jack was eager to start digging into the whereabouts of Alice Fremont, something told him not to decline the hospitality of the kind stranger who was now his neighbor.

"I'd like some," Jack replied. "Let me throw a few things into the trailer, and I'll head over."

Otto Finn smiled gently, inclined his head, then turned toward his own campsite.

Inside the trailer, Jack set the book down on the table. He drew his fingers over the cover. Alice had said he'd find the story familiar; he wondered why. He decided to read the book when he had time, then tossed it onto the bed.

Back outside, Jack called Crockett and the two made their way through the snow and trees to camp-site twenty-one.

Otto Finn was sitting in a folding chair pulled to one end of a picnic table. A small charcoal grill was set on the table in front of him, warming a speckled blue enamel coffeepot.

Jack eyed the pot skeptically, worried that Otto Finn's coffee might taste like road tar.

Otto handed him a tin cup. "Just about ready," he said. "Have a seat."

Jack threw a leg over one of the benches at the table and sat down, straddling it.

Crockett sniffed at the folding chair.

"What's his name?" Otto asked, scratching the dog behind the ears.

"Crockett."

Otto looked up. "As in Davy?"

Jack nodded. "As in Davy. I was told he was rescued from a shelter in Texas." He didn't want to go into the details about how he ended up with the dog. The body count in Aspen still haunted him.

They sat in silence for a while. The old man seemed content to merely have company, not needing to fill the quiet with talk. He pulled the coffeepot from the grill and filled Jack's cup, then his own.

"So what brings you to Telluride?" Otto asked. He blew steam off the top of his cup.

Jack wasn't sure how much he wanted to tell the old guy. "I'm looking for a friend." He took a sip of the coffee and raised his eyebrows, surprised. It was good.

"Is your friend from around here? Maybe I can help ya find him."

Jack set the cup down. "It's a she."

Otto looked at Jack. "She run out on you?"

Jack laughed once. "No, nothing like that." He told Otto about meeting Alice Fremont.

"And now she's missing?" Otto asked, a frown deepening the creases on his face. "Well, isn't that something? A famous author, you say? I read a lot of books—get them over at the library on Pacific. But I've never heard of an Alice Fremont."

"Probably not the type of books you'd be interested in," Jack said. "Society scandals. Stuff like that." Jack figured Otto probably read Westerns.

"And she's from around here?"

"Here and California. She splits her time between both."

Otto was quiet for a while. "And you're going to try and find out where she is?"

Jack thought about it for a moment. It was a difficult question to answer. He wasn't sure himself why he felt the need to find Alice. Maybe it was because he was one of the last people to see her before she disappeared. Maybe it was just curiosity.

Jack told Otto he was going to spend a few days in Telluride and see what he could dig up. If it didn't work out, if he wasn't getting anywhere, or if Alice showed back up, he'd move the trailer south to Santa Fe like he'd planned.

"You talk to anybody in town yet?" Otto asked.

Jack recounted his visit with Alice's son, Hugh.

Otto took a long drink of coffee, then set the cup down on the table, cradling it with calloused hands. "You go see Judith Hadley at Pandora Café. Nice woman. Lived here all her life like me. Judith knows everybody…and everybody's business."

Jack didn't have any better ideas, and he was hungry. "Is the café open for breakfast?"

Otto smiled. "Best breakfast in these parts. You're in for a treat."

By the time Jack left, the old man was finishing his second cup of coffee. Jack put Crockett in the trailer and headed for town.

It was a short walk.

CHAPTER 19

A FEW MINUTES later, Jack stepped out of the morning sun into Pandora Café. He took a moment to let his eyes adjust.

The café was a long open room, running front to back in the old building. An assortment of antique chairs and tables that looked decades old was scattered around the room. None of it matched. The plank flooring looked original to the building; it wasn't level and popped and creaked underfoot.

The smell of fresh pastries lured Jack farther inside.

His eyes adjusted. A glass counter ran the length of the room to his right. An antique silver cash register sat at the nearest end. Next to it was a black rotary phone—a model similar to one Jack's grandfather had kept on a side table beside his recliner years ago. Beneath the counter, glass display cases held an assortment of pastries and doughnuts, cookies, and several whole pies.

There was a murmur of conversation from patrons dining on omelets and pancakes. The room was filled with locals and a few outsiders. The tourists stood out in their barely worn designer ski clothes.

Jack chose an empty table next to a couple of guys talking about the weather while they downed coffee and eggs. He sat facing the door, then turned to his right and stared into the stone fireplace flickering with the flames from gas logs.

"The town outlawed woodburning in 1985." A medium-built middle-aged woman with a friendly face set a plate of cinnamon rolls and a menu down in front of him. She was wearing a burlap apron and had cropped gray hair with a pen tucked behind her ear. "Pollution and all."

Jack thought about what she'd said. "Makes sense, being in a canyon. Nowhere for the wind to blow the smoke."

The woman wiped her hands on her apron, then fished an order pad from its pocket.

"You must be new around here," she said. "Haven't seen you in the café before." She looked down at his scuffed cowboy boots. "And you don't look like you're in town to ski."

Her gentle prying gave her away.

"You wouldn't be Judith Hadley by chance, would you?" Jack asked.

She raised her eyebrows, surprised. "Speaking."

"Otto Finn said you had the best breakfast in town."

She stuck a hand on her hip and smiled. "How in the world do you know Otto? You're not local."

"How do you know I'm not?" Jack teased.

"I know everyone in town."

He laughed. "Otto told me that, too."

"I bet he did." She said it with an amused grin, then pointed at the menu with her pen. "I'm gonna give you a minute to decide what you want. But your first meal is on the house."

When Jack started to protest, she held up a hand. "Any friend of Otto's is a friend of mine." She started to walk away but turned back. "What's your name, stranger?"

"Jack Martin."

"Nice to meet you, Jack Martin. Now we're not strangers anymore."

Jack watched as she disappeared through a swinging door into the kitchen. He recognized the type. Judith Hadley was the sort of woman who befriended everyone she met. Jack liked her already.

A minute later, Judith reappeared and set a cup of coffee down in front of him. "Decide what you want?"

Jack ordered the Colorado breakfast—eggs, bacon, sausage, potatoes, and a side of fruit.

"I like a man with an appetite," Judith said, jotting down the order. When she finished, she looked him square in the eye. "Now, what else can I do for you,

Jack Martin? You didn't just come in for the breakfast—as good as it is."

How did she know? Was it written on his face?
Growing up, Jack's grandmother had a sort of sixth
sense, seeming to know what he was thinking before
he said it. Maybe Judith Hadley had the same intuition.

"I need to talk to you for a few minutes, when you
have time. About Alice Fremont."

She eyed him skeptically, then must have decided
his intentions were good. She glanced around the
café. "I tell you what. The breakfast rush is starting
to slow down. If you can wait about twenty minutes,
I'll get the girls to cover for me and I'll come talk to
you."

It was easier than Jack had expected. "That'd be
great," he said. "Thank you."

Exactly twenty minutes later, Judith untied her
apron, laid it across the back of the chair opposite
him, and sat down.

"How was the food?"

Jack had finished his breakfast in record time and
couldn't remember when he'd had a better one. "Otto
was right," he said, which made Judith smile.

"I've got about an hour and a half before the early
lunch crowd starts showing up," she said, laying her
hands down on the table. "Now, what's this about
Alice?"

Jack told her about his meeting with Alice on

Saturday, about the call from Sally Eagle, and his visit to see Hugh.

Judith sat thinking about what he'd said. "I agreed to talk to you about Alice because I'm concerned about her myself."

"Why?"

"She comes in every Sunday for brunch—never misses when she's in town." She pointed to the back of the room. "I keep the corner table open for her. But she didn't show this last Sunday."

"Did she mention anything the week before?" Jack asked. "Say something about a trip, maybe?"

Judith shook her head. "She tells me when she's leaving."

"Do you have any idea where she'd go?"

"None. When she's here, Alice practically barricades herself in that house of hers. We've taken food out to her. She has groceries delivered, even clothes and jewelry. I hear she runs the poor Waggoner sisters ragged keeping them running back and forth."

"The Waggoner sisters?"

"Opal and Ivy Waggoner. They own a store up the street—Waggoner Mercantile. They come in every few days for lunch. Opal is always complaining about having to take things out to Alice—jewelry mainly, from what I hear. Anyway, my point is, Alice almost never leaves the house—except on Sundays.

I was concerned when she didn't show up, but now I'm downright worried."

Except for a man sitting alone at a front table, the café was now empty. Two girls scurried about cleaning tables.

"I got nowhere with Alice's son, Hugh," Jack told her.

Judith leaned back in the chair and shook her head. "I'm not surprised. He's a bad seed. Always with his hand out, looking for money for some crazy scheme or another. I don't know how Alice tolerates him, but she does. I don't have children myself, so I guess that's what a mother would do."

"Does she have any other children?" Jack knew about Lars from Sally, but he wanted to hear what Judith would say.

"Yes. Another son. Another piece of work with his hand always out."

"Can you tell me anything else about him?"

"Lars has a reputation for being a playboy. Runs around with young Hollywood types. It drives Alice crazy. She wants him to get serious and settle down. He did a stint in a rehab clinic a few years back."

"Drugs?"

"Yep."

"Does he live here?"

"Not if he can help it. Alice complains he doesn't visit much anymore."

"Any other children?"

Judith shook her head. "That's it. Just the two boys. There's Hugh's wife, Eva. Alice's daughter-in-law."

"What's she like?"

"She comes in on occasion with Hugh. She's never been rude but seems a bit uppity. She's a foreigner—from Czechoslovakia or somewhere."

"Does Alice get along with her?"

"Alice doesn't talk much about Eva. I think she's nice to Alice, though—nicer than her sons. Probably does it to stay in her good graces for Hugh's future inheritance, but you didn't hear that from me. Hugh's not much of a looker—you've met him, you know. The scuttlebutt around town is that Eva married him for his money. The son of Alice Fremont and the late movie producer Warren Sheppard *should* be a good catch." She shook her head. "But you didn't hear that from me, either."

"What about Sally and Johnny Eagle?"

"Good people." She didn't hesitate with the answer.

From the little time Jack had spent with them, he agreed with Judith about Sally, but he wasn't as sure yet about her husband. He would look closer at the elusive Johnny Eagle before he reached a conclusion.

"What about friends?" he asked. "Is there anyone in town that I can talk to?"

She thought about it for a moment. "Alice can be

a difficult woman. She doesn't really have friends. She has acquaintances...business colleagues...employees. But not really any friends that I know of."

"Except you."

Judith gave him an easy smile. "Except me."

Jack could imagine everyone, at some point, ending up at Pandora Café for the friendly service and comfort food.

"Where are you staying?" Judith asked him.

"Town Park Campground."

"Ah, that's how you know Otto."

"Let me ask you something. Do you know of anyone who would want to hurt Alice?"

She blew out a breath.

"That bad?" he asked.

Judith nodded, a solemn look on her face. "That bad."

They talked a while longer about the past threats and attacks against Alice, Judith filling him in on the details that weren't reported in the media. The stories dated back decades. It seemed that with each new novel Alice published, there had been a flurry of new threats.

Judith stood up and put her apron back on. "I need to get back to work. It's been nice visiting with you, Jack Martin. Promise me you'll come back and tell me what you find out about Alice. If she comes into the café before I hear from you, I'll let you know. I know where to find you."

She started for the kitchen but turned back. "You might talk to Pastor Stan. He's at Wildwood Chapel on Pine Street. That's her church."

Jack thanked her for the food and the information, then dug a few dollars out of his pocket and left them on the table for a tip.

It was obvious that Alice trusted Judith Hadley and considered her a friend—maybe her only one. And after talking with Judith, it was clear that Alice burned bridges at every turn. Jack worried that one of those bridges might have fallen and crushed her as it burned.

CHAPTER 20

HUGH SHEPPARD WAS nervous. He sat alone, sipping a martini and wondering where Eva was. He was having a bad morning and wanted someone to talk to. Eva had gotten home after he'd gone to bed the night before and had left the house before he got up. It was impossible to keep up with her schedule.

The day before had started with that pesky detective interrogating him about his mother. Hugh didn't let on when Jack Martin introduced himself, but he recognized him. Like the rest of Colorado, Hugh had been riveted by stories of the Hermes Strangler in Aspen, then about Elliot Banks's murder in Vail. Hugh knew Martin had solved both cases, but he wouldn't let Martin know that. No sense in giving the man a big head. His ego was probably large enough already. But why was he in Telluride? And why had his mother called him?

Where is the blasted woman? Hugh thought to himself. He needed to talk to her.

Soon after Jack Martin left, the potential investors he'd met with the week before had finally gotten back with him. They'd told Hugh that they weren't interested in funding the subdivision project. "We just don't see enough growth to warrant a development as large as what you're proposing," they'd said.

Idiots, Hugh thought, swirling the martini in the glass. He plucked out the olive and ate it. *Of course they don't see it. They're all idiots.*

But Hugh was running out of options. He needed money, and he needed it fast. There was one more group of possible investors to pitch the project to. If they said no, it would leave only his mother.

Hugh stood up and padded across the white shag rug in his bare feet to the bar. He was shaking another martini when he saw Eva's white G-Wagon pull into the driveway and disappear around the side of the house.

"Finally," he said to himself, carrying the martini and dropping back down onto the sofa. He stuck his feet on the glass coffee table and waited for Eva.

"Hello, sweetheart," she said, sweeping into the room, carrying what looked like a painting wrapped in butcher paper.

Hugh let her kiss him on each cheek. "A little early for shopping already, don't you think?"

She laid the painting on the sofa next to him, pulled off her coat, and sat down. "Look at it, sweetheart," she said, unwrapping the brown paper.

It was a small oil painting, a snowy landscape

almost completely gray and white, with just a hint of a distant mountain in the center.

"I picked it up at Quinn Gallery," she said, thrusting it toward him. "Isn't it beautiful? It is called *Snowstorm in the Mountains*."

"How original."

She ignored the comment, holding the painting up, admiring it. "It is fabulous."

Hugh leaned in and squinted. "We have several by that artist already, don't we?"

Eva set the painting on the floor. "Maybe. I do not remember."

Hugh got off the couch and carried his martini with him to the bar. "I've had a bad day."

"Already?" Eva asked. "It's not even time for lunch."

Hugh ignored the remark. He told her about the investment group declining to back his project, but she didn't seem interested. Talking about business bored her, which irritated him.

He then told her about his visit the day before from Jack Martin.

"*The* Jack Martin?" Eva asked, suddenly interested. "The handsome detective from Texas?"

Hugh swirled his martini. "He wasn't that handsome," he said. "But yeah, the one that's been in the news."

"What did he want?" She was sitting on the edge of the sofa.

By bringing up Jack Martin, Hugh now had her full attention, and that annoyed him. Still swirling the martini, he glanced down and saw the tracksuit pulled tight around his waist. He sucked in his gut to see if it would make a difference but gave up and let it out again, straining the zipper.

"What did he want?" Eva asked again, impatient.

"He asked about Mother."

Eva frowned. "What about her?"

"Apparently, Mother called him, and he went to visit her Saturday. Then Sally called him yesterday morning and told him that Mother hasn't been at the house for the last two days."

"What do you mean? Where is she?"

Hugh shrugged. "Who knows." He took a sip of the martini.

"You never talked to her?"

The judgment in her voice irritated him.

"I didn't. I called twice, but she didn't answer."

"You have to go out and check on her, then. Something is wrong."

Hugh knew Eva was right, but it was almost time for lunch, and he didn't feel like leaving the house. He would call her again later.

"What's for lunch?" he asked.

"It's still too early."

"I'm hungry."

Eva stood up and snatched the painting from the floor. "Your mother never leaves without telling us," she said. "You need to drive out there today, Hugh. If she is not home and you still cannot reach her, you need to report her missing. What did Jack Martin say?"

"About what?"

"About your mother," Eva shot back.

"He was asking questions, looking for her."

"At least someone is." Eva walked toward the foyer, then stopped. "If you do not go to see her today, I will go myself in the morning. Someone needs to find out what is going on."

She left the room, the heels of her stiletto boots clicking on the marble floor in the foyer as she headed for the stairs.

Hugh finished the last of the martini and set the glass down on the coffee table. It was true. His mother never left town without telling them first. He thought about what he'd do if something terrible had happened to her, if she never turned up.

He pulled a hand across his mouth, wiping martini from his moist lips, and smiled.

CHAPTER 21

JACK STEPPED OUT of the café into the late-morning sun. He was happy to see that although the air coming off the mountains was cold, there was no sign of more snow.

Alice's agent, Douglass Townsend, was due in that afternoon. Jack was eager to talk to him, but he didn't plan to sit around all day and wait. His visit with Judith Hadley had given him a couple of ideas about where to turn next.

First, he wanted to pay a visit to Wildwood Chapel. He hoped to catch the preacher there. Alice hadn't shown up at the café on Sunday, and Jack wanted to know if she'd been to church.

He walked the three blocks to the chapel, his toes aching from the cold. Judith had eyed his cowboy boots dubiously, and the patches of ice on the sidewalks had Jack rethinking them himself. But his hiking boots weren't insulated. They'd have more grip on the ice but wouldn't be any warmer than the boots he was wearing.

At the base of the steps, he gazed up at the little

church. The building was old. Petite but pretty. It was clad in a stone that must have been quarried locally; he'd seen the same rock on several of the buildings in town. At the top of the steps, two wooden doors were set in a shallow vestibule, with an arched window set to either side. The gabled roof was topped with a steeple, its thin metal spire pointing toward the heavens.

Jack held on to the handrail as he ascended the steps. He wiped his boots on the mat, found the front door unlocked, and stepped inside.

"Hello." It was a woman's voice.

It took a moment for his eyes to adjust, and then he saw her. She was standing in an open doorway to one side of the tiny sanctuary. Tall and thin, probably in her early forties, wearing a floral dress and snow boots. She stepped closer. Jack could see she wasn't wearing any makeup, but she was pretty.

"Can I help you?" Her voice was friendly.

Jack felt a gust of cold wind and closed the door behind him. "I'm looking for Pastor Stan. Is he around?"

"He is. Did you have an appointment?"

"No. I was hoping to catch him, but I can come back if it's not a convenient time."

She smiled and waved a hand. "No, no, it's perfectly all right. I thought maybe he had forgotten about an appointment. He's out back—in the shed."

She led Jack through a short hallway to the back door and opened it for him. "Down the steps and to the left." She didn't follow Jack out but closed the door behind him.

Jack found Pastor Stan in a small, enclosed garage, working on a Harley-Davidson. The bike was jacked up on a metal lift. The pastor was bald and had biceps the size of river rocks. Tattoos crawled up both arms. He was faced away from Jack but turned at the rush of cold air when the door opened.

"Pastor Stan?"

"Guilty," the preacher said, standing up and wiping his hands on a dirty grease rag. He held a hand out for Jack to shake.

Pastor Stan was nothing like any of the preachers Jack had known growing up. Gone were the black robe and wing-tipped shoes. Pastor Stan wore oil-stained jeans. A faded denim jacket was tossed across the bike's handlebars. A flaming cross patch on the sleeve read HOLY ROLLER.

Jack introduced himself. "Can I ask you a couple questions about Alice Fremont?"

The preacher eyed him skeptically. "Why?"

Jack told him about his meeting with Alice and that she was now missing. "Was she in church on Sunday?"

The pastor shook his head. "She wasn't. I didn't

think much of it at the time, but now you've got me concerned."

"Does Alice tell you before she leaves town?"

"Not usually. But I'd be surprised if she's left on a trip already—she hasn't been back that long. I'd know—she comes to church faithfully every Sunday when she's in town." He snatched a wrench from the concrete floor and tossed it into a toolbox. "She came for the Christmas service. That was the first time I'd seen her in a few months, so she must have gotten into town the week before."

Jack thought about it. Alice hadn't been in church on Sunday. The information narrowed the timeline for when she went missing. Sally Eagle swore Alice was at home when she and Johnny left Saturday evening but wasn't there when they returned the next morning to take her to church. And Alice's bed hadn't been slept in. She disappeared sometime Saturday night.

"Can I tell you something in confidence?" the pastor asked, throwing another tool into the toolbox and breaking Jack's train of thought.

"Of course."

Pastor Stan brushed something from the leather seat of the motorcycle, then dragged his hand over the top of his bald head. "I know what some people say about Alice, but that's only one side of the story." He paused for a moment. "Alice Fremont is a very complex woman. She's outspoken. Some people say she can be harsh at times, but she's honest. And she's been very generous to the church."

He pulled the grease rag from his pocket and wiped his nose, searching again for the right words. "Alice is surrounded by people who want something from her." He stuck the rag back in his pocket. "What I'm trying to say is, despite what some people say, deep down, Alice is a good person." He stopped talking. For some reason, the conversation was difficult for him.

"I'll find her," Jack said.

The pastor nodded. "I hope you do."

Talking to Judith Hadley and Pastor Stan changed Jack's opinion of Alice. He thought of her living in the huge old house, isolated from town, and wondered what it was like to be that wealthy, that misunderstood...and that alone.

As he walked back toward Main Street, Jack racked his brain, wondering where in the world she could be. How could a seventy-something-year-old woman vanish in the Rocky Mountains in the dead of winter?

He turned the corner and was smacked with a blast of cold air. He folded his arms tight in front of him, ducking into the wind.

It was then he had an idea.

CHAPTER 22

As Sally Eagle was leaving the house the night before, Alice Fremont's youngest son, Lars, returned from a day spent snowboarding. He told Sally he'd be in town just long enough to talk to his mother.

When Sally told him she'd been missing for two days, Lars didn't seem to care. He had shrugged, said, "She'll turn up," then gone upstairs to shower.

When Sally left that evening, Lars had been digging through the refrigerator for something to eat like he didn't have a care in the world.

Alice's oldest son, Hugh, still hadn't returned Sally's call from Sunday morning. She was beginning to think she was the only one worrying about what could have happened to her. Sally couldn't think of where to turn next and desperately hoped Jack Martin would help her.

When Sally got to work that morning, it was the first time in twenty-three years she didn't make coffee but went straight upstairs to the master suite and found it empty. It had now been three days since Mrs. Fremont went missing.

After the master suite, Sally checked the guest room Lars was using, but he was gone again.

She couldn't think of anything else to do. She spent the rest of the morning like any other—she cleaned. She beat the heavy velvet curtains with a broom handle, then dusted the furniture and vacuumed the rugs on the first floor. As she worked, she looked for anything out of the ordinary, anything missing or out of place. If only she could find something—a note that had fallen onto the floor, something new or missing that would explain where Alice had gone.

When she was finished on the first floor, Sally decided to dust upstairs. She could check the master suite again, look behind the curtains and under the furniture.

She grabbed the newel post and had just started up the stairs when her cell phone rang. She pulled it from the pocket of her dress and looked at the number. She recognized the 713 area code and answered the call immediately.

"Mr. Jack Martin?"

"Sally, I need you to do something for me." He sounded out of breath, like he was walking uphill.

"Yes?"

"Check Alice's coats. See if they're still there."

"Her coats?" Sally was confused.

"Yes, check them all."

Sally didn't understand why he wanted her to look for Alice's coats, but she would.

"Then I want you to check her boots," Jack said. "Or shoes she wears in the snow."

Sally checked the downstairs closet near the back door and found Alice's tattered trench coat she wore when she was on the estate. On the floor below sat the tall rubber boots she used to feed the ducks that summered on the small lake just past the barn.

Sally still held the phone to her ear as she continued up the stairs. She thought Jack Martin was a strange man. "I am inside Mrs. Fremont's closet," she told him, switching on the light.

She went immediately to the back of the closet, where an assortment of winter coats was kept. There was a window that looked toward the mountain behind the house. Everything outside was blanketed in snow. It was then Sally understood what Jack Martin wanted to know. If Alice had left on her own the night of the storm, she would have taken one of her coats.

Sally held her breath and ran a hand across them, taking inventory. The wool cape. The down jacket. The full-length mink. There were a few others— Sally knew them all. Near them sat a pair of winter boots, suede with fur trim at the top, that Alice wore to church on Sundays when it was cold.

She felt nauseated. "Mr. Jack Martin," she said, her voice quaking. "The coats…"

"Yes. What about them?"

"They are all here."

CHAPTER 23

TWENTY MINUTES LATER, Jack pulled through the entrance onto Alice Fremont's estate.

Sally met him at the front door.

Inside, a tall kid in his late twenties was making his way down the stairs, sticking his arms into a sweatshirt and pulling it on. He had on jeans, and his feet were bare. His blond hair was still wet from a shower.

"Who are you?" he asked, looking at Jack. "And why are you here?"

"Jack Martin. I'm looking for Alice Fremont."

"What do you want with her?" The kid stood at the bottom of the stairs.

"You must be Lars."

"I know who I am," he replied in a sarcastic tone. "But again, who are you and why are you here?" The kid was smug.

Jack could feel his temper rising but kept it in check. "I'm a detective. Your mother offered me a job several days ago."

Recognition showed on Lars Fremont's face. "Ah. Jack Martin. The detective that solved the Hermes

Strangler case in Aspen last spring." When Jack didn't respond, Lars continued. "The last I heard, you were solving some case in Vail. Are you playing cops and robbers in Telluride now?"

Jack's jaw hardened. "Your mother is missing—"

"She's fine," Lars said, waving a hand. "She's on a trip somewhere for one of her books. She'll be back."

What was it with Alice Fremont's sons? Jack wondered. She'd been missing for three days, and neither seemed to care.

Sally was standing to the side, uncomfortable, listening to the exchange. Jack wanted to speak to her in private. But first he had a few questions for Alice's arrogant youngest son.

"When was the last time you talked to your mother?" Jack asked.

"Oh, I don't know," Lars answered, pretending to think. "Let me see…"

He was stalling, deliberately making Jack wait for an answer.

"I believe the last time I talked to her was on the phone Saturday."

Jack remembered seeing the dirty guest bedroom the day before. "You got to town on Sunday. Sunday afternoon or evening."

He pointed at Jack and winked. "Uncanny deductive skills, Detective." His smile was insolent.

Jack ignored the remark. He decided he couldn't

stand Alice's youngest son, but he needed information from him.

"When you talked to your mother on Saturday, did you tell her you were coming?"

"Of course I did."

"But she wasn't at the house when you got here?"

Some of the insolence left his face. "No, she wasn't."

He was surprised or hurt that Alice hadn't been there. Jack couldn't tell which.

"Where were you yesterday?" Jack asked.

"That's none of your business, but if you must know, I was snowboarding."

"When Sally got here yesterday morning, the back door was unlocked. Were you the one who left it open?"

Lars sighed as if he was tiring of the conversation. "I left it open because I didn't have a key. There was no way for me to lock it."

"If you didn't have a key, how did you get in the night before?"

He was silent a moment. "I used a key that's kept hidden outside. But I'd left it upstairs."

"And you didn't want to go all the way back up to get it, even though you know Alice insists on keeping the doors locked?"

Lars shrugged. "Arrest me. Now, if that's all, Sherlock, I've been snowboarding all day and I'm

hungry." Without waiting for a reply, he walked out
of the room and disappeared in the direction of the
kitchen.

Jack was glad to be rid of him.

Sally had said that none of Alice's coats was
missing, but Jack wanted to see for himself. He had
learned from experience that immersing himself in
the scene of a crime sometimes helped him think.

He followed Sally up the stairs and into Alice's
closet. It was big but much smaller than what Jack
expected for such a large house. He was struck by
how organized it was. Alice's clothes were arranged
neatly according to style and color. Casual clothes
were hung near the front. Dresses and caftans similar to the one she'd been wearing the day he met her
hung farther down. Shoes and luggage were arranged
neatly along the back wall. A window provided natural light, but Sally turned on an overhead fixture.

"Mrs. Fremont's coats," she said, stepping to the
back of the closet and pointing.

"And they're all here?"

She nodded.

Jack looked at the coats. There were several, all
neatly hung equally spaced, one from the other.
"You're sure these are all she has?"

Sally nodded.

"I'm surprised," Jack said, looking over the closet.

"I expected a woman as wealthy as Alice to have more clothes."

"No. Mrs. Fremont has only these."

"What about winter shoes or snow boots?"

Sally turned and pointed to the floor, where Jack saw a pair of suede boots with fur trim. "These she uses in the snow. She has a coat and boots she uses only on the estate. I checked, and they are still in the closet downstairs."

Nothing was missing. Jack thought for a moment and remembered the turquoise necklace Alice had been wearing when he met her. He remembered Judith Hadley's comment about Alice having jewelry brought out to the house.

"What about her jewelry?" he asked. "Is anything missing?"

Jack followed Sally out of the closet to an armoire in the bedroom. She opened the doors, exposing an array of shelves, and pulled one open. It was filled with silver jewelry. Most of it turquoise, but a few of the pieces were coral and other colorful stones Jack didn't recognize.

Sally closed the drawer and opened another, full of more silver and turquoise. It was an impressive collection.

"Nothing's missing?" he asked.

Sally opened and closed the remaining drawers, looking. "It is all here."

"Someone mentioned Alice buys jewelry from two sisters."

Sally nodded. "Yes, Miss Opal Waggoner and Miss Ivy Waggoner."

"They bring it out to Alice?"

"Yes." Sally crossed the room to a bureau set between two windows. "They brought these for Mrs. Fremont on Sunday. I put them here for her return."

Jack opened the velvet box and studied the two necklaces, both silver with large turquoise stones set in similar geometric patterns. He turned and looked out a window, taking in the snowy landscape while he thought.

Alice disappeared the night the record storm hit, yet neither her winter boots nor any of her coats were missing. All of her jewelry was still there, which ruled out the possibility of theft. If she had left on her own, she would have taken *something* with her.

It came to him. "Her luggage?" he asked. "Is any of it missing?"

Sally went back into the closet, and Jack followed her. Near the back, she drew up and pointed to an empty spot on the floor.

"There is one missing," she said.

Jack rubbed his chin while he thought. No coats were missing; Alice would have worn one if she'd left of her own volition. If she was abducted, had her kidnappers let her pack a suitcase? But what would she have packed in it?

Jack walked out of the closet and back through the bedroom, then into Alice's study, still thinking. None of it made any sense.

On the way out of the room, his gaze drifted across Alice's desk, nothing on it except a lamp and her old typewriter. He pulled up abruptly.

The manuscript. It was the only thing missing other than her suitcase. Had Alice taken the manuscript with her in the suitcase? Had someone else taken it?

Jack stuck a hand on his hip, staring at the desk. It was then he noticed two paintings sitting on the floor, propped against the wall next to the desk. He had seen them the day before but hadn't paid much attention.

The paintings were two nearly identical land-scapes of mountains that looked to be somewhere in the Rockies. The foregrounds of both were dark, a forest of pines surrounding a small lake set to one side. Behind the trees were snowcapped mountains painted in more vibrant tones, which drew Jack closer. He looked from one to the other. They were small but stunning.

"Why are these on the floor?"

Sally shrugged.

Jack bent closer and squinted, reading the artist's signature. It was the same on both. ABierstadt. Jack took the notebook from his coat pocket and jotted down the name. He'd research it later.

Back downstairs, he turned to Sally. "Is there anything else you can think of? Anything unusual Alice might have said or done in the days before she went missing?"

Sally thought for a moment, then shook her head.

"Was there anyone she was angry with? Maybe someone angry with *her*?"

Sally glanced at the hallway that led to the kitchen, then back at Jack. She seemed to want to say something but changed her mind.

"I can think of nothing." There was something she wasn't telling him.

Lars reappeared, a sandwich in his hands. "You're still here?"

Jack looked from Lars to Sally, who had dropped her eyes to the floor.

"I was just leaving," Jack said. He wrote his cell phone number in the notebook, tore out the sheet and handed it to Lars. "Call me if you can think of anything that might help me find your mother."

Lars stuck the number in his pocket without looking at it.

Jack turned to Sally. "I'll be in touch," he said, opening the door.

Lars followed him and leaned on the jamb. "Why

do you care where my mother is, anyway? You're not law enforcement anymore."

Jack stared at him, not sure what to say. He still didn't understand it himself. There wouldn't be any money in it; nobody was paying him. And he barely knew Alice, having met her only once. Maybe it was guilt. But maybe it was because he had nothing better to do.

Jack stared at Lars a moment longer, then turned and left him standing at the door, his question unanswered.

CHAPTER 24

As Jack approached Telluride, he saw gray clouds looming over the ridge above town to the north. It was his second winter in Colorado, and he knew they were in for more snow.

He would go back to the trailer and let Crockett out. Next, he'd make a trip into town to see the Waggoner sisters. If they were frequently taking things out to Alice, "running them ragged" as Judith had put it, Jack wanted to talk to them, see if there was anything they knew.

At the trailer, he let Crockett out. The dog jumped on him, then immediately loped through the snow toward Otto Finn's tent.

Jack followed and found Otto sitting cross-legged on a worn wool blanket that had been laid over a tarp on the riverbank. The edges of the river were frozen, but in the center, the water ran, making a peaceful sound as it splashed over river rocks.

Crockett lay down on the blanket next to Otto. The old man held a pocketknife in one hand, a small aspen branch in the other, and was whittling on the wood. He pointed to an empty spot on the blanket, and Jack sat.

"Find that writer woman you're looking for?"

"Not yet."

The two men sat in silence and listened to the river.

Jack was frustrated. He didn't feel like he'd made any progress in finding Alice. Her own sons didn't seem concerned about her, so maybe he shouldn't be, either. He could be wasting his time. The thought ran through his mind that maybe Alice didn't want to be found.

Jack looked down at his watch. Alice's agent, Douglas Townsend, was probably already in Telluride. It was still possible that Alice would show up for their scheduled meeting as if nothing had ever happened. Jack's gut told him that wasn't going to happen, but he would be at the restaurant just in case.

Jack twisted on the blanket. "Otto, can I ask you something?"

"It's a free country."

"How long have you lived here?"

"Might near all my life."

"Here at the campground?"

"No." The old man chuckled and stopped whittling. "I had a cabin once. Up there." He pointed toward the mountains with his knife, then dropped his head and cut at the stick again.

Jack thought about it. He wasn't one to pry. He didn't like being on the receiving end himself, but he wanted to know Otto's story.

"Why'd you move to town?"

"Got too old."

Jack understood. He didn't like to think about it, but he knew that one day he'd have to settle down somewhere, too. But not yet.

Otto laid the stick and knife on the blanket, dug into his tattered coat, and pulled out a pack of Camels and a plastic Bic lighter. He offered Jack a cigarette, but Jack declined.

"So, what are you planning to do about it?" Otto asked, blowing out smoke and damp breath as he spoke.

"Do about what?"

"The woman."

Jack figured it was the old guy's turn to pry. "I'm going to keep looking for her. She'll either turn up or she won't, but somebody knows where she is or what's happened to her."

"Sounds like it could be a bag of nails." Otto brought the cigarette back to his lips. "Something you best not be getting into." He blew out more smoke.

Jack stood up and smoothed the front of his jeans. "Otto, can I ask for a favor?"

"Free country, remember?" He was cutting shavings from the stick again.

"I've got to go into town for a bit—"

"Want me to watch Crockett for ya?" He stopped whittling and patted the dog on the head.

"I've had him cooped up in the trailer already today."

"You go on ahead. The two of us will get along just fine."

"Thank you." Jack bent and gave Crockett a quick pat. "Be good."

He took several steps toward town, then turned back. Otto and Crockett were in the same spot, both facing the river, looking peaceful and content. Jack watched them for a moment, envious.

The spark of curiosity about what had happened to Alice Fremont had ignited a fire in him he didn't understand. He hoped the Waggoner sisters or Douglas Townsend could shed some light on where she was.

CHAPTER 25

LARS WAS GLAD when Sally finally left. He would snoop through his mother's things again, but he had to wait until the nosy housekeeper was gone. He watched Johnny Eagle's truck as it disappeared into the trees, then turned his attention to the house.

Two nights earlier, his search had been for money. This time it was to find a copy of his mother's will.

Less than a year earlier, when Lars had asked his mother for an increase in his allowance, he'd made the mistake of doing it over the phone. She had threatened to disinherit him, calling it "tough love." Lars knew better this time and had shown up to ask her in person.

He resented how difficult it was to get distributions from his own trust fund. His yearly allowance was a pittance—an insult—and nowhere near what he needed to live on, much less help finance his fledgling music career.

He was Alice's favorite son. His father had been her favorite husband. And it wasn't as if he was asking for large sums like Hugh. Hugh came to her for *millions* at a time. Lars knew Alice had lost a ton of money over the years investing in Hugh's overly ambitious real estate projects.

When Alice had threatened to take Lars out of her will, he hadn't taken her seriously. There was no way Alice would cut out her favorite son. But recently he'd started to wonder. His birthday had come and gone a month earlier without so much as a card. She had called, but it was the first time she hadn't sent money.

He couldn't help that his career hadn't taken off yet, that the first band he signed had broken up only a month later. But now Lars had a lead on a solo artist, one he knew he could make a star and who would make him millions.

The eviction couldn't have come at a worse time. He'd just had business cards and letterhead made to show off his new logo. He'd paid the designer a small fortune for it all. But with his old address printed on them, they were worthless, and he'd thrown them out with the trash.

Lars needed a new place to live, and fast. How could he be expected to project a professional image without a proper office address?

He started the search for his mother's will in the walk-in pantry. For as long as he could remember, she had kept a filing cabinet tucked in a corner. He riffled through it for several minutes, but the only papers he found were invoices and receipts related to the house.

Next he tried the downstairs parlor, rummaging through the fancy Victorian desk his mother never used. Lars didn't find a will, but he discovered a few more Franklins he hadn't found in his first search. He counted the money—five hundred dollars—then folded the bills and stuck them into his pocket. Alice would never notice. If she did, he would blame it on Sally.

After that he went to the second floor. He grabbed the thick oak banister, took the stairs two at a time, and was winded when he reached the top. Damn altitude.

Castle in the Clouds sat just over 9,700 feet above sea level. When Lars visited, it took him several days to get used to the thin air. As if being isolated in the middle of nowhere wasn't bad enough, it was hard to breathe. He couldn't wait to get back to LA.

Lars had always hated the house. His mother bought the estate the year after his father died. She didn't say it, but Lars knew it was her retreat, a place to get away and escape the memories after the death of her fourth—and favorite—husband nearly devastated her.

After she purchased the estate, she spent less time in California each year, preferring Colorado. And by the time Lars was in high school, she lived at Castle in the Clouds almost year-round, leaving Lars in California, under the supervision of a revolving door of housekeepers. While still in school, Lars was expected to spend summer vacations with her in Colorado. Thankfully, the obligatory trips ended when he graduated.

Lars rarely traveled to Telluride anymore. And when he did, it was usually because he needed money. Except for his allowance, his trust fund was off-limits until he was thirty-five; he would have to tolerate his mother until then.

In the master suite, Lars sat down at her desk and pulled open the top drawer. An assortment of pens and pencils was neatly stowed in an organizer, a datebook set to one side. Lars noticed half a dozen hundred-dollar bills near the back of the drawer and stuck them in his pocket with the others. But when a nagging voice in his head told him not to be greedy, he put two of the bills back.

He opened the next drawer—a file drawer. *Now we're getting somewhere*, he thought. He went through each of the folders one by one. Halfway through the drawer, Lars pulled out a folder labeled INVESTMENTS. As he flipped through its contents, his jaw went slack.

The folder included stock and bond certificates, account statements, deeds for real estate properties he didn't know his mother owned. It took him several minutes to go through it all.

When he finished, he did a rough total of the sums in his head and was stunned to realize his mother was worth nearly half a billion dollars. Lars reopened the top drawer, took out the remaining two bills and stuffed them into his pocket.

He then continued through the drawer. The last folder was labeled PERSONAL. He riffled through papers, surprised to find the ones on top were Hugh's financial statements. *Interesting reading for later,* Lars thought, continuing through the folder.

The last thing he found was a photocopy of Alice's will. He scanned it, then let out a sigh of relief. Despite her threats, she *hadn't* disinherited him. In fact, after princely sums bequeathed to Johnny and Sally Eagle and what Lars thought was a ridiculously large amount to be donated to Wildwood Chapel, *he* was the largest benefactor. Hugh would get a significant chunk of it, but the bulk of Alice Fremont's estate would go to Lars.

He replaced the papers, put the folder back in the drawer, and shoved it closed. Only then did he notice the typewriter sitting on the desk.

That's odd, he thought, staring at it. *She hauls that old thing around with her everywhere.*

He felt his body tense as he stared at the typewriter.

Maybe she *wasn't* on a trip like he thought. Maybe something had happened to her. He thought about the detective who'd been at the house asking questions.

For some reason his mother had called him, and now he was looking for her.

Could she have taken a walk in the woods and gotten lost? Had she run into a bear? Maybe walked in on an intruder? Or a kidnapper? Someone she'd insulted in one of her books? They had threatened her before.

Lars stared at the typewriter a moment longer, then glanced at the closed file drawer and thought about the will, the half a billion dollars.

His muscles slowly relaxed.

CHAPTER 26

JACK HAD AN hour before Alice was to meet her agent, Douglas Townsend. But the more Jack thought about it, the more convinced he was that Alice wouldn't show.

He walked out of the campground and toward town. The sidewalks were crowded with tourists hitting the restaurants and bars after a day on the slopes. It was an uphill walk, and Jack's breath fogged in front of him.

After a few blocks, he saw a metal sign hanging over the sidewalk, the words WAGGONER MERCANTILE spelled out in block letters. A bell rang above the door as he stepped inside.

"We're about to close." An old woman hobbled toward him using a cane. She had cropped gray hair and wore large round glasses and a vest that looked like it had been cut from a Navajo blanket.

Jack suspected she was one of the sisters. "I'd like to talk to Opal or Ivy Waggoner."

"Speaking," the woman said, rapping her cane on

the floor and eyeing Jack suspiciously. "I'm Opal, the older and wiser one. Who are you?"

Jack explained his connection to Alice Fremont and told them he was looking for her. As he talked, another woman emerged from the back of the store. She was shorter than Opal, around the same age, but with a friendlier face and a head of soft curly gray-blue hair.

Jack could hear someone else in the back room, cutting open or breaking down boxes.

"I have no idea where Alice Fremont is," Opal said with another rap of her cane. "But when you find her, tell her we need our necklaces back."

"We don't need them back." It was the other woman. She smiled at Jack. "I'm Ivy."

"Nice to meet you." Jack tipped his head.

He remembered the turquoise necklaces on Alice's bureau, then thought of the missing suitcase. "Do you know if Alice was planning on going somewhere?" he asked them.

"If she was, she didn't tell us. We wasted half the day Sunday because she insisted—"

"She didn't *insist*," Ivy interrupted, rolling her eyes.

Opal glared at her sister, then continued. "She *insisted* we bring her a couple of necklaces to look at. Then we drove all the way out to her house and she wasn't even there."

"Has she done that before? Asked you to bring something but then wasn't there?"

"Never," Ivy answered.

Opal harrumphed. "It doesn't matter. That woman has ordered us around like hired help for years. Treats everyone poorly. If she's missing, I wouldn't be surprised."

Ivy shot her sister a cautious look, and Opal stopped talking.

"Why?" Jack asked.

Opal glanced at her sister, considering what to say. "Let's just put it this way," she said. "Alice Fremont's not well liked around this town. Or probably *any* town, for that matter, writing those trashy novels of hers."

Jack thought of the missing manuscript and wondered if the rumor Judith Hadley had told him was true. Was Alice's next book really going to be about people she knew in Telluride?

He turned to Ivy, hoping the seemingly nicer of the two sisters might answer his question truthfully. "Have either of you heard that Alice was writing a book about Telluride?"

Ivy drew in a quick breath and held it.

Opal took a step toward him, drawing his attention to her. "There have been rumors. But at Waggoner Mercantile, we don't peddle in gossip."

Ivy was looking at the floor. It was obvious Jack

had hit a nerve. The sisters *had* heard about Alice's next book, and for some reason, they were nervous about it.

Jack hoped Douglas Townsend could shed some light on the missing manuscript, on what—and *who*—might be in it.

Jack glanced around the store. It was organized chaos—merchandise stuffed on shelves, into cabinets, and hanging on the walls. There wasn't an inch of space that didn't display something for sale.

An oil painting of an Indian chief wrapped in a blanket caught Jack's eye. Other paintings dotted the walls throughout the store. He remembered the landscapes that sat on the floor next to Alice's desk.

"Have you ever sold Alice any art?"

The sisters were silent.

"I don't believe we have," Opal finally said, blinking behind her black-framed glasses.

She was lying. But why?

"Now, if that is all, Mr. Martin."

"You've been there," Jack said. "Her house is full of art. From what I saw, it looked mostly regional—mountain scenes and wildlife. If she's never bought art here, where else in town would she have purchased it from?"

Ivy Waggoner looked visibly distraught, made a quiet excuse about not feeling well, and pushed her way through a back door.

"Tell Sam not to leave yet," Opal instructed her sister as the door swung shut. "I need to talk to him."

Jack felt sorry for any employee of Opal Waggoner's.

She turned to Jack and put both hands on the top of her cane, pressing it into the floor and causing her knuckles to go white. "There are several galleries in town," she said slowly. "But I would suggest a visit to Gordon Quinn. Now, if that is all..."

Jack made a note of the name and decided to follow up the next day. Something was going on between Alice and the Waggoner sisters, and he hoped Gordon Quinn could shed some light on it.

"Thank you for your time, Ms. Waggoner."

"When you see Alice, you tell her she owes me for the necklaces." Opal followed him to the door, her cane clicking on the wood planks.

"I will," Jack said, stepping outside. "But if she's not back in a few days, I'll check back and see if you've heard from her."

"Do whatever you have to, Detective." Opal Waggoner, turning a sign from OPEN to CLOSED. "Damnable woman, that one. It's a wonder she's made it this long."

"What do you mean?"

"I mean, it's a wonder someone hasn't killed her yet," Opal said, then shut the door on him and locked it.

CHAPTER 27

THE RESTAURANT WHERE Alice was supposed to meet Douglas Townsend was just across Main Street from Waggoner Mercantile.

It had started to snow. Jack pulled his coat closed and stuck his hands in his pockets as he walked. The streets swarmed with the night crowd.

Jack started across the street with a rowdy group that had just stepped out of a corner bar. One of the men bumped into him.

"Sorry, pal." The guy was drunk.

Jack gave the group space and raised a hand to the driver that had stopped to let them cross. He stepped onto the sidewalk, careful to avoid a patch of ice in front of the restaurant.

Inside, Jack brushed snow from his coat and took it off. He stood at the hostess stand and peered down a hallway into the restaurant. It was nice—too nice. White tablecloths, china, and silverware. He glanced down at his wet boots. They needed a polish.

A pretty twentysomething watched him. "May I help you, sir?"

Jack cleared his throat. "I'm meeting Douglas Townsend."

"Yes, sir. Mr. Townsend is already here. This way, please." She led him past the bar and pointed at a corner table in the back.

Jack saw a middle-aged man wearing a business suit, sipping a glass of wine. There was an expensive briefcase on the floor at his feet. He was alone.

"Douglas Townsend?" Jack asked, approaching the table.

"Yes?"

"Jack Martin." Jack held out his hand.

Townsend shook it, then gestured to an empty chair.

Jack pulled it out and sat. "I take it Alice hasn't shown up yet."

"Not yet."

"Is she ever late?"

"Never." Townsend raised a hand to get the attention of the waiter. "I've been traveling all day. I'm going to go ahead and order. Get yourself something if you want."

Jack was hungry, but he didn't bother opening the menu lying on the table, knowing the prices would be too high. "I'm good," he said, declining the offer.

"Suit yourself."

The waiter took Townsend's order. When he left, Townsend leaned back in his chair. "So, you're looking for Alice. I admit, I'm concerned that I haven't heard from her. I would have canceled my trip if this next book of hers weren't so important."

"You don't have a copy of it? An early draft?"

Townsend shook his head. "Just a few sections. As I told you over the phone, that's why I'm here." He gestured to the briefcase at his feet. "That's what this is for. She gives her manuscripts to me personally. I get them to the publisher after I've had a chance to look at them."

"Seems kind of an old-fashioned way of doing business."

Townsend chuckled. "It is. But Alice is old-fashioned. I think I told you—no computer, no email, not even a cell phone." He shook his head. "It'd make my life a lot easier if she weren't so behind the times, but with an author as successful as Alice Fremont, you do what you have to. She's too popular to insist on anything different. Her publishers and I *both* jump through hoops to keep her happy." He didn't say it with any resentment.

"I've heard she can be difficult to deal with."

"Yes, she is. But she's brilliant—knows exactly what her readers want from her. It's worth dealing with the woman to be able to work with the author."

Jack's eyes swept the room. "You've been here before?"

"Several times."

"And if she doesn't show?"

Townsend was lifting his wineglass but stopped. "She'll show." His tone was more hopeful than certain. Jack could tell he was getting nervous.

Townsend spent the next ten minutes talking, filling Jack in on how the publishing business typically worked, then how it worked for Alice. He explained how he'd gotten lucky early on in his career when his superior suddenly died and Townsend had inherited Alice as a client. It was early in her career as well.

"There's always a silver lining," Townsend said. "Even with the death of a colleague."

Jack thought the statement was crass, but he let him continue. The relationship between Alice and her agent sounded like an unusual one. Jack couldn't tell if Townsend actually liked Alice or merely tolerated her. But it was obvious he had no idea where she was.

When the waiter appeared with Townsend's order, Jack realized how hungry he was. He watched as Townsend cut a bite of filet and stuck it in his mouth. He hoped Townsend couldn't hear his stomach growl over the noise in the restaurant.

Jack let Townsend continue to talk about himself through most of the dinner, then grew impatient. He wanted to redirect the conversation.

"You don't have a copy of her latest book, but what do you know about it?"

Townsend drank the last of his wine and gestured to the waiter for more. "I know some, but not a lot," he said, dabbing his mouth with a napkin. "She sent just a few sections. But I could tell, like her previous novels, it's going to be explosive. It includes story lines about a crooked politician and a scandal that could potentially rock the art world. She didn't give me many details—she never does—but I told her that if the full story is as salacious as it sounds, I'd be able to negotiate her a bigger advance than before."

"I read online that she's getting a million-dollar advance and the book will be out in the fall."

Douglas Townsend blew out a laugh. "Not true. But my phone has been ringing off the hook because of that story. You read it in the *New York Post*, right?"

Jack couldn't remember where he'd read it.

"Alice is a master at public relations," Townsend said. "*And* at making sure she gets top dollar for her books. No, there's no contract yet, but leaking that bit of information to the media set off a bidding war. Everyone wants a chance at it now. Which is fine with me."

"You think Alice leaked the false information herself?"

"I *know* she did. She's done it before."

Jack shifted in his chair, processing the information. If it was true, and Alice had leaked the information to the media herself, who else had she told?

"There's a rumor going around town that the new book is set in Telluride."

Townsend appeared alarmed but recovered quickly. "How? None of the excerpts have been released for publicity yet."

Jack shook his head. "I don't know, but that's the rumor. And my sense is that some people around here are getting jumpy."

Townsend adjusted the napkin in his lap, then pulled up his sleeve to check his watch. "I guess she's not coming."

He tried to hide it, but Jack could tell he was worried. Worried about Alice? Or about his portion of the future royalties?

No sense in pulling punches, Jack thought. He would throw out the question he really wanted answered. "Do you know anyone who would want to hurt Alice?"

"I can think of at least a dozen people off the top of my head."

"People she's included in her books?"

"Yes," Townsend replied. "But they would have gotten to her before now—some *have* gotten to her before now."

"Speaking theoretically," Jack said, trying to be tactful. "If something has happened to her, is there anyone in particular you think could have done it?"

Townsend shook his head. "Alice writes a book

roughly every two years. It's been almost that long since her last one was published. Too much time has passed. If they were going to do something, they would have done it by now."

He paused a moment. "I still think she's going to turn up. But to answer your question, if something *has* happened to her, and if what you say is true, that word has gotten around that the upcoming novel is set in Telluride—and I'm not saying it is—I would think whoever is responsible could be someone who suspects they're going to be in it."

That made sense.

Jack needed to get his hands on Alice's manuscript.

Townsend must have been reading his mind. He leaned across the table and dropped his voice. "I have a proposition for you, Detective. Keep looking for Alice, but if you find her manuscript first, you call me. It could help us find Alice, but even if it doesn't, I'll reward you handsomely." He leaned back in his chair and added, "Start with the house. Unless she took it with her, the manuscript is there."

Jack was silent, not sure how to respond. The question of whether Douglas Townsend's loyalties lay with Alice or his wallet had been answered. The guy was a snake.

"Look at it this way," Townsend said, still leaning in. "You'd be doing Alice a favor. She's going to turn up. I'd bet you money on it. And wherever she is—vacation, sabbatical, wherever—she'd want that book published." He sat back in his chair.

Jack wanted to be rid of the slimy agent, but he had one last question. "What about her typewriter?"

Townsend took a sip of wine before he answered. "Alice's typewriter? What about it?"

"Does she travel with it?"

"She's superstitious. She takes it everywhere she goes."

"Well, it's sitting on her desk."

Townsend raised his brows. "At the house?"

"Yes."

"But no manuscript?"

"No."

"And no Alice," he said quietly. Douglas Townsend thought about it, then gently set his wineglass on the table. "That's a problem."

CHAPTER 28

Wednesday, January 12

ON WEDNESDAY MORNING Celeste Bailey woke before dawn to fresh snow. She hadn't skied in days and was eager to spend the morning on the Nordic track just past Trout Lake, near the entrance to Alice Fremont's estate. It was a twenty-minute drive from Mountain Village. She hoped that by the time she got dressed and out the door, the roads would be cleared.

Before suffering a nasty ACL tear a decade earlier, at the age of fifty, she had skied downhill for years and was proficient at even the most difficult black diamond runs. But after the injury, she had decided that, at her age, it was no longer worth the risk.

The next season, she gave cross-country skiing a try. After her first outing with a guide and rented equipment, she was hooked and hadn't skied downhill since.

Celeste pulled back the covers and got out of bed, careful not to wake Buckley, who was snoring beside her. In the closet, she dressed for the cold morning temperatures, pulling on a pair of stretch ski pants and a turtleneck sweater. Downstairs in the ski room, she took her favorite Moncler jacket from her locker, grabbed her Nordic skis and poles and loaded them into the Range Rover.

It was a beautiful drive to Trout Lake, the early sun casting everything in a pinkish glow. On the highway, Celeste cracked open the window, letting the cold heighten her senses before she closed it.

The mornings she spent skiing were her sanctuary. Life with Buckley was never dull; a lot of times she wished it were. Wherever they went, Buckley was the life of the party, but he was controversial. People either gravitated to him or were repelled by him. But they were always fascinated by him. Buckley's image as a larger-than-life swashbuckling Texan had, for some reason, resonated with a lot of Texas voters.

And Buckley had been a good governor, accomplishing most of what he'd promised to do for the state during his campaigns. Under his leadership, Texas's economy had thrived. But the rumors of scandal and the brutal media coverage that had started with the *Dallas Morning News* article had cost him reelection. Celeste spent the following year nursing his ego, but she had been secretly relieved their stint in the public eye was over. Or so she had thought.

Now Buckley had set his political sights even higher. And although Celeste had enjoyed the time she'd spent in the governor's mansion in Austin, she was leery of going to Washington. She would never admit it to Buckley, but she secretly hoped he would change his mind about running.

At the top of a rise in the highway, Celeste turned onto the gravel road that skirted the northern bank of Trout Lake. She cracked the window a second time, once again drawing in a breath of frigid air. It was going to be a glorious morning spent in quiet solitude in the forest, a break from talk of politics and campaign funds.

The small parking area adjacent to the track and near the historic railroad bridge was empty. At least for a while, she would have the mountains to herself.

Celeste pulled into the lot and shut off the ignition. She spent the next two hours sliding across the snow, climbing the gently sloping terrain along the abandoned railroad line, through the thickly forested mountainside, then circling back.

After the sun rose, the sky had turned a brilliant turquoise. All morning, there had been only one other skier, a woman who'd moved from Wisconsin to Norwood several years earlier. Celeste had met her at the track once before.

By the time Celeste finished skiing, she was exhausted—and exhilarated. It had been a fabulous morning.

As she was loading her gear back into the Range Rover, she heard a vehicle and turned in time to see

Eva Sheppard pull through the standing logs that marked the entrance to Alice Fremont's estate.

She thought of Buckley's rants about Alice not returning his calls. Alice must have returned from her trip, Celeste decided. She would mention it to Buckley when she got home.

Sitting on the tailgate, Celeste pulled off her boots and placed them next to the skis in the back. As she slipped on a pair of leather Tod's, she heard a second car approach. A truck slowed as it passed the parking lot, the driver glancing in her direction as he went by. There was something familiar about him. Celeste had seen the man before. But where?

She watched the truck pull through the entrance onto Alice's estate, then closed the tailgate, got in the driver's side, and started the car. As she pulled out of the parking lot, she glanced again at the standing log entrance, wondering who the man was. Then it dawned on her. He was the detective she'd seen on the news, the one who'd solved the murder cases in Aspen and Vail. Jack Martin. But why was he going to visit Alice?

As she drove the tilted curves of the highway back to Mountain Village, Celeste wondered about the detective. Something must be wrong. She thought again about Buckley's unreturned calls. Could something have happened to Alice?

Eva Sheppard had arrived just minutes before

Jack Martin. Was he meeting her there? Maybe Hugh had gotten to the house earlier, and the detective was meeting both of them.

Celeste's imagination was running away from her. As she drove, she tightened and relaxed her grip on the steering wheel.

It was a stretch, but she wondered about the hollow threats Buckley had made against Alice in the past. Maybe they weren't just threats after all. Celeste knew that Buckley resented Alice—even hated her on occasion. Buckley was ambitious and proud, and he resented Alice for the times she had openly insulted him. But Alice insulted almost everyone at some time or another. Celeste knew that Buckley tolerated her for the campaign donations.

In the last couple of weeks, Buckley had made several late-night calls, and he'd made excuses for not telling Celeste what they were about. "Campaign stuff, Celeste. You wouldn't be interested."

Buckley was an ambitious man. Celeste knew he pushed the envelope when it came to ethics and in the past had done things he shouldn't have to get what he wanted. But how far would he go?

Celeste glanced down at the speedometer and realized she was speeding. Her pulse had quickened. She took in several slow breaths, willing herself to calm down.

But why was Jack Martin there?

Celeste was now sure something had happened to Alice. And as much as she tried not to think it, she couldn't help wondering if Buckley had something to do with it.

CHAPTER 29

JACK WAS ON Alice's estate. He steered the truck through the trees, then over a slow rise that allowed a glimpse of the mountains in the distance. The country was beautiful, everything blanketed in a couple of inches of fresh snow.

He was tired. He'd stayed up for hours the night before, going over everything Douglas Townsend had said.

He agreed with Townsend. It made sense that if Alice had been harmed because of her books, it would more likely be by someone who would be exposed in her upcoming novel, not someone still angry two years after the last one was published. Revenge was a crime of emotion, and usually not a patient one.

Late into the night, he had wondered what could have happened to Alice, making a list of scenarios. He had carefully considered each one, then one by one had crossed them off his list.

There was no evidence of a break-in. No signs of forced entry. The house hadn't been ransacked, and nothing—including Alice's jewelry—appeared to be missing. Except Alice, a suitcase, and the manuscript.

Jack thought about how, ahead of a blizzard, Alice hadn't taken a coat or boots. And her Suburban was still in the barn. Jack had called the handful of local drivers and shuttle services in town; none had picked her up. Yet she was gone.

As hard as he tried to think of other plausible explanations for Alice leaving on her own, he couldn't come up with any. Jack was convinced someone had taken her.

Earlier that morning, he'd called Hugh Sheppard. Hugh said that he still hadn't talked to his mother and didn't know where she was. When Jack mentioned the manuscript, Hugh had said, "I'm not surprised it's not at the house. Frankly, I'd be surprised if it *were.*" He said his mother would never leave a manuscript she was working on. He still seemed unconcerned, insisting that Alice would turn up with some outlandish excuse for where she'd been. He seemed no more concerned than when Jack had talked to him two days before.

But then Jack had told him that Alice's typewriter was still at the house. Like Douglas Townsend, Hugh had balked. Jack could tell by the change in his voice that Hugh Sheppard was worried. Jack told Hugh he was going to search the house. He would look for clues, but he was convinced the answer to what had happened to her would be in the book Alice had yet to publish. He needed to find the missing manuscript.

CHAPTER 30

WHEN JACK ARRIVED at the house, he was surprised to find a Mercedes G-Wagon already there. As he walked toward the front door, a tall, good-looking blonde came out to greet him.

"I'm Eva Sheppard, Alice's daughter-in-law," the woman said with a strong Slavic accent. She sounded like Melania Trump.

"Jack Martin," he said, shaking her hand. Her grip was confident and strong.

"My husband told me you were looking for Alice." They stepped inside. "He said you were coming to the house to search for something. I thought I could help. I am very worried about her."

Jack wondered why Hugh—Alice's own son—hadn't cared enough to come himself, yet his wife had. He remembered what Judith Hadley had called him. *A bad seed.*

Sally Eagle was in the room, and Jack asked her about Lars.

"I'm here, Sherlock, not that it's any business of yours," Lars said, bounding down the stairs. "But not for long." He was wearing ski pants and a turtleneck and had a ski jacket draped over his arm.

"Eva." Lars gave his sister-in-law a disinterested nod. She didn't reply.

Jack wanted to keep him close. He might have questions. "Where are you going?"

"Well, that's none of your business either," Lars shot back. He turned to Sally, heading in the direction of the kitchen. "I'll be back in time for dinner." With that, he was gone.

Jack looked at Sally.

"Mr. Lars goes to the resort every day," she said.

"Snowboarding?"

She nodded.

Jack told Sally and Eva that he was looking for Alice's manuscript. He asked Sally to search the first floor and Eva the third, knowing that if the manuscript were still in the house, it would likely be somewhere in Alice's suite on the second floor. He would search those rooms himself.

As before, the suite was immaculate. Everything in its place. Everything clean and dusted. According to Sally, there was never a sign of a struggle in the room, or anywhere else in the house.

Jack went into the bathroom. The walls were painted white. Small white tiles were laid in a simple herringbone pattern on the floor. A white towel hung from a hook; another was folded and lay perfectly across a claw-foot tub.

He opened a mirrored cabinet over the sink. It was nearly empty, but a comb and hair spray, toothbrush and toothpaste—things Alice would have taken with her on a trip—were arranged neatly on two shelves. He shut the door.

In the bedroom, Jack noticed a book on her bedside table and picked it up. A Ruth Ware novel—*One by One*. He could tell by the placement of a bookmark that Alice had nearly finished reading it. If she had left of her own volition, she would have taken the book she was reading with her.

Jack opened the front cover and was surprised to find his name and cell number written on a sticky note tucked inside. Something stirred in him, and he set the novel back down.

He went into the sitting room and sat at the desk. Eva walked in as he slid open the top drawer.

"Find anything?" she asked. "There is nothing upstairs. Just a few old pieces of furniture. I have told Alice many times the house is too big for one person, but she does not listen…"

Jack quit listening. Inside the drawer was an assortment of pens and pencils. He found a datebook bound in leather. The year was embossed on the cover in gold numbers. Jack pulled it from the drawer and opened it. Handwritten notes were scrawled in the squares for several of the dates. Squiggles and small drawings edged the pages. Alice was a doodler.

Eva was still talking. "I do not feel comfortable searching through the private affairs of my mother-in-law."

He flipped through the pages and stopped at the previous week. "Lars home" was written in bold handwriting in Sunday's square. Alice knew her son was coming, making it even more impossible to believe that she had left on her own.

Gordon Quinn's name was scribbled in a square the week before. Opal Waggoner had suggested Jack speak to him; he now made a point to.

"What do you know about Gordon Quinn?" he asked Eva.

"He owns the most exclusive gallery in town. My house is full of art I purchased from him. It is spectacular." She paused, then added, "You should come to see it sometime."

The way she said it made Jack uncomfortable. He'd steer clear of Eva Sheppard in the future if he could help it.

"I have a fabulous collection," she continued. "It is not as large as my collection in Brentwood, of course, but still one of the *most* impressive in Tellur—"

Jack cut her off. "It looks like Alice had an appointment with Quinn a couple weeks ago. Do you have any idea why?"

Eva thought for a moment. "Maybe it was about some art she was thinking to purchase."

In the square the day before her meeting with Quinn, Alice had written down a name of a gallery.

"Have you ever heard of the Lamston Gallery?" Jack asked.

Eva shook her head. "It does not sound familiar."

"It's not one in town?"

"I do not think so,"

Jack pulled his notebook from a pocket and wrote it down.

There was only one other thing written in the squares for the week. A name. Buckley Bailey.

Bailey, again? Jack decided he would talk to the former governor next.

He flipped back to the current week and saw that she had written "Douglas Townsend, Chop House 7:00" in the square for Tuesday. She had planned to give Townsend the manuscript, but now both she and the book were missing.

He flipped forward, saw there was nothing scheduled farther out, then skimmed through the pages of the previous months. Large blocks of time had been drawn through, with "Finish Manuscript" written above the line. Days Alice must have been writing.

He flipped again to the week Alice disappeared, turned his attention to the random doodles around the edges of the page. On the bottom were rows of stars and pine trees. Above and below were notes about things to order for the house and sets of random numbers crossed out and then changed.

Jack noticed a name scrawled among the ordered mess.

"Who is Ryan Oliver?" he asked.

Eva hesitated. "Ryan is…uh…a local artist." She struggled for the words but then caught her stride. "A fabulous one—the best in Telluride. His art is sold exclusively at Quinn Gallery but sent all over the world. I have several of his pieces myself. They are beautiful. You must come to see them…"

Jack tuned her out and wrote the name in his notebook.

He scanned the pages once more, then stuck the datebook back in the drawer and shut it. He opened the drawer below. Files, dozens of them. He shut the drawer.

He studied the two paintings sitting on the floor next to the desk.

Eva noticed him looking. "They are by Bierstadt." She pointed to a signature at the bottom right corner. "He was a famous German American artist who painted scenes of mountains in Europe, but also many of the Rocky Mountains."

"They're identical."

"Yes. They are beautiful," she said. "But his work is too traditional for my taste. But not for Alice."

"Do you know anything about these? Why would she have two?"

Eva was looking closer at them. "I—I do not know." She straightened and started for the door. "We should look now in another room."

Jack tilted one painting away from the wall. A yellow sticky note tacked to the back had "Lamston Gallery" written on it in Alice's handwriting. Jack set the painting carefully back against the wall, then tilted the second one forward and saw a similar note. But this one read "Quinn."

CHAPTER 31

GORDON QUINN ARRIVED at the gallery on Main Street at ten o'clock Wednesday morning. As he always did, he had walked from his condo along the river. But today he passed a black Suburban parked at the curb. Inside were two men dressed in suits. They looked out of place in Telluride, where, unless there was a formal wedding, no one ever wore a suit.

Gordon cut through the gallery, ignoring the greetings from his young apprentice as he passed her reception desk. He took the stairs to the second-floor office and went straight to a window that overlooked Main Street.

The Suburban was still there, the men still sitting inside. He watched them for a moment, then turned away. He was being paranoid.

He shrugged off his wool trench coat, hung it on the antique stand next to the desk, and took a seat. He swiveled slowly from side to side, taking in the office, admiring the sophisticated atmosphere he had designed for himself. The tooled-leather sofa and matching club chair, the Scandinavian acrylic coffee table, the forty-inch Dave McGary sculpture of a Sioux warrior perched on the ledge that ran below the windows.

Architectural Digest had called the gallery "A seamless juxtaposition of contemporary and mountain traditional, and considered by many to be as impressive as any gallery in nearby Aspen." Gordon loved the exposé the magazine had done several years earlier. The article was framed and hung on the wall beside his desk.

It *was* a stunning gallery, Gordon thought. He was proud of what he'd accomplished. But because of Alice Fremont, he could lose it all. He leaned back in the chair and frowned.

He remembered working alongside his father, a street painter in Central Park. Amos Quinn had been talented, but he'd squandered his life selling park scenes to tourists. Gordon and his four siblings had grown up living hand to mouth, too many mouths for their bedraggled mother to feed.

At an early age, Gordon had vowed to escape poverty, and he had. First it was a scholarship to City College, then to NYU, where he'd worked his way through school and amassed a pile of student debt. After graduation, he'd worked for years at a swanky gallery in SoHo before a chance trip to Telluride had changed his life.

The client was a Chicago resident with a mansion

in Mountain Village and a proclivity for fine art. At the age of thirty-three, Gordon Quinn had never been farther west than Newark, but he was assigned the task of delivering a particularly valuable Impressionist painting to the sleepy mountain town.

The ski resort in Telluride was still young, and the buzz was that the town was going to be the next Aspen. Although Gordon had never been to Aspen, many of the gallery's New York clients had homes there. At the time, there was already a smattering of high-end galleries in Aspen, but none in Telluride.

His first trip to the Rockies sparked a dream that took Gordon eight years to realize. But after working weekends and nights, scrambling to secure a handful of investors and a sizable bank loan, the result was Quinn Gallery. It had opened to fanfare, including an article in the *New York Times* that had provided the springboard he needed. Articles in *Architectural Digest, Mountain Living,* and *Town & Country* had followed.

He reached for a packet of cigarettes on the desk, pulled an engraved silver lighter from a drawer, walked to the window and pushed the sash open several inches. He sat down on the ledge, enjoying the rush of frozen air as he lit a cigarette.

The Suburban was still there. He watched it as he smoked.

He knew that all the Feds needed was to get their

hands on one of the forged paintings he'd sold. Thankfully, there hadn't been many.

He'd set up the operation on the side. Most of the gallery's business was legitimate, but Gordon had let Ryan Oliver talk him into getting greedy. Ryan was a masterful painter, not very imaginative when the work was his own, but his forgeries were masterpieces.

If only the Telluride art market had actually grown to match that of Aspen's, but it hadn't. Since he'd been there, the town had grown, but it had attracted the type of wealthy patrons and celebrities looking for anonymity.

Telluride never reached Aspen's level of notoriety, nor had it aspired to. Instead, the town had clung to its historic past, valuing strict architectural controls that maintained its mining-town heritage over ritzy condos and boutiques.

There were no Prada and Gucci stores on Telluride's main street, no Valentino or Ralph Lauren—even though Lauren's Rocky Mountain ranch was less than an hour away. But there was Quinn Gallery.

Although Gordon made a decent living selling and trading art, his level of income never reached that of his colleagues in Aspen or Vail. It left him vulnerable to Ryan Oliver's suggestions for expanding the business. He knew now that it had been a mistake.

Gordon reached through the window, stubbed out the cigarette on the brick wall, pulled the sash down, and took a seat back at the desk. If only he hadn't gotten greedy, but it was too late.

Weeks earlier, he'd decided to quit selling the forgeries, but Alice Fremont had already started snooping.

She was a miserable woman, and Gordon regretted doing business with her. It started with the purchase of a large oil—a herd of elk grazing in a mountain meadow. Alice had seemed content and didn't have any suspicions that the painting was a forgery. Then she had come into the gallery a second time. She had taken a smaller—more expensive—painting out on loan. That was months ago. Alice never paid for the painting. And for weeks, his inquiries went unanswered.

Gordon stuck the cigarette lighter back in the desk and shoved the drawer closed. He could still see Alice's face mocking him—threatening him—just two weeks earlier when she had come into the gallery. At first Gordon thought the visit was to finally pay for the painting she had on loan, but it was to accuse him of forgery. Somehow, she had found out.

At the time, Alice had baited him, trying to get Gordon to admit the forgeries. His offers to buy back the original painting he'd sold her were rebuffed. The maddening woman vowed to find out exactly what was going on.

She had called it "wonderful, salacious fodder for my next book." Gordon wasn't sure what she meant, but he knew he couldn't let her keep digging into his affairs. He had thrown her out of the gallery, physically shoving her to the door.

Although it had happened weeks earlier, Gordon's pulse raced as he remembered. He should have gotten the paintings back before throwing her out. That had been another mistake.

The intercom on the desk phone buzzed.

"Mr. Quinn?" It was Macy, downstairs.

"Yes. What is it?"

"There are two men here to see you." She paused. "They say they're from the FBI."

CHAPTER 32

BY AFTERNOON, JACK was exhausted. He'd spent several hours searching Alice's house for the manuscript. With Sally's and Eva's help, he had scoured the mansion top to bottom with no luck.

Afterward, he had enlisted the help of a reluctant Johnny Eagle, and the two had searched the barn and Alice's Suburban. But the manuscript was nowhere to be found.

On his way to town, Jack realized he was hungry. He had forgotten to eat that morning. He'd left Crockett with Otto and wanted to get back, but he decided to stop at a place called Smugglers. He'd seen their flyer tacked up in the office at the campground.

Jack drank a couple of beers on tap and had the best fish and chips he'd eaten in a long time. The waitstaff was attentive and friendly. The longer Jack stayed in Telluride, the more he liked it.

By the time he started for the campground, the afternoon sun had started its trek toward the horizon. As he pulled through the trees, winding his way toward campsite twenty, he noticed a hooded figure in the distance, walking quickly toward him. He was tall and wore a dark coat that came down almost to his knees.

As Jack approached, the man changed direction and disappeared into the trees. Something about the encounter was unsettling.

Jack parked the truck next to the Airstream and got out, then went straight to Otto's campsite. He called into the tent, but there was no reply. He unzipped the door flap and peered inside. No Otto. And no Crockett.

Jack stood listening to the rushing water in the creek with growing anxiety. Where was Otto? And where was Crockett?

Maybe Otto had gone into town and had taken the dog with him. Jack would wait an hour. If there was still no sign of them, he'd go see Judith Hadley at Pandora Café.

Jack made his way through the trees back to the trailer. The instant he pulled open the door, he knew something was wrong.

The camper was cold, like the door had been left open for a while. Jack checked the thermostat, but the heater was running.

With his hands on his hips, he stood in the trailer, eyeing every inch of the interior. Nothing appeared to be missing, but a cabinet door was ajar. It had been closed when he'd left earlier that morning. Someone had been there.

Jack was used to remote campgrounds. He'd gotten lazy and hadn't locked the door. It was a mistake he wouldn't make again.

He opened the door and looked outside. Most of the fresh snow had melted, leaving a muddy slush. There were no discernible footprints. He wondered who'd been in the trailer.

Jack shut the door, pulled the cushion off a bench, and opened the storage compartment underneath. His laptop and portable printer were still there. He pulled them both out and set them on the table, switched on his laptop, and opened his emails.

The night before, he had asked Douglas Townsend to send him the portions of Alice's manuscript he had in his possession. At first Townsend had balked at the request, claiming confidentiality. Then, under threat of lawsuit, Jack promising to use it only to find Alice and not share it with anyone, Townsend had agreed.

Jack clicked on the email he'd received from Townsend several hours earlier, then opened the attachment. He was disappointed to find it was only twelve pages. But it was the only thing he had to go on.

He plugged in the printer and printed the attachment, then read through the pages. They were snippets of scenes from the book Alice intended to publish. The story was set in a fictitious resort town in the Rockies, but from the description, Jack recognized it as Telluride.

There were brief mentions of the story's characters: a crooked politician, an illicit affair, money laundering, art theft, and forgery. The partial manuscript was salacious—titillating glimpses into the lives of the über-rich. It wasn't at all the type of book Jack was interested in reading, but then again, he didn't read much.

He glanced over his shoulder at the novel Alice had given him. It was lying on the bed beside one of Crockett's rawhide chews.

When he'd started the book, he had never expected to like it, but a hundred and twenty pages in, he was surprised to find that he did. It was the story of a Spaniard who wandered the land in search of adventure, seeking out ways to right the world's wrongs. It was a tale of conflict and morality—so different from the drivel Alice wrote.

She had said he would find something in it familiar, but he hadn't, and he still didn't know why she'd given it to him to read. He hoped that one day he could ask her.

Jack checked the time on his phone. It hadn't been an hour, but he was growing impatient. He stood up from the bench and glanced through a window toward Otto's campsite.

Where was his dog?

CHAPTER 33

JACK PULLED ON his coat, gathered the manuscript pages together, folded them, then stuffed them into his pocket. He went to leave but stopped and grabbed his keys from the countertop before he stepped outside and locked the door.

The wind had picked up and blew snow at him as he started for town. But he heard a dog bark and turned back. It sounded like Crockett. He looked in the direction of a footbridge that crossed the creek near Otto's tent and was disappointed to see a woman, followed by a black Lab, emerge from the trees. Jack glanced again at campsite twenty-one. It was quiet. And empty.

Starting for town again, he drew in and released a frustrated breath, the fog he exhaled disappearing with the wind.

At Pandora Café, Judith Hadley was waiting on a table of rowdy teenagers—loud, rich kids in designer ski clothes. Judith looked up and saw him, pointed to the empty table near the fireplace he'd sat at before.

Jack pulled the folded manuscript from his pocket,

stepped around the table, and took a seat facing the door. He was glad the restaurant wasn't busy. It was a small, in-between crowd—after lunch, but before après ski.

He unfolded the manuscript and laid it on the table, then stared into the yellow-orange flames of the gas logs. He felt weary. Who were the people in Alice's book? Could one of them have something to do with Alice's disappearance? He needed answers and hoped Judith could help. And he wanted reassurance that Otto would bring his dog back.

Judith set a small plate of chocolate chip cookies down in front of him. "You look like a man who could use a cookie," she said and sat down.

"Is it that obvious?"

Judith smiled, her expression one of friendly concern. "Nah, we just baked them. I need someone to try one and tell me they're all right."

Jack picked up a cookie and took a bite. They were still warm. "Delicious."

Judith leaned back in the chair and studied him. "Why the long face?"

"Do you know where Otto is?"

She shook her head. "No one ever knows where Otto is. He comes and goes as he pleases."

It wasn't the answer Jack was looking for. "He has my dog."

Judith reached across the table and laid a hand

on his. "Your dog will be fine. If Otto left, he'll be back. He's got an old placer claim somewhere above Ballard Mountain."

Jack frowned. "A placer claim?"

"An old mining claim, left over from his father—probably his father's father. Who knows. But Otto will disappear up there from time to time, dig around, come down with enough gold or silver to hold him over until his next trip up."

"He makes a living that way?"

Judith chuckled. "You've met Otto. I'm sure he doesn't make much, but it's as much as he needs."

Jack thought about the rusted bike and the surplus tent pitched by the river. "How long is he usually gone?"

"A week or so, maybe longer." She patted Jack's hand, then drew hers away. "Don't worry about it. He'll be back. He's probably just around town somewhere—maybe picking up groceries. If he comes into the café, I'll tell him you're looking for him."

Jack was still worried, but Judith's confidence eased his worry a bit.

"I need your help with something." He pushed the pages across the table to her.

"What's this?"

"Portions of Alice's latest book."

Judith picked them up, raising her eyebrows. "How did you get them?"

"I can't say. But if anyone asks, I never showed them to you."

Judith stared at him a moment, then nodded. "Got it." She skimmed the first few pages while Jack waited. "Well, I'll be darned," she said after a few minutes.

"What?" Jack leaned forward in his chair.

"The rumors were true. She *is* writing about Telluride. You can tell by the description of Main Street looking toward the end of a canyon and a waterfall. Her description of the courthouse matches ours, too."

Jack had figured as much and hoped Judith could help further.

"And look here," she said, pointing. "This character—Mark Dailey—he's a dead ringer for Buckley Bailey. Corrupt politician with his hand always out for the next campaign contribution. There are a couple of other former politicians in town, but none as flamboyant as Buckley—it's got to be him." She laughed. "This isn't going to sit well with the esteemed ex-governor when he finds out."

Her tone was sarcastic. It was obvious Judith wasn't a fan of Buckley Bailey. She kept reading.

"And this is Gordon Quinn," she said, pointing at another page, then hesitated. "Maybe it's the Waggoner sisters. Or...maybe the guy who owns the smaller gallery at the edge of town." She thought about it, then shook her head. "No, it's Gordon."

"How can you be sure?"

Judith pointed to a line near the bottom of the page. "She calls him a 'pompous ass.' That can only be Gordon."

That was twice in one day that Quinn's name had come up. And Opal Waggoner had mentioned his name the day before. Jack thought of the paintings on the floor next to Alice's desk.

"What do you know about him?" Jack asked.

"Gordon? He's got a fancy art gallery up the street. I don't know him personally. He doesn't come in here—we're too casual. I hear he prefers the white-tablecloth establishments in town. But everyone knows who he is."

"Alice knows him?"

"I'm sure she does."

Judith flipped back through the pages and gave Jack the names of a few other people she thought she recognized.

As she talked, Jack watched her. There was something brutally honest about Judith Hadley—gossip and all. Nothing she said was vindictive or cruel—just an honest woman's frank opinion. He admired the quality.

"Where can I find addresses?" he asked.

"Telluride's a small town. Everyone knows where

the bigwigs live." She turned over the last page and wrote the street names and directions for the addresses she knew.

When she was finished, she slid the pages back across the table to him. "Alice isn't exactly one to win friends and influence people. And I can tell you, she's going to ruffle the feathers of some pretty prominent folks around town with this next book."

"How many people do you think have heard the rumor she's writing about Telluride?"

Judith thought a moment. "My guess is lots have. Gossip spreads like wildfire around here."

If something happened to Alice, the more people who knew about her book, the larger the suspect pool would be. But Jack couldn't worry about that now. He would start with the list of names he'd gotten from Judith.

Jack folded the pages and stuck them in a coat pocket. "Thank you for your help." He grabbed the last cookie and started to get up, but Judith touched his arm and he sat back down.

She spoke in a hushed tone. "Let me ask you something, Jack. I know you're looking for Alice. And I know you've asked me about the people in those pages because you want to find out who might have harmed her." She glanced around to make sure no one could hear, then continued. "If you really think someone could have hurt Alice, I would take a microscope to those wretched boys of hers."

"Her sons?"

Judith nodded. "Alice tells me things. She loves her boys in her own way, but they're greedy—always coming to her for money. And if she doesn't give it to them..." She leaned back and shook her head. "They freeze her out for a while, until they try again."

Judith released her hand from his arm and stood up. "You keep that between you and me."

"I will." He stood to go.

"Hold on a minute." Judith disappeared into the kitchen.

She had given Jack a lot to think about. If Alice didn't turn up, he now had a list of possible suspects. But Jack wasn't going to wait to see if she showed up. He made up his mind to talk to all of them, including Alice's sons, Hugh Sheppard and Lars Fremont, again soon. Somebody knew where Alice was.

Judith returned holding a brown paper bag. She folded over the top and held it out to him. "A turkey club for later." When Jack started to protest, she stopped him. "You're doing a good thing, Jack. Not many people around here like Alice, but I do." She pressed the bag into his hands. "If you don't want it, give it to Otto when he gets back."

Jack thought of Crockett and felt his heart clench.

She must have seen it in his face. "Don't you worry. Otto *will* come back. He always does."

Jack hoped to hell she was right.

CHAPTER 34

JACK STEPPED OUT of the café and checked the time
on his phone. It was nearly three o'clock. The sidewalks in Telluride were crowded. Cars crawled down
the street in both directions. While he was inside, a
snowplow had obviously made a pass down Main
Street, piling more snow onto the top of the berm
already mounded in the center lane.

Something across the street caught his eye—a tall
figure in a dark coat, the hood pulled down, hiding
the wearer's face. The man was walking in the same
direction as Jack, but had his head turned, watching
him. Jack knew instantly—it was the same man he'd
seen in the campground.

When the guy realized Jack had spotted him, he
casually changed direction and began walking away.
But Jack wasn't going to let him off that easy.

Jack dodged several tourists standing near the
café, stepped over a patch of ice, and started across
the street. A few seconds later, the man turned and
saw Jack following him. He started to run.

Jack lunged forward. A truck appeared from

nowhere and blew its horn. Without stopping, Jack threw up a hand and dashed for the curb.

The man was still running, pushing tourists aside. He collided with a small child and reached down and caught her before she fell. He looked back, then ducked into a nearby shop.

Jack wove through the crowd and into the store. Several customers stood looking toward the back. Jack saw the man dash out the door and leap over a handrail into the alley below.

By the time Jack reached the back of the store, the man was gone. Jack slammed a hand down on the metal railing.

Someone had been following him. It was the same man who had avoided him in the campground. Probably the person who had been inside his trailer.

CHAPTER 35

A HALF HOUR later, Jack was in Mountain Village, turning onto Buckley Bailey's driveway, eager to meet the former Texas governor.

It was a giant log home at the end of the road, deep in Mountain Village. It was beautiful, its stripped logs, stacked one on top of another, polished and glowing in the late-afternoon sun. It was two stories, with an assortment of steep gables, huge windows, and covered balconies. Snow-covered fir and bald aspens flanked both sides.

Jack parked in the circular drive and got out, took a set of wide rock stairs that led up to the front doors. A dog barked from somewhere inside, reminding him again of Crockett.

He knocked and within a few seconds saw a petite woman with short dark hair through the glass in the front door. She opened the door, and her eyes widened like she was startled by something. But she recovered quickly and cleared her throat.

"May I help you?" Her voice was smooth and polished, with a faint Texas drawl.

"I'm Jack Martin. I'd like to speak with Buckley Bailey."

"You're the detective?"

"Yes, ma'am." Jack wasn't sure if it was going to hurt or help that she recognized him.

She reached for a large gold coin dangling from her necklace and rolled it around in her hand. "Is he expecting you?" She was nervous.

"He's not. I'm sorry I didn't call first. But I'd like to ask him a few questions about Alice Fremont."

The woman hesitated, then opened the door wider. "Please come in." The smile on her face looked forced.

The dog he'd heard came to him, wagging its tail. A black Lab the same size as Crockett. Jack bent to pet it and felt another sting of worry.

"That's Bo," the woman said, then told the dog, "Place." It immediately went to a large plaid cushion on the far side of the room and lay down.

Jack glanced around. The house was beautiful. The walls, like on the exterior, were made from giant stacked logs. The two-story entry soared to a cathedral ceiling, where a chandelier made of elk antlers hung overhead. Navajo rugs in rich colors were laid over slate floors. Across the room, floor-to-ceiling windows offered stunning views of the mountains above town shrouded in snow clouds. The furnishings looked tasteful but lived in. It was the most magnificent home Jack had ever seen.

"Do you like it?"

"It's beautiful," he said.

Her smile relaxed. "Thank you. We do love it here." She paused a moment, then held out her hand. "I'm Celeste Bailey, Buckley's wife."

Jack shook it. "Nice to meet you."

"My husband is on a fundraising call in his study. Would you like to wait?" She gestured toward two sofas facing each other near the far windows.

"Thank you." Jack walked to one, waited for her to sit, then took a seat. He continued eyeing his surroundings.

A rock fireplace that was almost as large as Alice's stretched from the floor to the vaulted ceiling above. Inside it, flames danced above a huge set of gas logs. On the mantel was an oil painting of an Indian tribe making their way through a mountain pass in the snow, their belongings rolled up in rawhide and fastened to the backs of their horses. The bright colors beaded into their clothes, contrasting sharply with the stark white mountains.

Jack had never dreamed of being rich, never thought about money except as a means to get by. Through the years, he'd seen how wealth corrupted some people and crippled others. He'd vowed long ago never to become a slave to the almighty dollar.

But this house had him rethinking it. He shook his head gently, clearing it.

"Can I get you something to drink?" Celeste asked.

"Thank you, but no."

"Do you mind if I have something?"

"Not at all."

Jack watched as she walked across the room to the bar. Open shelves held an assortment of crystal glasses that sparkled against the log backdrop.

Celeste poured a glass of wine. "It's not my business, Detective, but I'm curious why you want to talk to Buckley about Alice. Is she all right?" She crossed the room and sat on the sofa facing him.

Jack hesitated, not sure how much he wanted to tell her, but he decided whatever he told Buckley would likely get back to his wife anyway. "She's missing."

Celeste clasped the coin on her necklace with her free hand. "Missing?" She appeared genuinely shocked.

"She's been missing since Saturday night."

"Have you talked to Hugh Sheppard, her son?"

Jack nodded. "He wasn't much help."

Celeste looked into her wine. "I'm not surprised."

"I was told Buckley is a friend of Alice's."

Celeste nodded. "That's correct. My husband is in politics, and she's been one of his biggest supporters for years."

She glanced nervously in the direction of a set of large wooden doors. *The study*, Jack thought.

"But, of course, Alice is our friend, not just a contributor to Buckley's campaign," she added, fidgeting with the necklace again.

Behind her were several more large paintings.

"You have a beautiful art collection," Jack said. Then, on a hunch, threw out: "Did you purchase any of it at the Quinn Gallery in town?"

Celeste relaxed into the sofa. "Oh, heavens no."

Jack was intrigued by the response. "I've heard it's one of the nicest art galleries in town."

"*The* nicest," Celeste replied, then took a sip of wine.

"But you don't buy from them?" Jack hoped she'd say more.

She hesitated. He could tell she was debating what to say.

"There are rumors…" she said quietly.

"What kind of rumors?"

"It's just hearsay."

"I'm a detective. You can tell me or I'll find out some other way." He was pretending to tease but was trying to bait her into revealing more information.

Celeste smiled. "I guess you would find out anyway." She took a moment. "The rumor is that he's being investigated."

"Quinn? For what?"

She slipped her shoes off and tucked her feet underneath her. "I'm not sure. But it's an art gallery; my guess is that if it's not for something like back taxes, it's for theft or forgery." She took another sip, studying him over the rim of her glass.

She was baiting *him* now, to see what he knew. Celeste Bailey was a shrewd and classy woman, but there was something she was holding back.

"Do you know if Alice was a customer of the gallery?" Jack asked.

Celeste thought about the question. "I'm not sure, but I believe so. I purchased a painting from Gordon several years ago that I later sold back to him. Buckley mentioned he saw it at Alice's later." She shrugged. "I wouldn't be surprised. She has a large collection—much larger than ours."

Jack tried asking another question about Quinn, but she tactfully deflected it. He could tell she wasn't comfortable talking about him. He decided a visit to the gallery would be next on his list.

They talked a while longer—about Telluride and the weather and about Texas. She told Jack how she and Buckley had met at the University of Texas in Austin and about what it was like being the wife of a politician. She asked Jack about his time spent in Aspen and about the Hermes Strangler case, mentioning she had followed the case closely in the media.

While they were talking, Jack caught her stealing

glances at the closed doors to the study. She seemed nervous. He wondered why.

Buckley was taking longer than she had expected, and she apologized. "I'm sorry, Detective, but my husband is a very busy man. He's considering running for office again."

After all the scandals, Jack was surprised. "Oh? Which office?"

"The presidency."

He raised his eyebrows. Celeste held his gaze with a cool, questioning expression. She wanted to know what Jack thought about it, but he didn't want to tell her. As far as he was concerned, the world had had enough of loudmouth Buckley Bailey and all the political scandals. Jack couldn't imagine the man as president.

Celeste was still watching him. He knew he had to say something. "Well, I wish him luck in making the right decision."

She stared a moment longer, then, seeming content with his answer, set her empty wineglass down and stood up—a clue it was time for Jack to go.

"Again, I'm sorry my husband is too busy to see you, Detective." Her smile was gracious but reserved.

He followed Celeste to the door, but before he left, he asked her for their cell phone numbers.

On the drive from Mountain Village to town, Jack ran through their conversation in his head. They had talked about art and the weather, Texas and Telluride. But although Celeste had said she and Alice were friends, after he told her Alice was missing, Celeste had never mentioned her again.

She had avoided talking about Alice. But why?

CHAPTER 36

CELESTE BAILEY WATCHED from a window as Jack Martin turned off the driveway and onto the street. Almost as soon as his truck disappeared from view, Buckley slid open the doors to the study.

"Is he gone?"

Celeste turned to face him. "You knew he was here?"

"Of course I did," Buckley replied.

"Then why didn't you come out? I thought you were still on the call."

"Why would I want to talk to him?" Buckley pulled a glass down from a shelf at the bar.

"It was Jack Martin. The detective from Aspen who caught the Hermes Strangler."

Buckley poured whiskey from a crystal decanter. "I heard."

The desk in the study was at the far end of the room. Celeste knew that the only way Buckley could have heard was if he had been listening through the door.

She frowned. "Why didn't you come out and talk to him? He was here about Alice."

"That's *exactly* why I didn't," Buckley said, waving the glass at her as he sank down on the couch. "As much as I'd like to help, I don't have a clue where Alice is." He took a long drink of whiskey, then called to Bo. The dog came and sat on the floor at his feet, and Buckley petted him. "Besides, I've got my hands full with the campaign."

"But he thinks Alice is *missing*." Celeste heard the rising frustration in her voice. She took in a deep breath, trying to steady herself.

"Celeste, calm down. We all know Alice isn't *missing*. She's just avoiding us—me because she knows I need campaign funds and Hugh probably because he's always begging her for money for one of his crazy real estate deals. The guy is a disaster. You remember when he came to us several years ago, wanting us to invest in one. What was it?" He thought about it, then pointed a finger at her. "The chain of rundown bowling alleys he was going to convert into *state-of-the-art* entertainment centers." He made air quotes with his fingers and blew out air as he said it.

Celeste knew it was pointless to argue with him. She got up from the couch and poured herself another glass of wine.

When she sat back down, Buckley said, "You shouldn't have told him about the painting you bought from Quinn. Hell, I should have never told you I saw it at Alice's after you returned the damn thing."

"How much of our conversation did you listen to?"

"Enough." Buckley bent forward and set the glass down on the coffee table. "Look, Celeste, I'm running for president. You're going to have to stop letting strangers in the house without consulting me first. No, I take that back; you're going to have to stop letting anyone into the house, period. I'm too well known. It's not safe."

Celeste couldn't stand it when Buckley acted pompous. She marveled at how easily he'd forgotten his humble roots. She wanted to remind him of his working-class beginnings in the Panhandle, but there was no sense in arguing. He wasn't going to change now, after all these years. Besides, there was a more pressing matter.

"Buckley, what about Alice?" she asked.

"What about her?"

"Something is wrong. You haven't been able to get ahold of her. Jack Martin said Hugh hasn't heard from her, either." Buckley looked bored with the conversation, and she was getting irritated. "Alice's disappearance doesn't concern you?"

Buckley took his time, considering how to answer the question. He was a career politician, a master at covering up his true feelings and putting on an act. It frustrated Celeste that it didn't bother him to tell a lie. She prepared herself for one.

"Alice is fine, honey," he said, reaching for the whiskey. "She'll turn up."

Celeste watched as he lifted the glass, but he swallowed once before it reached his lips.

Alice Fremont was missing, and Buckley refused to talk about it. But, for some reason, he was nervous.

CHAPTER 37

AT THE CAMPGROUND, Jack went straight to Otto's tent but found it empty. The old man and Crockett were still missing.

Next he checked the Airstream. He'd locked the door when he left, and it was ludicrous to think they'd be in there, but he checked anyway. It, too, was empty.

Standing in the doorway, he remembered the man in the dark jacket and glanced around the trailer. Everything appeared as he'd left it. Back outside, he circled the perimeter of the campsite, looking for footprints in the slush and mud, but didn't find any.

Jack stood on the trailer step, scanning the surrounding trees and wondering what to do next. It was cold. The night sky was clear and twinkled with a million stars. The snow had moved on, but the freezing wind bit through his Carhartt jacket, and he pulled it tighter.

He checked the time on his phone. Seven thirty. Quinn Gallery would probably be closed, but Jack was restless, so he decided to walk into town and check.

Only a handful of cars remained parked on Main Street, and the crowds had thinned. Bars and restaurants were still open, but most of the stores had closed for the night. He noticed Pandora Café was dark, then remembered Otto saying Judith closed early. But it would be one of the first places to open in the morning. Jack would pay her a visit tomorrow, thank her for providing the Baileys' address, then ask a few more questions about the evasive couple.

As he approached the gallery, Jack was surprised to see the lights still on. A short man with a thin mustache and a comb-over was inside, gesturing wildly. Jack noticed a second guy—younger, nice looking, with a tall, athletic build and sandy-blond hair. The two looked like they were arguing.

The sign in the window said CLOSED, but Jack tried the door and found it unlocked. As soon as he stepped inside, both men glanced his way. The older one looked at his companion, gave him a quick nod toward the back of the store, and the younger man disappeared.

The older one turned to Jack. "Welcome to Quinn Gallery. I'm Gordon Quinn. We're closed, but may I interest you in some art?" He said it with open arms and a broad smile.

It was a complete reversal of the body language Jack had seen through the window. The man was slick. And already Jack didn't trust him.

The gallery was classy, looked like an art museum. Landscapes of the Rocky Mountains hung next to paintings of Native Americans. Bronze sculptures of bears and elk sat on glass stands in the corners of the room. Behind a marble counter, there was a twisted mess of antlers in some sort of contemporary art piece that Jack was sure cost a fortune.

Gordon Quinn was still grinning at him, hopeful for a sale. Jack saw him glance down at his boots, and the smile faded.

"I'd like to ask you a couple of questions," Jack said.

Quinn's smile was replaced by a frown, his unctuous demeanor long gone. "How may I help you?"

"When was the last time you spoke with Alice Fremont?" Jack watched his reaction carefully.

Quinn stood quietly. The question had taken him by surprise.

"A-Alice?" he stuttered, breaking the silence.

"Yes. Alice Fremont," Jack repeated. "When was the last time you spoke with her?"

Quinn cleared his throat, recovering his composure. "Well, I'm not sure," he said. "Why do you ask?"

"She's missing." Jack needed answers and decided to stretch the truth. He added, "And I've been hired to find her."

"Missing?" Quinn raised his eyebrows. Jack

thought he saw the tiny hint of a grin. "And just who might you be?" he asked.

"My name is Jack Martin."

All traces of Quinn's smile vanished. "You're from Aspen?"

Jack nodded and saw the little man's mustache twitch. "When was the last time you spoke with her?" he repeated.

"I don't remember."

Jack wasn't buying it. "She had your name written down in her datebook a couple weeks ago."

Quinn acted as if he were trying to remember, then shook his head. "I can't imagine why."

"You didn't meet with her at her house?"

"No, I did not."

"What about here at the gallery? Did Alice come here?"

Quinn blinked, and Jack knew the next words out of his mouth would be a lie.

"She did not," Quinn said defiantly. "If she had come, I would not have let her in."

Why the hostility? Jack wondered. "I take it you don't like her?"

"Few people do."

"Why not?"

"If you have to ask, you've obviously never met her. The woman is demanding, yet grateful for nothing. And she makes a living ruining lives."

It was the opening Jack had hoped for. "Do you know about the book she's working on?"

When the color drained from the little man's face, Jack had his answer.

"I...No, I don't," Quinn lied.

Jack saw a shadow move under the door through which the other man had disappeared. He was listening.

On a hunch, Jack asked, "Was the man in here earlier your employee?"

Quinn's eyes darted briefly toward the door. "He is not."

"Who is he?"

"He is a local artist. I display his work from time to time."

A painter. Jack searched his memory for the name of the artist Eva Sheppard had mentioned. It was written in his notebook, but he didn't want to pull it out in front of Quinn. What was the name? Brian... Ryan...

"Ryan?" Jack said. Gordon Quinn's eyes grew wide. Bingo. "Ryan Oliver, isn't it?"

Quinn remained silent.

"I'd like to talk to him," Jack said.

The shadow under the door suddenly disappeared.

Quinn hesitated. "He has probably gone home. As I told you earlier, we are closed."

"Could you check for me?" Jack was sure that Ryan Oliver was still back there.

"One moment and I will check."

Gordon Quinn was gone for several seconds, then reappeared. "As I suspected, he has left for the evening."

Quinn stood defiant, an arrogant look on his face. But the quick rise and fall of his chest told another story. Gordon Quinn was scared.

Jack was beginning to think *everyone* in Telluride harbored secrets. And he was sure that at least one of them knew where Alice was.

CHAPTER 38

WHEN JACK GOT back to the campground, he parked the truck and trudged through the slush and snow to the trailer, using his cell phone to light the way.

As he got closer, he noticed footprints that hadn't been there before and quickly swept the campsite with the light from his phone. There were lots of prints. From a pair of man's boots…and a dog.

Jack jogged through the trees to Otto's tent. He saw a light on inside. Jack heard a man talking over music, Willie Nelson and Merle Haggard singing "Pancho and Lefty."

"Otto?" Jack called through the tent flap.

The voice went silent, and the music was lowered. Jack heard the excited panting of a dog.

He watched as the flap was slowly unzipped from the inside, and a brown muzzle pushed its way out.

"Crockett." Jack rubbed the dog furiously. "Where've you been, buddy?"

Otto finished unzipping the flap and came out to join them. "I hope you weren't worried, Jack. Crockett and I went into town and ran a few errands."

Jack was too relieved to be angry.

Crockett danced between the two men.

"You were a good boy today," Otto said, bending to pet the dog with a weathered hand. When he finished, he straightened up, holding his lower back as he did so. "I tried bringing him to you earlier, but your door was locked."

Jack could tell the old man meant well, and by the looks of Crockett, he had taken good care of his dog. "Thank you for watching him," Jack said. "I hope he wasn't any trouble."

"No trouble at all." Otto bent to pet the dog again. "He was good company."

Jack felt a stab of guilt for worrying that Otto had run off with him. It was obvious the old guy was lonely and liked the company.

"If it's all right," Jack said, "I might ask you to watch him again sometime."

Otto's eyes lit up, and his wrinkled lips curled at the edges. "Anytime." He gave Jack a nod, then looked down at Crockett. "Good night, friend."

As Jack made his way through the trees with Crockett at his heels, he turned back in time to see Otto finish zipping up the tent flap. For a moment Jack watched the dark silhouette moving slowly against the glowing lamplight inside. The music was turned back up.

Jack had never met anyone like Otto before. A

man who'd spent his life wandering the mountains. He wondered if Otto had always been alone. Jack was curious to know more.

As he settled into bed, Crockett lying on top of the covers near his feet, he thought of the people he'd met in Telluride. It was an eclectic bunch—a mix of haves and have-nots. Some he liked—he thought of Otto and Judith Hadley. But there were others he didn't. And some he still needed to meet.

He leaned over and switched off the lamp mounted to the wall beside the bed. He knew it would be a struggle to sleep, but he had to try. There was work to do in the morning.

CHAPTER 39

Thursday, January 13

JACK WOKE WITH a start to the sound of an explosion in the distance. The howitzer. Otto had told him it was how the ski resort dealt with buildups of snow on the uppermost slopes in order to prevent an avalanche.

After another boom, Jack gave up on sleep and rolled out of bed. He glanced out a window and saw the day had dawned overcast and gray, reflecting his mood.

He let Crockett out to relieve himself, then downed coffee and a bowl of oatmeal. When he was finished, he lay back down on the bed, resting the back of his head on an arm and staring through the window at the morning gloom.

He was frustrated he hadn't made more progress on finding Alice and wasn't sure where to turn next. His gut told him that when he found her, it wasn't going to be good. He'd worked enough missing persons cases to know.

He ran through the events from the day before.

The more he thought about it, the more convinced he was that Buckley Bailey had been avoiding him.

Jack sat up and grabbed his phone from the floor. He took his notebook from the pocket of his jacket and dialed Bailey's number, listening to it ring until the call went to voicemail. There was no sense in leaving a message. If Bailey was avoiding him, he wouldn't return his call. Jack tossed the phone onto the bed and leaned back again.

As he often did, Jack analyzed the problem like one of his old football plays. He had been a tight end, used to catching a pass and plowing forward, weaving and dodging, always striving for forward progress. It was how he approached investigations— meeting suspects head-on, relentlessly dogging them until the innocent ones eventually fell away, leaving him with the goal line—or perpetrator—in sight.

But Jack couldn't get ahold of Bailey to question him. And not being in law enforcement, he could no longer force the issue—especially with an ex-governor. His gut told him Bailey was hiding something. And with Bailey's history of political scandals, Jack wouldn't be surprised if what he was hiding was illegal. For some reason, Bailey was avoiding him, and Bailey's wife was nervous.

Jack swung his feet to the floor and stood up, then paced the trailer. If Bailey wouldn't talk to him, forward progress would be impossible. He needed an end-run play.

Jack grabbed his phone off the bed, flipped open his notebook again, and found the number he was looking for.

"Hello?" The voice was rich and cultured.

"Celeste, it's Jack Martin."

"Hello again, Detective."

"I'm sorry to bother you. I tried Buckley's number first, but he didn't answer. Is he available? I still need to talk to him about Alice."

Except for a rattling noise, there was silence on the other end of the line.

When Celeste finally replied, her voice was shaky. "Uh…I believe he's in meetings all day. He's on a call now and has a slew of them scheduled later. Calls soliciting campaign funds. I'm sure you understand how busy he is. Is there something I can help you with instead?"

The gatekeeper was keeping the gate closed. If Jack wanted to get closer to Buckley Bailey, he was going to have to go through Celeste.

"I know it's early, but could I stop by this morning?"

Jack heard the rattling noise in the background again.

"I'm just loading my skis. Would you want to meet me at the Nordic track past Trout Lake? It's actually very close to the entrance to Alice's estate."

Jack knew where it was. And although he wasn't excited about driving all the way out there, he wanted to talk to Celeste. He was positive that if he was careful, he could get more information out of her. And after his visit to the gallery the night before, he had a few more questions to ask her about Gordon Quinn.

"I know where the track is," he replied. "Are you leaving now?"

"I am."

"Then I'll see you there."

Mountain Village was on the way to Trout Lake, so she would have a head start on him. Jack pulled on jeans and boots, grabbed his coat and keys to the truck on his way out the door.

"Let's go, Crockett."

CHAPTER 40

BY THE TIME Jack reached the track, Celeste Bailey was carrying skis and poles out onto the snow. Jack parked the truck next to her Range Rover and got out. Crockett followed, then dashed for the mounds of snow.

The sky was still overcast, but there were gaps in the clouds to the west, exposing bits of turquoise sky.

Celeste waved.

Jack made his way onto the icy track, careful to step over the parallel grooves carved into the snow.

"Thank you for that," she said, smiling. "Most people would trudge right through them. You must cross-country ski."

Jack had never skied in his life—cross-country *or* downhill. He watched as she slipped her boots into the grips on the skis and wondered if it was something he'd like to do.

"I met Gordon Quinn last night."

Celeste raised an eyebrow. "And? Did you catch him on a good day or bad?"

"A good day, I guess, until he found out I wasn't a customer."

She laughed. "I'm not surprised."

"You don't like him," Jack said. "Why?"

Celeste pushed her ski poles into the ground, making small holes in the snow. "Like I told you yesterday, there're rumors."

"You mentioned an investigation," he said. "But what else?" The hesitant look on her face relaxed, and Jack knew she was about to open up.

She still poked at the snow. "He sold us a painting last year, but there was something not quite right with it. It was a Bierstadt—a rendering of a lake outside of Idaho Springs near Mount Evans. It was gorgeous—a stunning dark forest with bright snowy peaks in the background. But a couple of months later I read an article about Bierstadt in *Southwest Art*— it's a magazine. Anyway, the article included photographs of several of Bierstadt's works. I noticed that all the paintings in the article were similar to ours, but different."

"How so?"

She frowned, trying to find the right words. "The colors. Artists favor certain hues—some have even attempted to copyright their favorite color palettes. But I noticed that the colors in our Bierstadt were slightly different from the ones in the magazine. The average buyer would probably never notice, but a connoisseur…" Her voice trailed off, and Jack knew she was embarrassed.

"A connoisseur such as yourself would," he finished for her.

She nodded with a shy smile. "The signature was expertly done. But to me, at least, there was a possibility the painting could be a forgery."

"Did you report it to anyone?"

"No. With my husband's position in politics, the last thing we need is to be pulled into another scandal."

"So what did you do?"

She looked down, poking at the snow again. "I took it back to Gordon. I confronted him."

"What'd he say?"

"He got irate. Asked me to leave the gallery. I did. I told him I would never buy anything from his gallery again." She looked uncomfortable remembering the confrontation. "And I haven't."

"But if he's being investigated," Jack said, "then *someone* must have reported him to the Feds?" Jack made a mental note to check with a couple of his buddies still with the bureau.

Celeste stared into the distance before turning her attention back to him. "It could have been Alice who reported him."

Jack remembered the paintings on the floor next to Alice's desk. Had she purchased the painting Celeste returned, found out it was a forgery, and reported Quinn? It would make sense. Jack decided to pay another visit to the arrogant Gordon Quinn.

Crockett was loping in the snow, but he stopped abruptly and held his nose aloft, sniffing. Beside him was a bridge spanning a ravine. Several warning signs were fixed to a pole, instructing people to keep off. Snow had piled on each of the crossties.

Jack watched as Crockett took a tentative step closer to the bridge.

"What's that?" Jack asked Celeste.

She turned. "That's the old trestle bridge. It was abandoned years ago."

"Railroad?"

Celeste nodded. "A spur from the old Rio Grande Southern line that ran all through these mountains back in the day."

Crockett suddenly barked and leaped from the bank, disappearing into the icy ravine.

Jack ran after him. "Crockett, come!" But the dog was gone. "Crockett!"

By the time Jack reached the edge, the dog had vanished into the snowy slopes below.

Jack turned frantically to Celeste. "What's down there?"

She had taken off her skis and was coming toward him. "A river. But it's frozen in winter."

Jack cupped his hands around his mouth.

"Crockett!" he hollered into the ravine. He looked around for help, trying to figure out what to do next.

Out of sight, Crockett barked frantically. It sounded more like a plea than a bark from pain. Seconds passed, but to Jack it seemed like an eternity.

Then he saw it, Crockett's brown body fighting the deep snow as he climbed his way back out. There was something in his mouth.

Jack took a couple of steps down the slope, sinking to his knees in the snow and helping the dog up. The struggle left Jack exhausted. He bent at the waist, and with his hands on his knees, tried to catch his breath. His jeans were soaked.

Crockett dropped what was in his mouth and stood panting, fogging the air around him.

"What's this?" Jack asked, picking it up. It was a woman's house slipper, silky material with an elastic band that would hold it snug to the ankle. It was similar to the ones his grandmother used to wear but more expensive.

Jack stared at it for a moment. Then he looked over his shoulder at the standing logs and realized they were less than a hundred yards from the entrance to Alice's estate.

He looked back down into the ravine.

Celeste must have known what he was thinking. "You can't go down there," she insisted. "It's too steep."

Crockett was dancing frantically at his feet. "Keep him here," Jack said, grabbing his collar and handing it to Celeste. "Crockett, stay!"

Jack wasn't sure how he would get out, but he slid down the snowy bank to the frozen river below. He could hear Crockett barking. Suddenly the dog was at his side. Celeste was small. He should have known she wouldn't be able to hold him.

Crockett barked once at Jack, then loped forward, disappearing in the snow with every leap. He stopped near the middle of the ravine.

Jack stumbled toward him and cried out when his shin hit a rock buried somewhere in the snow. Limping forward, he slipped on the ice and fell forward.

When he finally reached Crockett, Jack looked down at a small mound of snow and stared in silence at the frozen corpse of Alice Fremont, her unblinking eyes sheathed in ice.

CHAPTER 41

JACK'S CLOTHES WERE soaked. He shivered, standing next to Alice's body. He shoved his hand into a pocket, his fingers numb with cold, and pulled out his cell phone.

Please God, let there be service, he thought as he dialed 911, then let out a sigh of relief when he heard the call ringing on the other end.

A woman answered. "San Miguel County Sheriff's Office."

Jack gave her his location, then told her about finding Alice's body. The woman asked him to stay on the line until deputies arrived. Jack knew it was standard procedure, but he refused. They knew where he was, and he wasn't going anywhere. But he was cold and wet and wanted out of the frozen ravine.

Fifteen minutes later, after a nearly impossible struggle to climb up to where Celeste Bailey was still standing, Jack heard sirens wailing in the distance. As they came closer, he could see three Chevrolet Tahoes racing through the gravel and snow toward them.

Jack put Crockett in the truck to keep him out of the way and walked back to Celeste, stomping at the ground with his wet boots, trying to warm his swollen feet. Celeste had taken a towel from her car and gave it to him. It was little relief from the freezing cold, but Jack appreciated the gesture.

The Tahoes screamed to a stop behind Jack's truck, and several men in uniforms got out. A man about Jack's age who, by the insignia on his uniform, Jack identified as the sheriff, walked intently toward him.

"Jack Martin?" the man asked, holding out a hand for Jack to shake. "I'm Sheriff Tony Burns." He was short and stout, with the grip of an NFL fullback.

Jack explained how he'd found Alice's body. As he talked, a young deputy stood behind the sheriff, taking notes.

Within an hour, the scene was swarming with personnel. There were men under the bridge with Alice's body, others combing through the snow along the edge of the ravine, looking for clues. Sheriff Burns was in the distance, talking into a radio. An ambulance had arrived and sat waiting to whisk the body to the morgue.

Jack heard the deep rhythmic sound of an approaching helicopter and looked up, shielding his eyes from the sun that had emerged from behind the clouds. As it drew closer, Sheriff Burns waved it down onto the snow.

A few minutes later, as the chopper blades slowed, Jack heard a struggle. He looked in the direction of the ravine and saw a deputy fighting to climb out. Jack went to help.

"Thank you," the deputy said, brushing snow from his soaked uniform.

He was young, probably still in his twenties. Jack hoped the kid's inexperience would work to his benefit, and he'd be able to get some information out of him. A seasoned cop would likely be more suspicious and tight-lipped.

"Find anything else down there?" Jack asked casually.

"So far, just the body and a shoe matching the one you found."

"Where was it?"

"Approximately twenty feet from the deceased. Must have fallen off."

Jack studied the bridge. He didn't think for a minute that Alice would have voluntarily wandered out onto it during a storm in her nightclothes. She would have been taken against her will, maybe even dragged across it. It would explain the one shoe being found so far from her body.

Jack stepped closer, studying the mounds of snow covering each crosstie. There were no footprints or any evidence someone had been on the bridge. It helped narrow the timeline.

Alice had gone missing sometime after Sally and Johnny Eagle left Saturday evening, the night of the blizzard. Since then, there had been only a couple more inches of new snow—not enough to cover footprints or drag marks. Alice had to have been on the bridge sometime *before* the storm.

Jack watched the crime scene being worked and lost track of time. He heard the helicopter rotors starting up and watched it lift off the ground. It hovered above the bridge as a basket was lowered, sending a spray of snow in every direction. Jack turned his face from the stinging ice and noticed that Celeste Bailey was still there, sitting inside her car.

Sheriff Burns and a deputy walked toward her, and she got out. After a conversation that lasted less than a minute, Celeste backed out of the parking lot and left. From his experience at crime scenes, Jack knew she had been released.

He turned his attention back to the bridge and what was going on below. Shock waves pulsed through his chest in rhythm with the helicopter's blades. After several minutes, shielding his eyes from the blowing snow, he watched as Alice's body was lifted from under the bridge.

The helicopter swung the basket slowly toward the waiting ambulance, where two paramedics guided it to the ground and unhooked the cables. Sheriff Burns threw a thumbs-up to the pilot. The helicopter pivoted and flew away, leaving the scene eerily quiet.

Alice's body was covered with a white tarp and looked rigid as the paramedics transferred it from the basket to a gurney. Jack watched as they loaded her into the ambulance and shut the doors.

The hint of fear in Alice's voice when she'd offered him the job haunted him. He thought of the threats and assaults against her and was convinced she'd been murdered.

As he watched the ambulance pull away, the overwhelming need to find Alice's killer seized him like a vise. But it wasn't his case or his problem. Jack barely knew her. He looked back toward the bridge, trying to convince himself to walk away. He would take the trailer and Crockett and head south for the rest of the winter.

For several minutes, Jack watched law enforcement work the scene. He was done here. He'd given the sheriff his statement and his cell number. They could call him if they had any more questions.

But as hard as he tried, Jack couldn't convince himself to go. He was angry. And for some reason he didn't understand, he was determined to find Alice Fremont's killer.

CHAPTER 42

WHEN HUGH SHEPPARD woke on Thursday morning, he realized Eva hadn't come home the night before. Probably partying with friends downtown again.

He knew when he'd married her that she wasn't the type to sit at home, but he had thought that, after nearly ten years, she would have settled down. The longer he thought about it, the more he regretted marrying her. He should have married someone closer to his own age.

His trip to Los Angeles the afternoon before had been canceled due to weather. Hugh had been halfway to the Montrose airport when he regained cell service and was notified. *Damn airlines.* They were notoriously unreliable.

It was ridiculous he had to fly commercial anyway. For months on end, his mother's jet sat unused in its hangar at the Telluride airport. But he'd learned long ago not to bother asking to borrow it.

It was a beautiful Cessna Sovereign, white fuselage with stripes in deep red painted down the sides, the interior upholstered in a buttery tan leather. It made him angry just thinking about it. It sat just fifteen minutes from the house in Mountain Village, yet his mother expected him to drive an hour and a half through the mountains to Montrose, then fly shoulder-to-shoulder on a commercial flight like common riffraff.

He wondered why she still had the thing, since she rarely left town anymore. Only a few years earlier, she would spend most of her time in Los Angeles, coming to Telluride for summer vacations and the occasional holiday trip. But with each book she published, she had spent more time hidden away at the estate in the mountains.

It was just before lunch, but Hugh mixed himself a martini. He sat down on the white leather sofa, nearly sliding off. He hated the damn thing. If he'd gotten his way, they would have built a house that looked like Buckley Bailey's, a log home, with warm and inviting interiors—what a mountain house *should* look like.

Hugh repositioned himself on the sofa, the leather screeching in protest, then took a long swallow of the martini. *Where was she?* It was bad enough that she hadn't bothered to come home the night before, but his texts to her that morning had gone unanswered.

The doorbell rang. "About damn time," he said, standing up and starting for the front door. It would be Eva. The blasted woman still hadn't found her keys.

But when he opened the door, his heart lurched to his throat. It wasn't Eva but a young woman dressed in a law enforcement uniform.

"Mr. Hugh Sheppard?"

"Is she all right?" Hugh's mouth had gone dry. "Has something happened to Eva?"

"Mr. Sheppard, I'm Officer Kim O'Connor with the San Miguel County Sheriff's Office. I regret to inform you…"

Hugh sat in silence as the woman told him his mother's body had been found. He was relieved it wasn't Eva. As infuriating as he found her, she was his trophy.

When the woman left, Hugh stumbled back to the sofa and finished his drink in a single swallow, then got up and mixed himself another.

So that was it. Alice had finally made the wrong person angry. Hugh had warned her over and over that staying in that old house—alone in the middle of nowhere—wasn't safe. But she hadn't listened to him—she *never* listened to him. Now she was dead.

He sat staring out the window at the snow-covered mountains in the distance. He felt numb, not sure what to do next. A call to Lars would be the logical thing to do—he *was* his half brother. Hugh considered it a moment, then decided against it. He'd let the spoiled brat find out on his own.

Several minutes later, he heard the door to the

garage open and knew it would be Eva. He didn't bother to get up.

"You're here, sweetheart," she said, coming into the room. The surprise in her voice was obvious.

"Where've you been?" Hugh heard his speech slur. He'd had too much to drink, but he didn't care. His mother was dead.

"You weren't supposed to be back until tomorrow. I had dinner with friends last night. It got late, so I stayed in town with Anne. You know Anne."

Hugh didn't look at her. "No, I don't know Anne," he said and threw back another swallow.

Eva sauntered to him, her heels clicking on the marble floor. Her perfume was overwhelming, threatening to make him sick. She set a bag down on the floor, then bent and kissed the top of his head.

"What happened to the trip?" she asked in her strong Slavic accent. Her *the's* sounded like *zee's*. He used to think it was sexy, but after ten years, it grated on him. More and more, the things she did were beginning to annoy him.

He swirled what was left of the martini, then downed it. There was no point in beating around the bush. "Mother's dead."

Eva drew up and took a step back. "What?"

"She's dead."

"Alice?"

He heard the emotion that had crept into her voice and nodded without looking up.

"How do you know?"

"Someone from the sheriff's office came by."

Eva dropped onto the couch beside him, laying her hand on his thigh. "Oh, sweetheart. What did they say?"

"They found her—no, that detective found her."

"What detective?" She frowned. "The one that came to see you?"

He nodded, then got up and staggered toward the bar for another drink.

"Hugh, you're drunk."

"So what if I am?"

She was immediately at his side. She took the empty glass from him, set it on the bar, then steered him back to the sofa. "You cannot be drunk, Hugh. They will come here again. They will want to talk to you."

Hugh's head was spinning. He rested it on the back of the sofa and closed his eyes. "Who? Who will want to talk to me?"

"The sheriff."

The sheriff? He felt his chest constrict. Of course they'd want to talk to him—he was Alice's son.

Thinking about it made his head pound. He leaned forward, rubbing at his temples. What would they ask? Would they expect him to cry or throw a fit?

Demand justice for his mother? Did they think he'd done it—that he had killed her?

Hugh dragged a hand down his face, then wiped the sweat onto his pants. "Bring me some water."

CHAPTER 43

IT HAD BEEN the worst morning of Celeste's life. She couldn't believe Alice was dead. Why would she be under the bridge? What had happened to her?

The events of the morning were a nightmarish blur. Talking to Jack Martin, the dog, the ravine. The ski track swarming with law enforcement, lights flashing, a helicopter. She had wanted to run—get away—but was made to stay for what seemed like hours before the sheriff had eventually let her go.

She had called Buckley from Trout Lake and told him about Alice. Shocked by the news, he had insisted on coming to the lake to get her. She told him the road was cordoned off and argued he wouldn't be able to get through; the area east of the lake was a crime scene. The sheriff and his deputies were everywhere and would turn him away.

When Celeste finally pulled into the garage in Mountain Village, she thought Buckley would be waiting, ready to comfort or console her, but he wasn't.

She left the ski gear in the car and went into the house. The kitchen lights were off. Where was he?

"Buckley?" she called but got no answer.

Celeste pulled a glass from a cabinet and filled it with water, then sat down at the breakfast table and rested her head in her hands. When Bo appeared at her side, wagging his tail, she expected Buckley to be behind him. But he wasn't.

"I'm all right, sweet boy," she told the dog, patting the top of his head. "I just need a few minutes."

Bo wandered away, and Celeste sipped at the water. When she was done, she set the glass in the sink and started for the bedroom. She wanted to take a shower and lie down.

On the way to the stairs, she heard a muffled voice in the study and crossed through the living room to the open doors. Buckley was sitting at the desk, his back to her.

"I'm telling you one last time, Charlie, you find out what happened to her ASAP," Buckley barked into the phone. "And if your man screwed up, you sure as hell better make sure this doesn't lead back to me."

Celeste knew *Charlie* was Charlie Dungee. Through the years, Buckley often hired him to do odd jobs for his campaigns, but Celeste had never liked him. Charlie was a slick ex-con, the type who said one thing to your face and another behind your back.

Buckley ended the call and slammed the phone down on the desk. He swiveled the chair around and was startled to see her.

"You're home," he said, crossing the room to her. "I didn't know."

"What were you talking to Charlie about?"

Buckley wrapped his large arms around her and pulled her close. "Nothing you need to worry your pretty little head about," he replied. "Especially after the morning you've had. Why don't you tell me all about it. It'll make you feel better."

For hours, Celeste had managed to hold herself together, but now she felt like she would collapse. She buried her face in his large chest, fighting the urge to cry.

He squeezed her gently. "Honey, I'm sorry you had to be there."

"It was horrible," she said, her voice shaking.

"I'm sure it was."

She pushed back from him to collect herself. "At least I didn't see her. That poor detective was the one who found her."

"What?"

Celeste told him about the dog and the ravine, how it all happened.

"What was Jack Martin doing there?"

"Oh, darling, I forgot you didn't know. You were asleep when I left. He called you this morning, but when you didn't answer, he tried me. He had more questions about Gordon Quinn."

"Quinn? Why?"

"I'm not sure, but it doesn't matter now." She expected Buckley to agree, but from the look on his face, she could tell he didn't.

"What did you tell him?"

"Darling, Alice is dead. It doesn't matter now."

"It does," Buckley insisted. "I'm just trying to get the whole picture."

Celeste sighed, frustrated. "I told him that we suspected the Bierstadt we purchased from Gordon was a forgery. And that I insisted he buy it back from us."

"Shit, Celeste." Buckley dragged a hand down his face. "I told you not to talk to Martin."

"I don't understand what difference it makes." If Celeste's suspicions were right, that Alice was the one who had reported Gordon Quinn to the FBI, then so be it. None of it mattered anymore. She felt weary. "I'm taking a shower," she said, heading for the stairs.

Buckley followed her up. "What happened to Alice?"

At the top of the landing, Celeste turned to face him. "You finally want to know? Buckley, she was our friend."

He put a hand on her shoulder, but she shrugged it off and started for the bedroom.

"Honey, of course I'm upset about Alice. Tell me what happened. You mentioned the bridge. Do they know how she died?"

Celeste continued through the bedroom. "I don't think so," she said without looking back. She went into the closet and began to undress.

Buckley stood at the closet door. "What did they say?" When Celeste didn't answer, he hesitated. "Do they think it was murder?"

The question caught Celeste off guard. The events of the morning flashed through her mind. Of course she should have considered it. Alice wouldn't have wandered onto the bridge and fallen off—or jumped. It *had* to be murder.

Celeste looked up at him, the enormity of it all now weighing on her even heavier. "They didn't say anything about murder," she said, clutching her throat. "But maybe it was."

Buckley blinked several times. "What about a suspect?" he asked, shifting his weight from one foot to the other. "Did they mention anything?"

Celeste frowned. "A suspect?"

"Never mind," Buckley said, waving a hand. He backed into the bathroom counter and leaned against it.

He was staring at her, but it was like he was staring *through* her. Celeste knew his thoughts were elsewhere. She had come home, hoping he'd somehow make it all better, but he'd only made it worse. She wanted him to leave.

She sat down on a tufted ottoman in the closet. "Buckley, I'd like to take a shower," she said, pulling off her socks. When he didn't reply, she added, "Would you mind leaving me alone for a while?"

Buckley pushed himself off the counter. "There goes the campaign donation," he said quietly.

"What?" Celeste thought she'd heard him wrong.

"The campaign donation," he repeated, raising his hands, then letting them fall. "Kaput. That's that."

"Buckley!"

He offered a weak smile. "I'm kidding, Celeste. I'm just trying to lighten the mood."

But he wasn't kidding. Celeste knew how important Alice's campaign donations were and how he'd been counting on an even larger one for his presidential run.

"I'd like to be alone now," she said, and was relieved when he turned and left.

Celeste thought about the phone call she'd overheard—*You find out what happened to her ASAP.* Could Buckley and Charlie Dungee have been talking about Alice?

Then she remembered what Buckley had said next: *Make sure this doesn't lead back to me.* If they had been talking about Alice, why would anything lead back to him?

She had known for years that Buckley was capable of violating ethics—even breaking the law on occasion—but could he be involved in what had happened to Alice?

Celeste suddenly felt it difficult to breathe. With a quivering hand, she pulled open the shower door and turned on the hot water. As she stepped inside, she wondered how well she really knew her husband.

CHAPTER 44

GORDON QUINN'S MORNING had gone from bad to worse. He'd started the day analyzing the gallery's profits. December was usually one of his best months, but not last year. And if the first couple of weeks of January were an indication of how the new year would go, Gordon was in trouble.

He was sitting at his desk, bent over ledgers and printouts, when he heard the downstairs telephone ring.

A few seconds later, Macy's voice came over the intercom. "Mr. Quinn, the FBI is on the line."

Gordon felt his heart thump in his chest. What did they want now? The Feds had questioned him the day before, asked about the art he displayed in the gallery. It had been difficult, but he'd kept his cool and had answered their questions without so much as a stutter.

When the rumors of forgeries got out, he knew it was a possibility the Feds would show up one day. But he was ready and had his script memorized. As far as he knew, it had worked. So why were they calling him?

Gordon leaned forward and pushed the intercom on the phone. "Did you tell them I was here?"

"Uh…yes, sir."

Gordon jerked his arm back, releasing the button. "Idiot girl," he said aloud.

He twisted his mustache as he thought about what to do next. Then he leaned forward and pressed the intercom. "Tell them you can't find me, that I must have left for lunch and that I'll be back later. Take a message and say that I'll call them back." He needed more time to think.

Gordon went to a window and looked out. The morning had started overcast, but the clouds had cleared and the sky was a bright shade of blue. It was a beautiful day, but Gordon couldn't enjoy it.

He noticed Ryan Oliver across the street and watched as he made his way toward the gallery. Ryan was the *last* person Gordon wanted to see at the moment. The mess he was in with the Feds was Ryan's fault.

Gordon took the stairs to the first floor. "What do you want?" he asked as Ryan stepped into the gallery.

"Alice Fremont is dead!"

Gordon felt the color drain from his face. "What?"

"Alice is dead! They found her body."

"How do you know?"

"The sheriff's office put out a tweet. They said the east end of the lake, including the Nordic track, was closed while they recovered a body."

"And they said it was Alice?"

Ryan shook his head. He started to speak, but Gordon stopped him.

"Shh!" Gordon held up a hand and turned his back. "Of course it was her. Who else would it be?" This was bad. He started for the stairs. "Ryan, get up here."

Ryan followed.

Upstairs, Gordon opened a storage closet and took out two paintings. "Get this crap out of my office."

Ryan stared at him, confused.

Gordon shoved the paintings at him. "Take them and get out. Your idiotic plan is going to cost me everything. You're lucky I had already put these in the closet when the Feds showed up yesterday morning. I want them out of my gallery."

Ryan took the paintings but didn't move.

"Go!" Gordon yelled. "And don't come back!"

After Ryan left, Gordon worked in a frenzy, rummaging through his desk and several filing cabinets, searching for anything connected to Ryan Oliver. He spent twenty minutes shredding correspondence and invoices—everything that had Ryan's name on it.

Next, Gordon booted up his computer and opened his email account, then searched and deleted any mail sent or received from Ryan. It took almost an hour.

When he was finished, Gordon settled back into his chair to think. There were no more forgeries left in the gallery, and everything connecting him to Ryan Oliver had been destroyed.

What next? Gordon thought. He remembered the painting he'd sold to Alice and the one she'd taken on loan that he'd first sold to Celeste Bailey. His mouth went dry. That could be a problem.

He remembered the heated exchange when Alice had come into the gallery a couple of weeks before. He went downstairs and approached Macy. She was sitting behind the reception desk, scrolling through social media on her phone. She looked up nervously when she realized he was standing there.

She's a stupid girl, Gordon thought. *This just might work.*

With his calm restored, Gordon studied her slack jaw of stupidity, the anxious, downcast eyes. He should have fired her months ago.

"Macy," he said. "You heard Ryan say that Alice Fremont is dead?"

Macy nodded.

Gordon talked slowly, like he was speaking to a child. "I need you to think about it, Macy. Think really hard. Was Alice here at the gallery a couple of weeks ago?"

Macy's brows creased. She studied Gordon for a clue on how to answer. "I—I think it was a week ago last Wednesday," she stuttered. "Maybe Thursday?"

Gordon smiled but shook his head. "Alice was never here, Macy."

She thought about it for a moment, still frowning, then shook her head slowly. "No, I guess she wasn't."

"That's right," Gordon said. He took her hand and stared at her. "Alice was never here. Do you understand, Macy?"

She eased her hand from his grip and nodded. "Yes, sir."

CHAPTER 45

LARS HAD LEFT the house early that morning to be at the front of the lift line when it opened. If he had to be stuck in the mountains, he was at least going to get in as much snowboarding as he could.

Waiting around for his mother was a drag. He'd give her a few more days, then split for California. Although he liked snowboarding, he preferred surfing—and warmer weather. But he needed cash from the old lady or he wouldn't have a place to stay when he got back.

Lars thought of the redheaded backup singer he'd met while trying to sign the band she sang for. She was nothing special to look at, but she had shown an interest in him. He could use it to his advantage. All he needed was a couch.

His first two runs that morning had been cold, the sky a frosty, overcast gray. But by his fourth trip up, the sun had broken through the clouds. He raced down the slopes on his board, sliding back and forth, dodging skiers, the wind freezing the exposed parts of his face.

At the bottom, as Lars waited in the lift line again, he felt his cell phone vibrate. It was buried deep in a pocket of his pants and would be difficult to reach under his jacket. He ignored it. But several minutes later, as he rode the chair up, it vibrated again.

Lars glanced down at his snowboard dangling below the chair and estimated he was at least thirty feet above the ground. He thought about digging the phone out of his pocket but decided against it. One mishap and the iPhone would be lost in the snow below.

Before he reached the top of the lift, the phone vibrated a third time. Someone was desperate to reach him.

At the top of the mountain, Lars hopped off the lift, hobbled on one foot, dragging his board behind him with the other. As he pulled the phone out of his pocket, the screen lit up. He saw the caller ID and frowned. There was a message from the sheriff's department.

"Mr. Fremont, I'm calling on behalf of Sheriff Tony Burns of the San Miguel County Sheriff's Office. We understand from Sally Eagle that you are currently staying in Telluride. The sheriff has requested that you return to your mother's house immediately."

Lars made his way down the mountain. In the parking lot, he tossed his snowboard and boots into the back of the Jeep. On his way to the house, he ran through all the scenarios he could think of for why the sheriff would want to talk to him.

Had the hot checks he'd written finally caught up with him? Or the fraudulent credit card charges? Had the LAPD called Sheriff Burns? Requested they arrest Lars so he could be extradited to California? It seemed a stretch. Lars had made sure the charges were below a thousand dollars, knowing petty theft was usually swept under the rug, not worth bothering with.

When Lars turned off the highway on Trout Lake Road, he knew immediately that whatever the sheriff wanted to talk to him about had nothing to do with credit card theft.

A deputy stood in the middle of the road with his hand up. A Tahoe was parked off to the side. Lars rolled his window down.

"Road's closed, buddy. You gotta turn around."

"I'm Lars Fremont. I got a call from the sheriff's office saying to come home."

The deputy's face was somber. He stepped away from the Jeep and turned his back, then said something into a radio. After a few seconds, he approached the Jeep again.

"You're cleared through. Sheriff Burns said to go directly to the house and wait for him there. He'll be up shortly to talk to you."

As Lars neared the eastern edge of the lake, he

noticed a flurry of activity. There were several Tahoes from the sheriff's office and a couple of unmarked trucks parked in the lot just off the cross-country track. The entire area had been cordoned off with yellow police tape. It looked like a scene out of a movie.

He drove slowly, taking it all in. A handful of men searched the snow along the bank of the ravine. Someone in uniform stood bent at the waist on the old trestle bridge, looking over the side.

Lars remembered playing on the abandoned bridge as a child. While stuck on the estate summer after summer, despite the warning signs, he'd spent hours walking across it and exploring the ravine and narrow river below. It was a wonder the old thing hadn't fallen out from underneath him.

The area was a crime scene now. Lars wondered what all the commotion was about, feeling a pit form in his stomach.

He pulled through the entrance to his mother's estate, wound his way to the house, and was surprised to see Johnny Eagle's truck parked there instead of down at the barn.

Lars went in through the back door and found Johnny and Sally sitting at the long table in the kitchen. Sally looked like she'd been crying.

"What's going on?" Lars asked.

Sally started to say something but then dropped her head and began to cry.

Johnny got up from the table. "A deputy came. They said to stay here. They will return and tell us what has happened."

It was the most words Lars had ever heard the Indian string together. And why was Sally crying? Something was going on.

But it was too much to think about before a shower. He took the stairs to his room and peeled off his wet clothes. In the bathroom, he stepped under the hot water, letting it warm him.

His thoughts turned again to the old bridge, the deputies, the crime scene tape. Why did the sheriff want to speak with him? Whatever it was, Lars had nothing to do with it.

Then it hit him like a sledgehammer. Something had happened to his mother.

CHAPTER 46

SALLY WAS AT the kitchen table, her head in her hands, struggling not to cry. Johnny was sitting across from her. He wouldn't approve of any display of emotion.

But something had happened to Alice. Sally had suspected it ever since she'd arrived at the house Sunday morning and found her missing. When the deputy had come earlier and instructed her and Johnny not to leave the house until the sheriff came and spoke to them, he'd all but confirmed it.

After the deputy left, Sally had run down to the barn and told Johnny. He'd driven them back up to the house, and they'd been in the kitchen ever since.

She stole a glance across the table at Johnny. He was sitting quietly, studying the backs of his hands, an empty coffee cup in front of him. Their life as they knew it would be over. Sally wondered what would happen to the estate. Would new buyers want her and Johnny to stay on? If not, they would have to find other jobs. But they were in their fifties now. Who would hire them? She and Johnny had scraped together small savings over the years, but not enough to live on.

Johnny was picking at a callus on the side of his hand. Sally knew he would be wondering and worrying about the same things.

Sally didn't want a new job. She liked working at Castle in the Clouds, liked working for Alice. She felt her eyes start to water and swallowed, fighting back the tears. She couldn't let herself cry.

When Lars came through the door, he had startled them. It wasn't until he left the kitchen that Sally thought of the conversation he'd had with his mother several months earlier. Sally had answered the call in the kitchen. Alice was in the parlor and had picked up the extension on a side table. Before Sally could leave the room, they were already arguing. On the way back to the kitchen, she had overheard Alice threaten to disinherit him.

Sally sat at the table, remembering. Alice had gone missing the day before Lars arrived. Had he actually gotten to the house a day earlier? Would Lars have hurt his mother? The timing of his visit troubled her.

She watched Johnny pick at the callus and felt her stomach twist into knots. She hadn't told him about the conversation she'd overheard and debated whether she should tell him now. Should she tell the sheriff?

Sally got up from the table, took the coffeepot

from the counter, then refilled Johnny's cup, agonizing over what to say. She sat back down and leaned across the table.

"I might know something," she said in a shaky whisper.

Johnny frowned, making her nervous. "Know what?"

Sally twisted her hands in her lap. "Something Mrs. Fremont told Lars." She paused, summoning the courage to continue. "Maybe it made him angry."

Johnny's gaze shot toward the hallway and back. He looked alarmed. He dropped his voice. "You tell them nothing," he insisted. "As the sun rises in the east, their laws will bite you if you interfere."

"But maybe it would help—"

"Leave it be, Sally. This is not our business." He snatched the coffee, then leaned back, watching her over the rim as he drank. He set the cup down with a thud. "When the sheriff comes, I will go to the door."

For as long as she'd known him, Johnny had fiercely guarded his privacy. People looked at him suspiciously, some even calling him a "recluse" or a "hermit." Sally knew his behavior stemmed from his run-in with the law years before. As a teenager, he'd been accused of stealing cattle from a ranch outside Cortez. It was a crime he hadn't committed. But an eyewitness had identified him, along with several men in a local cattle-rustling ring. Johnny had served nearly three years in jail before one of the others had laughingly told a cellmate that "the Indian was innocent." Less than a month later, Johnny was exonerated and let out of prison.

But even after he was released, Johnny wasn't able to shake the stigma of being a convict. He retreated from the world and had never trusted strangers or law enforcement again.

Johnny didn't want her to tell the sheriff about Alice's argument with Lars. But Johnny was wrong. Alice was one of the few people who trusted him. She'd given him a job when no one else would. Now something had happened to her.

Sally decided that despite what Johnny said, she would do what she could to help. If the sheriff had questions, she would answer them truthfully. She would tell him what she knew, about the missing manuscript and the suitcase. And about Lars.

CHAPTER 47

IT WAS SEVERAL hours before Jack left Trout Lake. He wanted to accompany Sheriff Burns to Alice's estate, be there as they searched the house and questioned Sally and Johnny Eagle, but the sheriff had said no. "You're not law enforcement anymore," Burns had said. "We can't have civilians involved in the investigation."

Jack had been angry, arguing that he was the one who had found Alice's body and that he had more experience than all of Burns's young deputies combined. But deep down Jack knew Burns was right—the sheriff's hands were tied. Jack had been investigating a missing person, but it was now a homicide. The case belonged to the San Miguel County Sheriff's Office.

In the end, Burns had agreed to keep him abreast of any significant discoveries. In turn, Jack agreed to share any information he thought of later that might be relevant to the case.

In his statement, Jack had told Burns and the county investigator about meeting Alice before she went missing, about her concern for her safety and the attempted break-in. The investigator had taken notes as Jack recounted his search of the house, with the help from Sally Eagle and Eva Sheppard, for Alice's missing manuscript and told him about the missing suitcase.

They asked Jack where he'd been the night she went missing, then requested he remain in the area until further notice. He knew that because he had found and reported the body, at least for a while, he'd be a suspect.

At the campground, Jack parked the truck and followed Crockett through the snow. They found Otto sitting at the picnic table, warming his gloved hands over the charcoal grill. Crockett ambled up beside him, wagging his tail.

"Hello, friend," Otto said, reaching to pet the dog.

"Would you mind keeping him for me again?" Jack asked. "I won't be as long this time. I just need a bite to eat." He wanted to talk to Judith Hadley.

"You go on," Otto said, waving toward town. "Crockett and I'll be here when you get back."

"Thank you." Jack started to go.

"You gonna find that woman's killer?"

Jack turned back. It had been only a few hours. How did he know? "You heard?"

Otto poked at the charcoal with the blunt end of

a stick, sending sparks airborne. "Word travels fast in a small town."

Jack looked around them. There wasn't another person in sight. "Did you go into town today?"

Otto stared into the charcoal and shook his head, still poking at the fire.

The rusted bicycle was still propped against the tent, buried in a foot of snow. It hadn't moved in days, maybe longer.

Otto noticed Jack looking and grinned. "Think maybe I did it?" There was a menacing twinkle in his old eyes.

"Did it"? Jack wondered. Was he talking about killing Alice?

Jack stared back at him, considering the possibility. It was ridiculous. But he knew from experience that underestimating someone could be a deadly mistake.

He saw Otto reach into the pocket of his tattered old coat.

Weapon. It screamed through Jack's mind. His instinct was to go for his own. But it was in the trailer, hidden in the compartment under the bed.

Otto pulled something from his pocket, and Jack flinched, ready to take cover in the trees. The old man busted out laughing and held up what was in his hand.

"Take it easy, son." Otto started to cough, then laughed some more. "It's a police scanner."

Jack let out the breath he'd been holding. He was about to let Otto have it but watched the old man pet Crockett, still chuckling.

"We got him good, boy, didn't we?" Otto bounced in his chair, still giggling like a child. He sat up and wiped his eyes. "I'm sorry, Jack. You've got to indulge an old codger. That was more fun than I've had in a long time."

Jack didn't reply, and the two men stared at each other for several awkward seconds. Jack held the look as long as he could, then felt it start low in his gut. Soon the two men were howling in laughter together.

"What in the world do you have a scanner for?"

Otto shrugged. "Keeps me company."

Jack eyed him suspiciously, knowing there would be more to the story.

"All right, all right," Otto finally said. "I told you, sometimes I do a little prospecting."

Jack didn't understand how it explained the scanner. "So?"

Otto shrugged again.

It was all Jack was going to get. He nodded toward Crockett. "Thank you again for keeping him."

Otto petted the dog. "Anytime. We're buddies, right, Crockett?"

Jack watched the two for a second, then shook his head and started again for town. Otto Finn was an odd bird, but Jack liked him. But he wondered what prank the crazy old guy would pull next.

CHAPTER 48

LARS STOOD AT the bathroom mirror, a towel wrapped around his waist. He leaned forward, studying the whites of his eyes.

He was sure of it. His mother was dead. It explained everything—why she hadn't returned his calls, why she hadn't been there when he arrived.

But why would she be at the Nordic track? Had she wandered out of the house and fallen into the ravine? Maybe she was sleepwalking? As hard as he tried, Lars couldn't come up with a plausible reason for her being there. His mother rarely left the estate, and he'd never heard of her being anywhere near the bridge except to drive past it.

Lars pulled back from the mirror and looked down into the sink, realizing that his mother was gone. He felt an unfamiliar lump form in his throat.

He had always been his mother's favorite. He knew it—even Hugh knew it. He wasn't sure if he ever loved her in return, but he was fond of her and her crazy antics. Through the years, the way she pissed people off had been entertaining to watch. Lars would miss her.

He might have loved her as a child; he couldn't remember. She was never just "Mom," but "Alice Fremont, famous author." From the beginning, while she traveled the world promoting her books, Lars had regularly been left in the care of nannies and housekeepers.

Her books, Lars thought. *Of course that's what happened.* He thought of the threats and attacks. Someone had finally gotten their revenge and murdered her.

He should call Hugh. Did he know? As quickly as the idea popped into his head, Lars dismissed it. He'd never liked his pompous half brother. He'd let him find out about Alice on his own.

At any minute, the sheriff was going to show up to tell Lars that his mother was dead. Would he expect him to rant and rave, demanding justice? Or even worse—cry?

Lars had seen enough true crime shows on television to know that relatives were always the first suspects. He'd have to show some sort of emotion.

Lars placed a hand on each side of the sink and leaned toward the mirror. He screwed up his face, trying to make himself cry. After several seconds, he gave up. It wasn't going to work.

He opened a drawer, pulled out a tube of toothpaste, and unscrewed the top. He squeezed a tiny amount onto the tip of his index finger, then dabbed the corner of each eye.

"Damn," he said aloud, rubbing his eyes. He threw the tube back into the drawer and shut it, then studied his eyes in the mirror. They were bloodshot and glassy with tears. "That's better."

He went into the bedroom and dug through his suitcase, tossing aside several concert tees until he found what he was looking for. He pulled on a plain, long-sleeved navy shirt and a pair of jeans.

As he started down the stairs, the doorbell rang. Before he reached the bottom, Johnny Eagle had emerged from the kitchen and opened it. It was Sheriff Burns and four deputies. Lars was surprised to see so many. It wasn't at all what he expected.

He recognized one of the deputies as the young upstart who'd arrested him for DWI the year before and was pretty sure one of the others had given him the MIP he'd received several years before that. Lars was no stranger to local law enforcement.

The sheriff stepped toward him. He was short but thick with a stern face. Lars had always been intimidated by him.

"Lars, I'm sorry to inform you that your mother's body was found below the trestle bridge earlier this morning."

Lars tried to look stunned, then dropped his head

in his hands, secretly poking his bloodshot eyes until he felt them start to water.

Burns gave him a moment.

When Lars looked back up, he stammered, "Wh-what happened?"

"We don't know yet. But I assure you, we're going to find out."

Sheriff Burns handed him a sheet of paper—a search warrant.

Lars stood stunned as the deputies filed into the house. Just behind them were several men in white jumpsuits carrying leather cases.

"These guys are from forensics," Sheriff Burns said. "We'll get this done as soon as we can and then get out of your way."

Burns introduced a plainclothes officer as an investigator with the department. "He'll have a few questions for you before we leave."

"Is this a homicide case?" Lars asked. "Did someone *kill* my mother?"

"We won't know for sure until we get the autopsy back, but we're assuming it is until we learn otherwise."

Soon, law enforcement was all over the house like ants.

Johnny and Sally Eagle were back at the kitchen table, but Lars wasn't about to sit still. He watched as the forensic team dusted surfaces for fingerprints and vacuumed rugs and furniture, collecting samples and sealing them in plastic bags.

He went upstairs and into his mother's suite. The desk had remnants of black powder scattered across the top. Lars realized they'd probably lifted his prints and felt his heart beat heavy in his chest. He would have to come up with an excuse for why he'd been at the desk.

The investigator rounded the corner of Alice's bedroom, startling him.

"Please step away from the desk," the investigator said. "Forensics is done with it, but I'm not."

Lars stepped to the side and pretended to study the wall of books on the opposite wall of the room. He watched out of the corner of his eye as the investigator pulled open the top drawer and carefully examined its contents with gloved hands.

He checked the file drawer next, taking his time to rummage through each of the files. Lars saw him pull out the one labeled PERSONAL INFORMATION. *The will.* Would they consider Lars a suspect when they found out how much he stood to inherit? Lars hoped he wouldn't find it.

But the investigator pulled it from the stack, holding it by a corner. "Have you ever seen this?"

Lars made a quick decision. "No. Those are my mother's private papers."

"Did she ever discuss her will with you?"

Lars shook his head. "I guess she figured it was none of my business."

The investigator scanned the pages. "Then you don't know that she's probably left you a sizable inheritance."

Lars sifted through possible responses like lightning. "Uh...I figured it'd be somewhat sizable." He swept a hand around the room. "My mother was a very wealthy woman."

The investigator stared at him for several excruciating seconds. When he finally nodded, seeming satisfied with the answer, Lars was relieved. He watched as the investigator started to put the will back into the folder but hesitated, then stood up and walked out into the hall.

"Frank?" he hollered down the corridor. One of the men in white emerged from another room. "Let's print this."

Lars felt his stomach lurch up to his throat.

CHAPTER 49

THE SUN WAS shining, but it was cold, the windchill hovering just above zero. Jack ducked his head and pulled his coat tight, trying to block the wind that blew at him, making the climb toward town a struggle.

He crossed the street, headed for Pandora Café, but a window display caught his eye. Several pairs of insulated boots in various shades of brown and gray were arranged in a row. They had thick rubber soles and laces. They looked peculiar but warm.

Jack glanced down at the scuffed Red Wings he'd bought years earlier. They were still wet from the ravine. He stepped into the store and was immediately greeted by a salesclerk.

"Can I help you find something?" He was a tall kid, with a friendly smile that stretched ear to ear.

Jack hesitated, then turned to the boots in the window and pointed to a brown pair. "I'd like to try on a pair of these."

"Good choice," the kid said, bobbing his head in approval. He asked for Jack's size, then disappeared into the back.

Jack took off the Red Wings and set them aside. They looked like he'd walked from Texas in them.

The clerk returned a few seconds later with a box and held out the boots. Jack pulled them on, then laced them up and stood in front of the mirror. He studied them from the front, then turned and looked from the side. There was one thing he was sure of: John Wayne—Jack's hero since he was a boy—wouldn't have been caught dead in them.

They were made of a waterproof material, their thick rubber soles wrapping slightly over the top. Jack thought they made him look like a duck. But his feet had never felt so warm.

He turned to the clerk. "I'll take them."

As Jack walked to Pandora Café, he was sure he saw several people glance down at his boots. Almost everyone wore something similar, but Jack was convinced that on him they looked ridiculous. But he didn't care; his feet were dry for the first time in hours.

At the café, he chose the same table next to the fireplace and pulled out a chair, its legs screeching in protest against the uneven wood floor. He set the bag with his wet boots down and turned toward the flames, letting them warm his face. The morning had finally caught up with him and he felt weary.

He thought of Alice. Death was something he'd never gotten used to. Whether it was a bullet-riddled body in the aftermath of gang violence, the corpse of a fugitive shot down in the pursuit of justice, or the frozen grimace of Alice Fremont, the sight of death chilled him.

The memory of finding his grandparents murdered still haunted him after twenty-four years.

"Been shopping?" Judith Hadley set a plate of pecan pralines on the table in front of him, then wiped her hands on her apron.

"Boots." Jack kicked a foot out from under the table.

Judith looked at them and nodded. "A wise choice. Those old cowboy things of yours weren't going to make it much longer in the snow." She noticed something in his face and frowned. "Another bad day?"

"You could say that."

She surveyed the remaining diners. "Give me ten minutes to get these last few tables out of here. You can tell me all about it."

Jack wasn't sure how much he wanted to tell her about finding Alice at the bottom of the ravine. But then he remembered what Otto had said. *Word travels fast in a small town.* She was going to find out anyway.

"I'd like that," he said.

Judith took his order. Several minutes later a waitress set a bowl of steaming chicken and dumplings down in front of him. He leaned in and sniffed. He was hungry.

As he scraped the bowl clean, Judith tossed her

apron over the back of an empty chair and sat down. "You're trying to hide it, but I can tell something's bothering you. So spill."

Jack wiped his mouth with a paper napkin. "Is it that obvious?"

He spent the next ten minutes telling her what had happened. As he talked, Judith sat motionless, her forearms propped on the table as she listened. When he finished, she sat back against the chair.

"Alice." Her voice caught in her throat. "I just can't believe it."

"I'm sorry to be the one to tell you. I know she was your friend."

Judith reached across the table and laid a hand on Jack's arm. "She *was* my friend. And this makes me madder than hell. But I'm glad you were the one who told me." She gave his arm a gentle squeeze, then released it.

"The sheriff's office is investigating it," Jack said. "They'll find out what happened."

"No." She shook her head. "There hasn't been a murder in Telluride since I've been here, Jack. And that's been a long time. *You* have to look into this. You're the one with experience."

"Tony Burns made it clear he didn't want my help."

"I don't care what he said."

"Burns seems like a good man."

She shook her head again. "Maybe he is, but if he doesn't want your help, then he's an idiot."

What Judith said was true, but Jack kept it to himself. It wasn't his case.

"Jack, I know Alice had a lot of enemies, but she didn't deserve this—thrown out in the snow like that. If you hadn't discovered her, who knows when her body would have been found?"

What had happened to Alice didn't sit well with Jack, either. He'd met her only once, didn't know her the way Judith had, but nobody deserved what had happened to her. Someone needed to be brought to justice.

And he shared Judith's concerns about law enforcement. If what she said was true, that they didn't have a lot of experience investigating a homicide, unless CBI, Colorado Bureau of Investigation got involved, they would need help.

Whoever had done this to Alice was smart. Jack had searched the estate himself. Experience told him that an amateur would have left clues—they always did. Whoever killed Alice knew what they were doing and was intelligent enough to know how to cover it up. Unless Burns called in help from CBI, Colorado Bureau of Investigation—they would need his help.

Judith stared into the gas logs, lost in her memories or grief—Jack wasn't sure which.

"Do they have any idea who did it?" she asked, breaking the silence.

"Not yet."

"What about you? Do you have any ideas?"

Jack had a handful of suspects, but he wasn't ready to reveal them yet.

When Judith realized he wasn't going to answer, she frowned. "Well, I hope those two wretched sons of hers are at the top of your list."

Relatives were always suspects until they could be ruled out. But it wasn't Jack's case, and he wasn't about to discuss suspects in public.

"It sounds like Alice had a lot of enemies," he said. "There's no telling who killed her."

Judith leaned in, dropping her voice. "Just don't leave this up to the local guys, Jack. Help them if you can. If not, investigate it on your own. But find out what happened to her."

"I'll think about it," he said to appease her, but he wasn't in any condition to make a decision yet. She held his gaze, and he added, "I promise I'll think about it."

Judith patted his hand. "That's all I can ask. You're a good man, Jack Martin." She stood up, then pushed her chair back under the table. "Did you get your dog back?"

"I did."

She smiled. "I told you you would." She turned and straightened the chairs at an adjacent table.

Jack thought about her request for him to find Alice's killer. He hadn't given Judith a definitive answer, but deep down he knew it would be hard to walk away. He needed to get back to the trailer and think.

He left cash on the table and put on his coat.

"Hold on a minute," Judith called from across the room, then disappeared into the kitchen. She emerged a moment later, holding a brown paper bag. "Take this to Otto for me. It's a turkey club, mustard instead of mayonnaise—just the way he likes it."

"I'll give it to him." Jack took a step to leave but stopped. "Did you know that Otto has a police scanner?"

Judith shot him a sly smile. "He's a prospector, Jack. But this time of year, he can't make it all the way up to his own claim." Jack didn't say anything, and she added, "Do you know how much of the land around here is owned by the government? A lot." She chuckled.

The old black phone on the counter rang, and she went to answer it.

Jack tucked the bag under his arm and started for the door. He was warming fast to the locals in Telluride. He liked Judith. And although he'd known her for only a few days, for some reason he didn't understand, he didn't want to disappoint her.

The mystery of who killed Alice gnawed at his gut. And by the time he stepped out of the café into the frigid wind, Jack knew what he had to do.

CHAPTER 50

BY MIDAFTERNOON, HUGH Sheppard had sobered up, but he couldn't calm his nerves. His hand shook every time he raised his glass of water to his lips, and he wasn't sure why.

His mother was dead. It was upsetting—and likely contributing to his anxiety—but he wasn't surprised. All the threats, the attacks, they were bound to catch up with her.

Thinking about his mother had set off a storm of mixed emotions. Hugh's relationship with her had never been the same after Lars was born. Following years of therapy, and insisting he didn't care that his younger brother was the favorite, he eventually realized it had actually wounded him deeply.

The few times Hugh had tried drawing closer to her, he'd been rebuffed. It was obvious that although Alice wanted him near, she didn't want him too close. It was as if she had liked the idea of having a family but hadn't really wanted one. And it wasn't just her sons; Alice had treated Eva with the same contempt. Although she had been thrilled when Hugh married her, soon after the wedding, Alice had turned a cold shoulder. As much as Eva grated on him, Hugh knew he needed her and appreciated her perseverance in tolerating his mother.

Hugh carried the empty water glass to the bar and stared at the bottle of vodka sitting on the counter. He'd give anything for another martini, but knew he'd have to wait until after the sheriff had been there. He stuck the empty glass into the sink for the housekeeper.

He paced the living room and lost track of time. A while later, he glanced at his watch. Eva had been upstairs for ages. Hugh wanted company. He started for the foyer and heard the familiar click of stiletto heels descending the marble stairs.

"Where've you been?"

"Lying down." She leaned in and kissed him, her blond hair brushing his cheek. "Are you feeling better? You still do not look well."

"I feel horrible."

Eva put a hand on his forehead and frowned. "You are hot." She took his hand and led him back into the living room. "Lie down. I am going to get you a glass of water."

"I've drunk gallons already," Hugh grumbled. "I feel like a damn fish."

"Well, lie down anyway. I am going to get you more."

Hugh didn't want water—he wanted answers. He wanted to know when the sheriff would call or stop by and what he was going to ask. Had they figured out what had happened to his mother? And more importantly, was Hugh a suspect?

He ran a hand over his bald head, a nervous habit from the days when he still had hair. "I should call Dennis Musk."

"The attorney?" Eva handed him a glass of water.

He took it, but annoyed she hadn't put ice in it, he set it on the coffee table. "Yes, the attorney. Do we know another Dennis Musk?"

"Sweetheart, I hate to tell you, but the news of your mother has already spread."

"Spread where?"

"Across town—across the internet. People are tweeting and putting it on Facebook. They must have took wind of it—"

"*Got* wind of it," Hugh corrected her.

"Anyway, they must have heard about it from the sheriff. But you know Shirley Newton—"

"The busybody who works at the spa?" He reached for the glass.

"Yes, but she is nice, Hugh. Anyway, Shirley posted a message on Facebook to say how shocked and sorry she was for our family. When I saw the post, it already had many comments from friends offering sympathy."

Hugh swirled the water in the glass but didn't drink it. "Why are you telling me this?"

"To let you know people are hearing about this, sweetheart. That the word is in that Alice—"

"*Out.* The word is *out.*"

She leaned over and took his hand. "Hugh?"

He stared into the swirling water, and she squeezed his hand.

"They are coming," she said.

"Who?"

"Someone to question us."

It would be someone from the sheriff's office. Hugh wished they'd hurry up. He wanted to get it over with so he could have another martini.

"You have to be ready, sweetheart. You look terrible."

"Thank you."

Eva let out an exaggerated sigh. "You can look upset, Hugh, but you can't look like you might be *guilty.*"

The doorbell rang.

Hugh felt his pulse quicken. Damned woman. It was the worst thing she could have said to him. His anxiety returned with a vengeance.

As Eva went to answer the door, Hugh stayed on the sofa, taking in and releasing deep breaths, willing his heart rate to slow. He could hear Eva talking to a man, their voices echoing in the marble foyer. But then there were more voices, not just two. It sounded as if a small army had descended on the house.

Eva marched back into the room, Sheriff Tony Burns following closely on her heels. Eva looked angry.

She held out a sheet of paper. "They have a search warrant."

Hugh felt the color drain from his face. They thought he was guilty.

CHAPTER 51

As a struggling artist, Ryan Oliver couldn't afford to live where he wanted or where he thought he deserved. Home was a studio apartment in a second-rate complex on the west side of town.

There was no view of the box canyon or Ingram Falls to the east, or the sprawling valley floor to the west. When Ryan opened his door, he looked directly into the dark brown siding of the adjacent building.

His Telluride digs didn't look much different from the apartment he'd had in Tampa, Florida. If he thought about it, it depressed him. But after what had happened at the gallery that morning, it now made him angry.

Gordon had no right to talk to him that way, practically throwing his paintings at him and ordering him out of the gallery. For almost two years, Gordon had let Ryan display his work at Quinn Gallery, while he painted forgeries on the side. But not anymore.

Everything had been going fine until Gordon loaned Alice Fremont the painting that Celeste Bailey had returned. Celeste was a sophisticated collector, a connoisseur. It was a mistake for Gordon to sell it to her in the first place.

The landscape was one of Ryan's best works—a near-perfect forgery of an Albert Bierstadt original.

But after Celeste insisted Gordon take it back, giving her a refund, he let Alice take it out on loan. If only he had sold it to some unsuspecting tourist, or even a wealthy part-time resident who had more money than art sense.

But they had been Gordon's mistakes, not his.

Ryan still wondered what it was about the painting that had raised Celeste's suspicions. He had taken great care in selecting just the right Bierstadts to copy.

Albert Bierstadt had been a prolific artist, painting hundreds, some say thousands, of landscapes of the American West. Ryan had researched his works until he felt his eyeballs would fall out. He had carefully chosen a handful to forge—landscapes of the Rocky Mountains, pieces that would appeal to the gallery's rich clientele. Ryan knew better than to forge one of Bierstadt's famous pieces, which someone might recognize.

There had been other forgeries, oils from lesser-known artists. Alice Fremont had purchased one of Ryan's early ones, a herd of elk. It was one of his favorites.

He and Gordon had started out small, but when

the scheme proved profitable, they had moved on and forged more prominent artists.

The plan had been nearly foolproof. Sell the forged art at the six-figure prices an original Bierstadt would command, with little risk that any of the gallery's customers were educated enough to spot them as fakes.

When Ryan had pitched Gordon the plan, he had leaped at the opportunity to shore up the gallery's sagging profits. Ryan had done Gordon a favor yet had been repaid by being thrown out like the day's trash. The more Ryan thought about it, the angrier he got.

The television in his tiny apartment was tuned into a Denver news station. Ryan was parked on the tattered couch staring at it but not paying any attention.

Earlier, as he'd walked home, Eva had called. Ryan had told her how Gordon had treated him, about his threats and being thrown out. He should have kept the story to himself, but he'd needed to vent.

The week before, he'd come clean with her. Told her about the forgeries, how Alice had confronted Gordon. And how afterward Gordon had taken his frustrations out on Ryan, threatening to ruin him if their scam was exposed.

He now knew that telling Eva about their scheme had been a mistake. The more people who knew about their scam, the greater chance it would be uncovered.

He had a good thing going with Eva. She was beautiful and married to an entitled pompous ass—easy pickings for a good-looking, young artist. He enjoyed their time together, but mostly he had enjoyed the free meals and occasional gifts. The fact that Eva had purchased several of his paintings from the gallery was icing on the cake.

They'd been seeing each other for almost a year. But now, like his side hustle forging Bierstadts, the gig was over. Eva hadn't taken the news well, alternating between screaming and crying into the phone, her tirade lasting almost the entire walk home.

Ryan was exhausted. He turned off the television and laid his head back against the couch, covering his face with his hands. Nothing was going as planned.

He didn't know how he was going to make a living. Winter wasn't kind to artists in Telluride. He needed warm days and a place off Main Street to set up his easel, somewhere in the path of tourists flushed with vacation euphoria and cash.

What he *did* know was that he wasn't going to spend one day longer than he had to living in low-income housing. If there wasn't money to be made in Telluride, he'd take his talents elsewhere—Aspen maybe, or Jackson Hole.

But he couldn't think about that yet.

Gordon Quinn had given him one last job to do and had threatened him with his life if he screwed it up.

CHAPTER 52

HUGH SAT ON the white leather sofa for nearly an hour, listening to them search his house. He heard their footsteps on the stairs as they went up and down, heard them going through closets and the kitchen cabinets. The alarm beeped every time someone opened an exterior door.

He watched through the living room windows as officers trekked through the snow, poking at the drifts with long metal rods.

Eva had disappeared soon after she announced their arrival, probably supervising—making sure nothing was damaged as they rummaged through her things and under her precious furniture.

Hugh sat alone on the sofa, having switched from water to diet soda, downing one after another. He was itching for a martini.

Sheriff Burns walked into the living room, a young deputy close behind.

"Hugh, let's go into the kitchen," Burns said.

Hugh got up and followed him out of the room.

When they got to the kitchen, Burns said, "We're

finished in here." He pulled out a stool from under the white marble island and took a seat. "I thought you'd be more comfortable out of the way while they checked the living room."

Hugh didn't reply. He set his soda down, yanked a stool from under the island, and sat.

Burns laid his hands on the cool marble surface. "Look, Hugh. I'm real sorry about this. But it's procedure. Like I told Eva, we got an anonymous call saying there was evidence somewhere in or around the house that would help us find out what happened to your mother."

Hugh kept quiet. He'd already answered dozens of questions, telling the sheriff over and over that he didn't know anything about his mother's death or what might have happened to her. And that there would be no evidence found in his house. He was ready for all of them to leave.

"Sheriff Burns?" The voice came from upstairs. "I've got something you need to see."

Burns slid off the stool and disappeared around the corner into the foyer.

Eva marched into the kitchen and dug through the wine refrigerator. "They're searching the house like we are common criminals. It is demeaning, and I will file a complaint. The least they can do is help me find our car keys—I cannot imagine where they are. But they wouldn't even listen to me, Hugh. I tried to give them the description—an expensive red Bvlgari key ring with pavé diamonds—but they did not care. They acted like it was of no significance. It is a small courtesy to let me know if they find it while they are groping my personal things."

When Hugh didn't respond, he saw her shut the refrigerator and turn to him out of the corner of his eye. She gave him a few more seconds to say something, then came around the bar. She leaned over and whispered harshly into his ear.

"You look like the shits, Hugh. Pull yourself together like a man. They are going to see your face and see that you have written guilty all over it."

Sometimes Hugh hated his Eurotrash wife. He turned to her, his face screwed into a snarl, ready to unleash his frustration, but Sheriff Burns was back in the room.

Eva straightened up and took a step away from Hugh, plastering a dazzling fake smile on her face for the sheriff.

"I've got a few more questions for you, Hugh," Burns said, his amiable tone now gone.

Sensing the tension, Eva stood silent and ramrod straight.

Burns studied Hugh closely. "We understand the manuscript for your mother's new book is missing."

"You already asked me about that. I have no idea where it is."

"The only other thing that we know of that's missing is one of her suitcases."

Hugh let out a frustrated sigh. "Again, I already told you. I don't know anything about that, either."

The sheriff stared at him, making Hugh nervous.

Burns leaned closer. "We just found your mother's suitcase in the back of your closet. The luggage tag has her name on it."

Eva brought her hand to her throat. "H-Hugh?"

Hugh looked from the sheriff to Eva, then back to the sheriff again. As he did, he broke out in a cold sweat, his vision closing in until he could only see two pinpricks of light. He opened his mouth, but his throat had constricted and he was unable to speak.

The last thing he remembered was sliding off the stool and crashing to the cold marble floor.

CHAPTER 53

AFTER HE LEFT the café, Jack went back to the camp-ground, determined to begin his own investigation. He'd take a few minutes to clear his head, then sort through all his notes and analyze everything he knew with fresh eyes.

After grabbing Crockett from Otto and taking him back to the trailer, Jack combed through his notes for almost an hour. As he stood to stretch, his cell phone buzzed. It was Judith Hadley.

Jack listened as Judith told him about the anonymous call she'd received as he was leaving the café. The caller had told her there was evidence regarding Alice's murder in the home of her son Hugh Sheppard. The caller then instructed her to relay the information to the sheriff's office.

"And did you?" Jack asked.

"Of course. They sent a couple of guys over to interview me. They poked around the café for a while, but I'm not sure what they were looking for. They must not have found anything interesting. They just left. I waited for them to go before I called you."

Jack was relieved she had. If he was going to look for Alice's murderer on his own—and he had no doubt that it *was* murder—the last thing he wanted was to have law enforcement think he was interfering in their investigation.

But why had the caller used Judith as an intermediary? Was it someone Judith knew? Then Jack remembered the old rotary phone at the end of the counter. There would be no caller ID. The caller was someone who must have known about the phone, someone who'd been in the café.

"Did you recognize the voice?" Jack asked.

"No. It was muffled, like they were talking through a T-shirt or a bath towel."

"Man or woman?"

"I couldn't tell."

"Young or old?"

"I'm sorry, Jack. I couldn't tell." She sounded frustrated that she couldn't be more help.

"It's all right," Jack said. "Thank you for letting me know."

"I told you one of those boys would have something to do with this," Judith said before she ended the call.

After he hung up, Jack sat at the table, his notes fanned out in front of him. It was a strange turn of events. He wrote "Anonymous tip—Hugh Sheppard evidence" on a clean sheet of paper and laid it on the table with the others.

Two hours later, he had gone through it all again multiple times, creating a list of viable suspects— people who had access to Alice, people she would have trusted. Next he'd listed their possible motives for wanting her dead.

When he was finished, Jack sat staring at the names. The list wasn't complete—someone he didn't know could have gotten to her—but it was a start.

He leaned across the trailer and pulled open the mini fridge for a beer. As he did, his cell phone vibrated on the table.

It was Eva Sheppard. She wanted to meet.

CHAPTER 54

THE HIGHWAY OUT of Telluride was blocked by an accident, and Jack couldn't get to Mountain Village. He turned the truck around, and after several minutes of circling, found a parking spot near the gondola. It would be his first time on it.

An elderly couple boarded the cabin with him.

"Are you in town on vacation?" the woman asked.

"Not exactly." Jack had hoped for a quiet ride, wanting to avoid small talk. No such luck.

"Do you live here, then?"

He had to say something that would satisfy her. "I'm in town on business."

"Oh, what do you do?"

"Edith, let the poor man be. Just look at these beautiful views, would you?" He gave Jack a wink.

As they rose higher, the box canyon came into view. Everything was blanketed in white, from the mountain peaks that loomed over the town to the rooftops of the buildings below. It looked like a village in a snow globe. And Jack thought it was stunning.

Edith was watching him. "It's beautiful, isn't it?"

"It is," Jack agreed.

"First time on the gondola?"

"Yes."

She seemed surprised. "Well, you're in for a treat. We're getting off at Allred's—that's at the top. The doors will open automatically at the next station, but don't get off. If you're going down to Mountain Village, you'll want to stay on."

Jack thanked her.

"Are you on your way to dinner?" she asked.

"Edith," her husband reprimanded.

"It's a simple question, Frank. It's not like I'm interrogating the man."

Jack smiled. "As a matter of fact, I'm meeting someone at a restaurant in Mountain Village."

"A special someone, I hope?" The woman had a mischievous gleam in her eyes.

Her husband sighed. "Edith—"

As each gondola cabin entered the station at the top of the mountain, it slowed and drew closer to the one ahead, allowing riders to get on or off safely. The old couple bid Jack farewell and stepped out.

As the cabin left the station, the doors closed automatically. Jack was glad no one else had gotten on. He spent the descent into Mountain Village wondering again why Eva Sheppard wanted to meet.

He thought of the anonymous tip about evidence hidden in the Sheppards' home. Jack hoped Hugh would be with her. He now had a few more questions for Alice's eldest son.

Jack stepped off the gondola in Mountain Village, asked the attendant for directions to Tomboy Tavern, and was relieved to learn it was only a short walk away.

The plaza was packed with people, kids running every which way. Someone was singing a rendition of "Ring of Fire" that didn't sound anything like the Johnny Cash song.

The restaurant's patio swarmed with raucous diners seeming oblivious to the cold, enjoying the waning sunlight as they sipped après ski cocktails and beer. Inside, the restaurant was full, many of the diners still clomping around in ski boots.

Eva waved at him from a booth near the back. When he reached the table, she stood up and gave him an unexpected hug. Her perfume was overwhelming.

"Thank you for coming," she said as they slid into opposite sides of the booth.

She was wearing a one-piece jumpsuit in some sort of animal print that hugged her curves. It looked ridiculous, but Jack was sure it had cost a fortune. A white fur coat was tossed on the bench beside her.

"Thank you for meeting me in Mountain Village. I have misplaced my keys," she said. "So I could not drive."

"What about the gondola?"

"The gondola?" From the look on her face, it was as if Jack had asked her why she didn't *walk* to Telluride.

"I was just on it," he said. "The views are amazing."

Her nose was crinkled in disgust. "I try to avoid it always," she said. "But I *never* take it during the peaks, when they put the strangers in with you."

Eva Sheppard might be beautiful, but she was a snob.

A waitress appeared, and Eva ordered a glass of champagne, Jack a beer. The two then settled back into the booth, studying each other from across the table. She was waiting for Jack to speak, but he kept silent, holding her stare. She was testing him, and Jack didn't like being tested.

She spoke first. "You are probably wondering why I asked you here." Jack remained quiet. "I want to help you."

"Help me with what?"

"To find out who did this horrible thing to my mother-in-law."

When Jack last saw Eva the day before, no one knew that Alice was dead. He'd been looking for clues in what he thought was a missing persons case. But it was now a homicide.

"The sheriff is investigating Alice's murder," he said. "It's *their* case."

Eva wasn't deterred. "You should look at Gordon

Quinn," she said, pointing a manicured fingernail at him. "Alice did not trust him. She was angry with him. He is probably the one who did this."

Jack wanted to know more. "Did Alice ever say *why* she was angry with him?"

"No." Eva shook her head, sending her platinum-blond hair swinging. "But I believe Gordon was going to be in her next book. And some of the people—after they are in the books—they want to kill her."

The waitress reappeared with their drinks.

"What about Buckley Bailey?" Jack asked. "Would Alice put someone like him in her book?"

"Of course," Eva said, setting the champagne flute down on the table after taking a sip. "A crooked politician is a perfect character. But Buckley did not do it."

"Why don't you think so?"

"Alice says he is—how do you say in English—he is tall hat and no cattle."

All *hat and no cattle*. Jack laughed to himself. Having lived in Texas, he knew the expression well.

So Alice didn't think there was any substance to the flamboyant Texas politician. But Alice might have been wrong. Jack would keep Bailey on his suspect list until he could question him and see for himself.

"It is Gordon Quinn," Eva insisted. "You look into him."

"What about your husband?"

She stared at Jack, surprised by the question. "Hugh? What about him?"

"What was his relationship with Alice like?"

Eva took a drink of the champagne. Jack suspected it was to buy her time to figure out what to say. He waited for her to answer.

"You think my husband did this?" She had regained her composure.

"I didn't say that."

"My husband is an old and boring man," she said, shaking her head. "He could not do something so extreme. He is not interesting like you." She said it in a flirtatious tone that he suspected was second nature to her.

Jack felt her foot brush his calf, and he pulled his leg back. He had known women like Eva Sheppard. They might be tempting, but they were vipers. And he'd been bitten before.

"I know what people say about me. That I am a beautiful woman who married a rich man. But I am much more. And my husband is much less. Do you know that I skied for the Slovenia Olympic team?"

Jack didn't care. "What about the missing manuscript and suitcase?"

It was a bluff. The anonymous caller had made reference to evidence at the Sheppards' house, and the manuscript and suitcase were the only things Jack knew were missing. The call to Judith had been hours ago. The sheriff's office should have already searched the house.

"I do not know what you are talking about," she said. But the look on her face told Jack he'd hit a nerve. The sheriff must have found something.

As they drank a second round, Eva steered the conversation back to Gordon Quinn, insisting there was bad blood between him and Alice.

Before they left, she reached into her bag and pulled out a velvet box. "I hoped you would do a small errand for me, since I do not have my keys."

Jack took the box from her, looked inside, and saw two turquoise necklaces.

"There is a store," she said. "Waggoner Mercantile—"

"I know it."

"Opal Waggoner is a terrible woman. Sally says she has called the house many times to get the necklaces. And she has now even called Hugh. She says Alice never paid for them, and she wants them back. I do not know why she is so concerned. They are ugly necklaces. I would never wear one. But they look like Alice, no?"

They were similar to the one Alice had been wearing the day Jack had met her and similar to several others Sally had shown him in the cabinet in the bedroom. Alice obviously had a fetish for turquoise jewelry.

"If you do me this favor, I will be forever grateful."

The line dangled like a fishhook, but Jack didn't bite.

He remembered Opal Waggoner's disdain for Gordon Quinn and decided to pay the sisters another visit.

"That terrible woman must stop calling my husband. He is now so upset with his mother dead. You will take the hideous things back for me?"

Jack told her he would.

As they exited the restaurant, Jack noticed several men looking at her. Eva Sheppard was beautiful but toxic. A smart man would stay away.

Outside, the sky had grown dark. They said goodbye and Jack started for the gondola but turned back. "Eva, how are you getting home if you didn't drive?"

"The shuttle. It is complimentary if you own a home."

Eva Sheppard on public transportation? Jack didn't think so.

She saw the skeptical look on his face and laughed. "They take me alone. Never with the strangers. I give them a big tip."

Jack watched her walk away. She tossed her platinum-blond hair over her shoulder. The light from a streetlamp filtered through it, causing it to look like a halo. But there was one thing Jack was sure of—Eva Sheppard was no angel.

She had insisted Jack look at Gordon Quinn, convinced he was involved with Alice's murder. Was she covering for Hugh?

But she'd made several disparaging remarks about him. And there was her flirtatious manner—the clothes, the perfume, her foot on his leg. It had been a long time—too long—but Jack knew when a woman was propositioning him.

He didn't think Eva Sheppard gave a damn about her husband.

But if it wasn't Hugh, then who was she protecting?

CHAPTER 55

As JACK CLIMBED the stairs toward the gondola station, he noticed someone peering at him from around the corner of a small shop. Jack stared ahead, pretending not to notice but watching the man out of the corner of his eye.

He was tall. The hood of his dark jacket was pulled over his head, concealing his face, but he could tell it was the man from the campground. The same man Jack had chased through town. He was sure of it.

When Jack reached the top of the steps, he bolted toward the guy, sending him scrambling and causing him to knock over a rack of sweatshirts set up outside the tiny store.

The man stumbled, then righted himself and pushed his way through the crowd toward the front of the line. There was nowhere else for him to go. Several men hollered at him, but he shoved them aside.

Jack followed, apologizing as he made his way through the crowd. When he entered the station, he saw the attendant reach out a hand to stop the man.

But he leaped onto a cabin just as the doors were closing. Jack watched as it launched into the darkness, headed up the mountain toward Allred's, then down to Telluride.

Jack hesitated, wondering what to do. The next gondola cabin drifted past him, and several people got on.

Who was the guy? He must have followed Jack to Tomboy Tavern. Had he followed him inside? The restaurant was crowded, but it was no excuse. Curious about Eva Sheppard, Jack had dropped his guard. He'd made a mistake.

The guy was waiting for him when he came out. Would he have followed Jack back down to Telluride? Maybe to the campground? What did he want?

The doors to the next cabin began to close. Jack ran for it. The attendant started toward him and raised his hand.

Jack yelled, "Police!" and jumped inside as the cabin left the station. He was immediately struck by the darkness—and the silence.

Three teenagers stared at him, their faces illuminated by the light of their cell phones.

"Dude, that was sick," one of them said, bobbing his head in approval.

"Are you really a cop?" another asked.

Jack was catching his breath. "Used to be."

The three stared at him.

Jack peered through the dark at the cabin ahead, wondering if the guy had seen him follow.

"Are you Jeff?"

It was a female voice. With all the bulky jackets and scarves, Jack hadn't realized the third teenager was a girl.

"It's dark, but you look pretty hot," she said, turning her phone screen in his direction, lighting his face.

Jack squinted at the glare.

"Sierra, don't be an idiot. This guy's too old. No offense, dude."

Jack had no idea what the kids were talking about but gathered from bits of their conversation that it had something to do with a video that had gone viral. Something about a Telluride cop chasing a bear. No, he wasn't Jeff. No one had ever accused Jack of being a coward, but he damn sure wouldn't chase a bear.

As the gondola crawled slowly up the mountain, Jack's frustration grew. When they finally reached the station at the top, before the doors opened automatically, Jack pulled them apart, jumped out, and started for the cabin ahead. Jack knew it was his chance to catch the guy following him.

"Good luck, dude!" one of the teenagers hollered. "Badass!"

Jack saw the hooded figure turn and look, then quickly push his way out of the cabin. The overhead lights illuminated the bottom half of his face. He was young.

The kid darted ahead for the gaping black hole where the line dropped toward Telluride. He was fast.

A cabin neared the far edge of the station.

The kid hesitated.

Jack closed the gap and thought he had him.

But the kid jumped, sending the cabin rocking from side to side. A woman inside it screamed. Somehow, the kid managed to squeeze between the doors as they closed. Jack watched as the cabin plunged toward town.

The next cabin was slowly making its way to the edge. As the doors began to close, Jack jumped on.

He had missed the guy again, and he was angry. His heart pounded like a jackhammer, not from fear but from adrenaline. He wanted to catch the guy, but it would be nearly impossible to catch him once they reached town.

The ride down was slow. The light from a crescent moon cast a faint glow, reflecting off the snow underneath them as they glided past.

Jack squinted into the night, at the cabin ahead. As it slid over a crest in the ski slope below, it began to rock. The light from several cell phones danced wildly inside.

Jack watched in stunned silence as the kid climbed out of the rocking cabin and hung from the open doors, then dropped to the snowy slope below. He tumbled and slid several feet but somehow righted himself, then scrambled out from under the gondola line and disappeared into the darkness.

Jack shoved open the doors, filling the cabin with an icy cold that brought immediate protests and curses from the other passengers. Ignoring their cries, he stared down at the snow beneath the gondola, glowing in the moonlight. At forty-three, with football injuries and a bum knee, the jump would be suicide. Jack yanked the doors shut and banged a fist against the metal frame.

He spent the rest of the ride down thinking about what little he knew. Somebody hated Alice Freeman enough to throw her from a bridge. That same person would now be hell-bent on self-preservation, wanting to keep their identity a secret. Was the guy following him Alice's killer? Was Jack his next target?

Jack knew he should take the trailer and head south to Santa Fe, let the local guys find out who had murdered Alice. He kept telling himself it wasn't his case; he could walk away at any time. If he stayed in Telluride, he could be putting himself in danger.

But none of that mattered. Jack was angry.

CHAPTER 56

Friday, January 14

FRIDAY MORNING, JACK woke before dawn after another night of fitful sleep. Fragments of dreams about Alice and the hooded kid still swirled in his head.

He rolled over and pulled back the curtains. The mountains were invisible in the darkness, blending with the night sky. It was early—too early to get up—but he couldn't sleep.

After a quick circle around campsite twenty to let Crockett take care of his morning business, both were glad to return to the warmth of the Airstream.

Jack made coffee and sat at the table, then mentally ran through the list of people he wanted to talk to.

The Waggoner sisters. He would take them the necklaces Eva had given him the night before, use the return as a ruse to question them again. What did they know about Alice's relationship with Gordon Quinn? Three days earlier, when Jack had stopped in the store, Opal had willingly expressed her disdain for Quinn. Jack hoped it wouldn't take much to get her to reveal what she knew about his contentious relationship with Alice.

Gordon Quinn. Jack wanted to talk to him again and, depending on what he learned from the Waggoner sisters, would confront him about his relationship with Alice. He would study Quinn closely when he did, watching his body language for clues. The man was slick, but he also wore his sentiments on his sleeve, which made it easier to detect a lie.

Sally and Johnny Eagle. The revelation of Alice's death would have come as a shock to her longtime employees. Or had it?

Lars Sheppard. Now that they knew Alice was dead, Jack had a list of follow-up questions for her overindulged youngest son. Jack wanted to hear Lars's version of the timeline of events again. When had he last spoken with his mother? When had he arrived at the house? Did he notice any evidence of foul play— any indication that something was wrong? With it known that his mother was dead, Jack was curious if Lars would change any of his answers.

Hugh Sheppard. What evidence had the sheriff found in the Sheppards' house? When Jack had asked Eva about it the night before, her reaction had verified that *something* had been found. Was it the manuscript? The suitcase? Maybe it was something else. Jack didn't want to call Sheriff Burns, knowing it would be tricky to get information about an ongoing investigation out of law enforcement. First he would try to get the answer from Hugh.

But there was someone else Jack wanted to talk to first: Buckley Bailey.

CHAPTER 57

CELESTE BAILEY ANSWERED the door with a nervous smile. "Detective Martin? This is a surprise."

"I was hoping it would be. Is Buckley home?"

She glanced over her shoulder. "Um…he is. Come in." Any semblance of the smile had disappeared. "It's early. Can I offer you a cup of coffee?"

"Thank you, but no. Just a word with your husband."

She hesitated a moment. Jack was sure she was trying to come up with an excuse for why Buckley couldn't see him, but it was too late.

"Celeste! Where'd you hide that damned dog?" Buckley asked, clomping into the room holding a shredded tie. He looked up, startled to see Jack standing there.

"Buckley—" Celeste began, but Jack cut her off.

"Mr. Bailey, I'm Jack Martin." Jack stepped toward him and reached out a hand.

Buckley switched the tie to his left hand. "Nice to meet you," he said, pumping Jack's hand and flashing a million-dollar smile, punctuated by a slew of white, Chiclet-like false teeth. He took a step into Jack's personal space—a cheap trick at intimidation. "Now, what's this all about?"

Jack stood his ground, looking him square in the eye. Buckley Bailey might intimidate some people, but Jack wanted him to know it wouldn't work on him.

"I need to ask you a few questions."

Buckley returned Jack's stare for a beat; then his stiff posture softened. "Sure, sure," he said, handing Celeste what was left of the tie. "Take this, honey. You might as well give the rest of it to Bo anyway. Have a seat, Martin."

Jack followed him to the far end of the room. The view through the windows revealed a stunning sunrise. Daylight was beginning to pour over the peaks.

Buckley dropped onto one of the sofas and indicated for Jack to have a seat in the other. "Now, what can I do for you, Detective?" His smile stretched from ear to ear, but Jack suspected it was forced—a natural reflex for a seasoned politician.

Jack peppered him with questions. How long had he known Alice? How did they meet? When was the last time he saw her?

Buckley was forthcoming with his answers, but he sounded guarded, like a man used to gotcha questions. Jack knew of the political scandals. The media had put him through the wringer for years. Buckley

Bailey was a loudmouthed politician, but he was no idiot.

"Did you hear that Alice was writing a book about people in Telluride?" Jack asked him.

Buckley threw a long leg over the other, resting an ankle on the opposite knee. "I had—everyone had. The rumor was out there, but who knows if it was true."

"You were friends with Alice, but she never told you?"

He shook his head. "Wasn't any of my business."

"You weren't curious to know if the rumor was true?"

He shook his head.

"What if she had a character modeled after you in it?"

Buckley laughed. "Well, she sure as hell better have. Who in town is more interesting than Buckley Bailey?" He raised his palms to the ceiling.

It was off-putting that he talked about himself in the third person. But Jack had dealt with politicians before and knew some had a weird sense of detachment when talking about themselves or their careers.

"It might have been an unflattering portrayal," Jack said. "That doesn't bother you?"

"Son, if there's a character modeled after me anywhere, I have no doubt it's going to be an unflattering portrayal." Buckley laughed again.

"And you wouldn't be upset by it?"

He waved his hand like he was batting away a housefly. "You probably already know this, but I'm considering running for office again. And you know the old saying: There's no such thing as bad publicity."

Buckley acted like he didn't care, but Jack wasn't buying it.

"Being lampooned in a bestselling novel doesn't seem like a winning political strategy. It sounds more like a way to ruin a career."

The look on Buckley's face gave him away. As much as he pretended not to care, it was all an act. Jack saw him swallow.

When Buckley didn't reply, Jack asked, "You never saw the manuscript?"

"How in the holy hell would I have seen that?"

"It's missing."

Buckley sat quietly for a while. "Well…that could be a problem for her publisher, but I don't see how it concerns me."

From the look on his face, it was obvious Buckley didn't know anything about the missing manuscript. It was then Jack knew he wasn't the one who'd stolen it.

The two men spent the next twenty minutes talking about Texas—its weather and its politics. When Jack admitted to voting for him in his last two gubernatorial elections, Buckley dropped the last layers of pretense. He peppered Jack with questions, wanting to know about his time playing football at Texas A&M and his tenure with the FBI.

"Celeste followed your case in Aspen," Buckley said. "She kept me up to date. Damned fine work, son." He nodded his approval.

Jack fielded several more questions about the cases in Aspen and Vail, then decided it was time to go. He stood up.

Buckley unfolded himself from the sofa and walked Jack to the door. He swung it open, letting in a blast of cold morning air. "Listen, Martin, if you want a job with the Texas Rangers, you let me know. I worked closely with them for years when I was governor. Good guys. I think you'd fit in nice." He winked at Jack and added a slap on his back.

Jack wondered if Buckley was sincere in offering to help him get a job or just looking for a way to get him out of town. But he was surprised to find that he liked Buckley and that the flamboyant public image was actually the mask of an insecure man.

The career politician was self-deprecating and friendly. He also had one hell of a motive for murder.

CHAPTER 58

Jack's next stop was Waggoner Mercantile. He wanted to talk to the sisters. But it was nine forty-five, and the store didn't open until ten.

He sat on a bench off Main Street, watching skiers march toward the base of the gondola for a day on the slopes. He thought of Lars Fremont. Lars would have been instructed to remain in town for a while. Would the kid snowboard the day after his mother was found dead? Something told Jack he probably would.

Jack turned his phone over and over in his hands. He was procrastinating, putting off a call to Burns, not wanting to come across as the pushy ex-cop nosing around in another guy's case. But there were several things Jack wanted to ask him, and he hoped Burns would be receptive when he called.

Through the window, Jack saw Opal Waggoner flip the CLOSED sign to OPEN. He got up from the bench and made his way to the door. As he stepped inside, the overhead bell jingled, announcing his arrival.

Opal was giving instructions to the lanky teenager Jack had seen in the store the time before.

She turned and saw Jack. "You again."

"Nice to see you, too, Opal."

The teenager looked nervously at Opal, then disappeared through a back door. *Damn kids these days. They don't know how to speak, much less look someone in the eye.*

"You obviously haven't found Alice yet, have you?" Opal asked.

"You haven't heard?"

"Heard what?"

Ivy Waggoner walked in from the back room. "Hello again, Detective." Her greeting was warm and sincere.

Jack tipped his head. "Ivy."

"Heard what?" Opal repeated.

Jack looked from one sister to the other. There was no polite way to put it. "Alice was found dead yesterday."

The sisters gasped.

"I don't believe it," Ivy exclaimed.

Opal thumped her cane against the wood floor. "What happened?"

Jack explained how he'd found her under the old railroad bridge.

"What on earth was she doing there?" Ivy asked.

"Well, it's obvious," Opal replied. "Someone *threw* her off."

"Opal!" Ivy shook her head, then turned to Jack. "Detective?"

They both looked to him for an answer.

"They don't know what happened yet," Jack told them. "The sheriff's office is investigating it."

"But it was murder, wasn't it?" Opal asked. "I knew it. That woman drove *everyone* crazy. It was bound to happen sooner or later. She practically asked for it."

"No one heals thyself by wounding another, sister," Ivy scolded.

Opal stabbed the floor with her cane again. "Hells bells, Ivy. If I wanted your opinion, I'd've asked for it." She looked at Jack. "That's terrible news about Alice, but why are you here?"

"I want to know about Alice's relationship with Gordon Quinn."

Opal raised her brows. "As I told you before, at Waggoner Mercantile, we don't peddle in gossip."

Ivy dropped her gaze to the floor.

Jack stuck his hands on his hips, flaring the sides of his coat. "Listen, ladies. I need help. What can you tell me about Gordon Quinn?"

Opal spoke first. "All we can tell you is that Gordon Quinn is the most unlikable, arrogant little man we've ever met. Isn't that right, Ivy?"

Jack glanced again at Ivy, her old eyes bulging

at Opal's brutal honesty. The sisters might discuss Quinn in private, but it was clear Ivy was shocked by her sister's public revelation.

Opal was still talking. "Have you met the wee sprite of a man for yourself, Detective?"

"I have."

"Well, then, you already know what I'm talking about. Quinn burns bridges at nearly every turn." She nodded in self-satisfaction. "Come to think of it, Alice is a lot like him in that way."

"*Was*," Ivy corrected her.

Opal gave the floor a gentle rap with her cane. "You're right," she said, her tone softer. "Alice *was* a lot like him in that way."

Jack saw Opal visibly deflate as she said it. As much as Opal Waggoner had professed to dislike Alice, he could tell the realization of her death weighed on her.

"I almost forgot." Jack pulled the velvet box from inside his coat. "Eva Sheppard asked me to bring this to you."

Opal took it from him and looked inside. She blinked several times, then cleared her throat. "The necklaces."

Jack watched as Opal passed Ivy the box, her old hand quivering.

CHAPTER 59

JACK WAS ON his way to see Gordon Quinn when his cell phone vibrated. He dug it from the pocket of his jeans, stepped into the recessed stoop of a vacant building, out of the wind and the path of tourists.

He glanced at the caller ID and couldn't believe his luck. "Sheriff Burns, what can I do for you?"

"One thing you can do is call me 'Tony.' I made it a policy a long time ago—unless he's a superior, it's first names with another lawman."

"*Former* lawman," Jack corrected him.

"Doesn't matter."

"All right, Tony." Jack liked him. "What can I do for you?"

Jack spent a couple of minutes answering some of the same questions he had the day before. What were you doing at the Nordic track? What prompted you to go down into the ravine? How did you find the body?

Jack gave him the same answers as before, knowing the follow-up questions were meant to assess whether he could recall anything new. Witnesses often remembered things after the initial adrenaline rush was over. Questioning them a second time, even a third time, was standard procedure.

When the sheriff was finished, Jack spoke up. "Now can I ask *you* a question?"

It took a while for Burns to reply. "Maybe."

"I heard that evidence was found at Hugh Sheppard's house." It was a bluff.

"Ah, hell. Who told you?"

"It's a small town."

"You're telling me." There was silence on the line. "Okay, but I don't have to tell you to keep this under wraps, do I?"

"No, you don't."

"We found the missing suitcase."

"What about the manuscript?"

"No manuscript, just the suitcase."

"You think Sheppard did it? He had access. Alice would have trusted him and let him in." Jack was thinking aloud, bouncing his ideas off Burns. "But what would be the motive? He would inherit a lot, but from what I can tell, he doesn't need it." Jack heard Burns sigh.

"There's something else," Burns said.

He had Jack's full attention.

"We found copies of Hugh Sheppard's financial records when we searched Alice's house."

"And?"

"Sheppard's broke."

The information was damning. Hugh needed the money. Even though the pieces fit, Jack still wasn't convinced Hugh had murdered his mother. But he wanted to know what Tony thought.

"That should be it, then," Jack replied, trying to coax more information from him. "Hugh's probably your guy."

"Maybe." By the tone of Tony Burns's voice, Jack knew the man also had doubts. "I've got Sheppard coming in any minute to answer more questions."

Jack would call Burns later, find out if Hugh confessed or changed his story. But while he had the sheriff on the phone, he wanted to get as much information out of him as he could. "What about the cause of death?"

"We couldn't tell when we pulled the body."

"Any blood?" Jack hadn't seen any when he found Alice, but she had been mostly covered in snow.

"No blood."

"So no visible signs of stab or gunshot wounds?"

"None."

Jack was irritated. "I didn't notice any blood, either. Must have been blunt force," he said, fishing for more information.

Burns sighed. "Listen, I don't normally share details about an investigation with civilians, but since you're not an *ordinary* civilian, I'll tell you." He paused. "On the agreement of strict confidentiality again."

"You've got my word." Jack turned his back to the sidewalk and stuck a finger in his ear, muffling the street sounds, not wanting to miss anything Burns said.

"I'm telling you this because we don't normally have homicides in San Miguel County. A couple in Norwood a few years back, but CBI was brought in. Before Telluride, I was in Ouray County—but we didn't have a single homicide case while I was there. So any information I give you...if you think of something...I'd appreciate it if you'd let me know."

Tony Burns was a good man. Jack could tell it was hard for him to admit that he didn't have a lot of experience with homicide. Asking a former lawman for help was swallowing a humble pill that most of the guys Jack had worked with in the past wouldn't do. Jack respected Burns for it. He also understood his raw desire to find the son of a bitch who'd killed Alice.

"I'll do what I can," Jack assured him.

"The coroner here is Mike Greenwald—a friend of mine." He hesitated before he continued. "Since we didn't see any wounds when we pulled her out, I asked Mike to put a rush on the autopsy to find out the cause of death. He got back with me this morning."

Jack held the phone still, waiting for him to continue.

"Like we thought, no wounds. I thought it would be blunt-force trauma of some sort, too, but Mike said the only bruises were postmortem. They were on the back of her head but occurred after Alice was already dead. So he ran a toxicology report." The sheriff fell silent.

"And?" Jack asked it as delicately as he could, not wanting to seem too pushy.

Burns cleared his throat. "He found tetrahydrozoline."

"Tetra what?"

"Tetrahydrozoline. It's a chemical in eye drops."

"Eye drops?" Jack pulled the finger from his ear and turned toward the street, as if facing the sun would shed light on his confusion. "Alice was poisoned?"

"That's what Mike thinks. But he hasn't done the full-blown autopsy yet. He stressed this is all preliminary and that he needs to do more tests before he knows for sure. But he said it was a concentration that was more than enough to kill her."

Jack had worked on poisoning cases before—arsenic and strychnine. Never tetra-whatever it was. But for some reason, it sounded familiar. He would google it later and find out why.

Jack's cell phone vibrated with an incoming call.

He pulled it away from his ear and glanced at the caller ID.

"Tony, can I call you back?"

"Sure thing," the sheriff said. "Just remember that everything we spoke about is official business."

"You have my word."

Jack ended the call, eager to answer the next one.

It was Sally Eagle.

CHAPTER 60

Sheriff Tony Burns placed his phone on his desk and laced his fingers behind his head, then tilted his chair back and thought about the conversation with Jack Martin.

He couldn't believe his luck that the person who'd found Alice Fremont's body was an experienced detective. Tony knew that discussing the case with Martin went against department policy, but he didn't care. It wasn't every day that he had a famous detective to bounce theories off. And depending on what he found out questioning Hugh Sheppard a second time, he might call Martin again.

Tony had known Alice Fremont since he was hired as a junior deputy nearly sixteen years earlier.

Every Christmas, Alice donated generously to the office's fundraising drive to purchase toys for the children on the reservation south of Durango. She wasn't stingy like a lot of the town's other millionaires, ones who wouldn't let go of a dollar if it didn't benefit them in some way to do so.

Despite Alice's reputation for being mean-spirited

and irascible, Tony had liked her. He couldn't remember a single time that she wasn't respectful. Not even the time they had arrested her youngest son, Lars, for DWI.

It was common knowledge in Telluride that Alice's sons were degenerates. Although Hugh didn't regularly run afoul of the law like his younger brother, everyone in town who knew him thought he was a conceited windbag. However, as bad as Alice's sons were, Tony wasn't convinced either one was capable of murder.

He came forward in his chair, laying his forearms down on the desk and drumming his fingers as he thought about the case.

It had been just over twenty-four hours since Alice's body was found—murdered and thrown from the historic bridge near the entrance to her estate. And although they didn't yet know what had happened, Tony was sure the perpetrator was no random thief. He might not have experience in homicide, but he was certain Alice had known her killer.

Although the evidence was mounting against her eldest son, Hugh, Tony wasn't convinced he was guilty.

Tony had studied enough high-profile cases to know that when a son killed his mother, it was typically violent. He thought of Ed Kemper, who in 1973 had struck his mother in the head with a hammer.

And there was Henry Lee Lucas, who'd launched his killing spree by stabbing his mother in the neck.

But Alice Fremont had been poisoned. It was too neat—too clean. Poison hadn't been used in any of the cases of familial homicides he had read about.

He snatched a pencil from the top of his desk, rolled it back and forth between his hands. Alice might have had a nasty reputation, but Tony liked her. Then again, he'd never been a target in one of her novels. Tony didn't read much, but he'd heard that her books were hit pieces on people she knew.

Several weeks earlier, while having lunch at Pandora Café, Tony had overheard Judith Hadley and a local preacher talking about Alice's latest novel. From the portions of their conversation he could hear, Tony gathered the book was going to be about people she knew in Telluride. He remembered thinking it would be the one book he'd be interested in reading.

Judith and the preacher had sounded concerned, not for themselves but for Alice. Tony listened as they talked about the previous attacks and death threats made against her. At the time, Tony had found their conversation interesting but thought the two were being dramatic, never imagining Alice would actually turn up dead.

The more Tony thought about it, the angrier he got. He squeezed the pencil with both hands until it broke in half. He was determined to find out who'd killed her. And if he had to skirt department policy to do it, he would. Jack Martin was a valuable asset to have around, one Tony intended to use to his advantage if he could.

The intercom on the desk phone sounded. "Sheriff, Hugh Sheppard is here to see you."

Tony pushed his chair back from the desk and stood up. "Send him in." He was going to grill Alice's eldest son, wring any valuable information or clues he could out of him . Lars Fremont would be next.

A few seconds later, Hugh Sheppard strolled into Tony's office, his demeanor as pompous and arrogant as ever. But his fleshy, round face gave him away. The look in his eyes was that of a guilty man about to be hanged.

CHAPTER 61

AFTER THE CONVERSATION with Tony Burns, Jack started in the direction of Quinn Gallery as he answered the incoming call.

"Hi, Sally."

"Mr. Jack Martin." She was talking fast. "Someone was in the house."

"Alice's?"

"Yes."

"Who?"

"I do not know. But the paintings, they are gone."

The paintings? Jack stopped on the sidewalk. "Which ones?" The house was full of art.

"The two that sat by her desk. And one more that was in the hallway."

Jack remembered the landscapes on the floor, propped against the wall. Who would take them?

"Is anything else missing?" Jack asked. "Any other artwork?"

"No."

He thought about it for a moment. "Did you see

any signs someone had been in the house when you got there?"

"No."

"Where's Johnny?"

"He is at the barn."

Jack glanced at his watch, then turned toward the campground, dodging tourists. "Stay in the house," he said. "But don't touch anything."

He would have to talk to Gordon Quinn later. He wanted to see for himself that the paintings were missing, look for any clues. Had the killer been back in the house? Was it the same person who'd tried to break in before? Had they been after the paintings all along?

"Sally, are you still there?"

"Yes."

Jack waited for a truck to turn, then started across the street.

A voice inside his head told him to call Tony Burns, let the sheriff deal with it. The voice was insisting he cut his losses, leave it to the local guys, and get on the road to Santa Fe. The voice was pissing him off.

Jack quickened his pace. "I'll be there in thirty minutes."

CHAPTER 62

IT WAS JUST past midday, but the manor was already cloaked in the shadow of the mountain behind it. As gloomy as it looked on the outside, Jack knew the house held even more darkness within.

He thought of the dark wood interiors, the heavy velvet curtains, the dead eyes that hung from the walls and followed him from room to room. It was a house where a murder had been committed and, Jack was convinced, committed by someone Alice knew.

He was certain the missing manuscript held the key to solving the case, but the stolen paintings could be a clue. He parked at the side of the house and got out. "Stay here, Crockett, I'll be ba—"

There was a whistle. The dog leaped from the truck and loped toward the barn. A man was standing in the distance. Johnny Eagle.

Jack watched as Johnny squatted down and held out his hand. Crockett sniffed it, then wagged his tail, letting Johnny pet him. He was talking to the dog, but Jack couldn't make out what he said.

Sally had come out of the house and saw Jack watching.

"My husband prefers to talk to the animals," she said, smiling as she watched them.

Johnny stood up and gave the dog a command in a language Jack didn't understand. He said it with a gesture toward the house, and Crockett ran back to them, panting, his warm exhales fogging the air around him.

When Johnny reached them, he looked at Jack, a stern expression on his face.

"Johnny," Jack said with a tilt of his head. He got a silent nod in return. A few moments of awkward silence passed. The only sounds were Crockett panting and the wind through the trees.

Sally was the first to speak. She turned to her husband. "I called him. There are paintings missing from the house." Her voice shook slightly as she spoke. She was nervous.

Jack knew that Johnny Eagle didn't trust him, but he probably didn't trust anyone. Jack wondered how he'd feel if their roles were reversed. Probably the same way.

Jack looked at Sally. "I need to search the house again. But first I want to look around outside." He turned to Johnny. "Will you help me?"

Johnny's gaze drifted from Jack to Sally, then back

again. He hesitated a moment, then gave Jack another silent nod.

Sally went back inside as the two men walked the perimeter of the house together. The first-floor windows and doors were all locked. No signs of past forced entry and no footprints in the snow.

The wind had picked up, blowing aspens together, their trunks making deep knocking sounds. They watched a bank of dark clouds boil over the peaks to the north like smoke from an enormous fire.

"Storm's coming," Johnny said.

Jack turned. It was the first thing he'd said since Jack got there. "Let's go inside and warm up."

Before they reached the door, Sally swung it open. Inside, the men shed their coats, then pulled off their wet boots and set them by the door. Jack studied the entrance hall, taking it all in. Nothing seemed different from the times he'd been there before. He asked Sally if she had noticed anything else missing, and she shook her head.

"What about Lars?" Jack asked. "Is he here?"

"He left this morning after he talked to the sheriff."

"Did he say where he was going?"

"To California. He said he did not want to stay in the house any longer."

"Do you know how to get ahold of him?"

"I heard him give his number to the sheriff."

Jack would ask Tony Burns about it later. He

pointed to the rug near the front door and told Crockett to lie down. Johnny stayed with the dog as Jack ascended the stairs, with Sally following behind him.

Jack asked her again not to touch anything, knowing that Burns would likely send in the forensic team to print the house again once they reported the burglary.

They walked toward Alice's suite on the second floor. Sally stopped in the hallway and pointed to an empty spot on the wall over a side table. There was a hook, but nothing hanging from it.

"There was one painting here," Sally said. "An elk herd in a valley."

They stepped into Alice's suite, and Jack stood in the center of the room. He looked down at the spot where the two Bierstadt paintings had previously sat on the floor. With no evidence of forced entry, whoever stole them had used a key to get into the house. But who? And why?

Jack thought of the sticky notes he'd seen on the backs. For some reason, Alice had written the name of a gallery on one and Quinn's name on the other.

He pulled his notebook from his pocket and flipped through it to where he had written down the name. Lamston Gallery. He googled it, found out it was located in New York City, and dialed the number.

A woman answered. "Good afternoon. Lamston

Gallery." She talked through her nose with a heavy accent.

Jack asked to speak to the manager.

"We are an art gallery, sir. We don't have a *manager*. We have a *director*."

"Then let me talk to your director." Jack was growing impatient.

"The gallery is about to close. Please call her back in the morning."

"No. I need to talk to her now. It's regarding a criminal investigation."

"Are you with the police?"

Jack didn't want to tell her the truth, that he hadn't worked in an official law enforcement capacity since he'd resigned from the Aspen Police Department nine months earlier.

On a hunch, he blurted, "It's regarding the murder of Alice Fremont. I believe she was a customer of your gallery."

There was silence on the other end of the line. "One moment, please."

It worked.

Several seconds later, another voice came on the line. "Ruth Winthrop speaking. How may I help you?"

They spoke for several minutes, with Jack first deflecting questions regarding Alice's murder.

"Are you with the FBI?"

It was an unusual question. Why had she asked if he was from the FBI? Jack told her it was a local investigation in Colorado, misleading her into thinking he was law enforcement—not quite the truth but not quite a lie.

Jack asked her about Alice's relationship with the gallery and found out that she was only a recent customer. She had never purchased art from the gallery before.

"Mrs. Fremont contacted us for the first time several weeks ago," Ruth said. "Of course I recognized her name immediately and was delighted to be of help. She was interested in one painting in particular—a Bierstadt. She has it out on loan." She fell silent. "Uh…?"

Jack knew it had dawned on her that with Alice being dead, she needed to find a way to get the painting back. He didn't want to tell her it had been stolen.

Jack had researched the artist and had a good idea of what the ridiculous thing was worth. When the Lamston Gallery found out it had been stolen, it would set off an insurance firestorm that would only complicate things.

Jack assured her he'd look into the painting's whereabouts and get back to her.

Before they hung up, he had one last question. "Have you ever heard of the Quinn Gallery in Telluride?"

"Not before yesterday."

That caught Jack off guard. "What happened yesterday?"

"I got a call," she said, "from the FBI."

CHAPTER 63

BUCKLEY BAILEY SAT in the study, drumming his fingers on the giant wood desk and staring out the window. It had been a hellacious morning. Ever since Celeste had gotten back from the Nordic track the day before, she had given him the cold shoulder. Whenever Buckley had tried making conversation, she'd ignored him.

He knew now that he should have picked her up from Trout Lake. To hell with her insistence that the road was closed. She'd said the lake was a crime scene, and they weren't letting anyone in. But he was certain that when they realized who he was, they would have let him through. He should have gone to her.

But that wasn't his only mistake. When she'd gotten home, he'd hounded her about Jack Martin. Why hadn't he waited, asked her about Alice first? But Celeste had no idea what a threat Jack Martin could be.

"Damn it," he said, dropping a fist onto the desk. He had screwed up.

Earlier that morning, when Celeste announced

that she was going to have lunch in town with friends, Buckley's knee-jerk reaction was to protest. He didn't like eating alone. But he realized that talking and gossiping with friends—or whatever women do to blow off steam—might snap her out of it.

In the meantime, with Celeste out of the house, he could call Charlie Dungee without worrying she might walk in on him again. But just in case, Buckley got up from his chair and pulled the wood doors shut.

Back at the desk, he reached for his cell phone and found the number.

"The contact insists he never went into the house," Charlie told him. "He got there Sunday, like you instructed, but there was someone there. You said there wouldn't be, but there *was*. He said he was close enough to the guy to be made—the guy could probably pick him out of a lineup."

"Shit."

"He said there wasn't even room to turn around with all the snow. He had to back out of the property. He's royally teed off now."

Buckley ran a hand through his hair. "Who'd he say the guy was?"

"Somebody who'd just finished plowing snow off the road by the house. Looked like some Indian. But the point is, the contact was angry enough to leave town and not get back to me. He knows the guy saw him, and he's furious. We're lucky he called back.

With screwups like this, we usually don't hear from a contact again."

Buckley thought of the cash he'd given Charlie to arrange the job. "What about the deposit?"

"Deposit?" Charlie spat. "Shit, Buckley. This isn't Walmart. There's no refund."

Damn. Buckley had been careful to siphon campaign funds from the account at a rate no one would notice. He had supplemented it with periodic withdrawals from petty cash, then finally with personal funds to get to the amount they needed to hire the guy. And now he had nothing to show for it.

There wasn't supposed to be anyone on the estate. When Alice was in Telluride, everyone knew she went to church on Sundays—she never missed. The man who worked on the estate would drive her, drop her off at the Wildwood Chapel on Pine Street. It was what they did every week like clockwork—except this past Sunday. What the hell had happened?

"I'm not saying it'll work," Charlie said, breaking into Buckley's thoughts. "And I'm sure it will cost us. But do you want me to see if the contact is willing to try again?"

"No," Buckley replied. "Keep him away. It's complicated now." He didn't want to tell Charlie that Alice was dead. It would spook him, maybe send Charlie underground, too. It could only make things worse.

Buckley ended the call and leaned back in his chair,

staring out the window. He had screwed up before but was always able to buy his way out of trouble. This blunder might have been too big.

Was the contact telling Charlie the truth? Had he gone to Alice's in search of the manuscript like he'd been hired to do? Found the maintenance guy plowing the driveway, abandoned the job, and ran? Or had he actually gotten in and found Alice there? And now Alice was dead.

Something moved in the distance, walking slowly through the snow. Buckley squinted. It was an animal, but too far away to tell what kind. He took binoculars from a desk drawer and stood at the window.

A coyote meandered through the deep snow, its nose close to the ground. Suddenly it stopped and started to dig. Buckley knew it had found prey. For several seconds, it dug furiously, sending sprays of snow into the air behind it. Soon the only thing visible was the animal's hindquarters and tail.

Buckley watched with bated breath and felt his pulse quicken. He had been on numerous large hunts in Texas, impressing hosts and campaign donors with his many kills—deer, feral hogs, even a mountain lion on a ranch in Big Bend. As a Texas politician, he knew it was important to project an image of virility and strength. He'd pretended to revel in the blood sport but had secretly loathed it. He hated participating, watching something die—especially at his own hands.

He should have been more careful, gone into Alice's house himself. If he had been caught, he could have come up with some excuse for why he was there—he was Alice's friend.

Friend. Buckley felt his chest constrict.

He should have done it himself, but he'd paid for a professional to go in looking for the damn book. Now Alice was dead.

Buckley watched through the binoculars as the coyote pulled something from the snow—a chipmunk or small marmot, its lifeless body hanging from the predator's jaws. The coyote sped away, disappearing into the shadows of the distant trees.

Buckley turned from the window and sank back down in the chair. He tossed the binoculars onto the top of the desk and sat rubbing his hands across the polished wood surface.

He thought of Alice, their hundreds of conversations, dozens of campaign events they'd attended. He thought of the money she had donated to his many campaigns over the years.

As much as Buckley had complained about her, even cussing her to Celeste, he was surprised to realize how upset he was now that she was gone.

They were kindred spirits of sorts—outcasts that had clawed their way into society and respectability through sheer grit and determination. But where Buckley courted public opinion, Alice had scorned it. She never cared what people thought or said about her. Buckley had secretly envied her for it.

He took in and released a long, slow breath. There would be a money trail that led from him to Charlie's contact. He worried it could come back to bite him, be used as evidence against him in a murder trial.

But he had an even bigger problem. Buckley wondered if he was responsible for Alice's murder.

CHAPTER 64

ON HIS WAY back to Telluride, Jack took a detour into Mountain Village. He wanted to catch Hugh Sheppard off guard, see if he knew anything about the missing artwork.

The housekeeper that answered the door told him that Hugh was at the bar at Allred's. When she told Jack that Eva was home and asked if he wanted to speak to her instead, Jack declined. He had decided the night before to steer clear of Eva Sheppard in the future. Women like her were nothing but trouble.

He parked his truck near the center of the village and scanned the crowd, looking for the hooded kid he'd lost the night before. But the plaza was packed, people jostling in every direction, many carrying skis or snowboards. It was the late-afternoon pandemonium, just after the slopes had closed.

Jack took the stairs to the gondola station and got in line. Twenty minutes later, he was finally headed up the mountain toward Allred's.

He found Hugh Sheppard in the bar, sitting alone at a table for four. He had his back to the room and was facing a floor-to-ceiling window that offered stunning views of Telluride below.

Jack approached the table, and Hugh looked up.

"You again," Hugh said. "With the morning I've had, you're the last person I want to see." He took the olive out of his martini and ate it.

Jack shrugged off his coat and pulled out a chair.

A waitress approached. "What can I get you?" she asked Jack.

Hugh waved a fat pink hand. "Nothing, honey. He's not staying."

"I'll have a beer," Jack said. "Anything you have on tap is fine. Put it on Mr. Sheppard's tab."

Hugh sank back into his chair. "What now?" he asked when the waitress had gone. "What do you want from me?"

"I want to ask you a few more questions."

Hugh raised and dropped his hands on the arms of the chair. "You have an insatiable appetite for badgering people, Detective. It's becoming quite annoying."

Jack ignored the comment. "What do you know about Alice's missing paintings?"

"What are you talking about?"

"There were three paintings stolen from the house last night."

Hugh frowned and came forward in his chair. "How do you know?"

"Sally called me."

"She should have called *me*." He thought about it for a moment. "Which ones were stolen?"

"One of some elks and two landscapes—nearly identical Bierstadts."

"Bierstadts?" Hugh's eyebrows shot up. "Those would be worth a small fortune."

Jack let him think about it for a moment, hoping he would offer some explanation, but he didn't. Hugh Sheppard either didn't know what had happened to the paintings, or he was a good liar.

The waitress brought Jack's beer. He took a sip, taking his time to let Hugh digest the information.

"Well, what happened to them? What did Sally say?"

Jack set his glass down and watched him closely. "Do you know why someone would steal them?"

"I have no clue, but you're the famous detective—you tell me." His impatience was morphing into anger. "I didn't know she owned one Bierstadt, much less two. I don't remember seeing *any*. Where were they hanging?"

"They weren't on the wall. They were on the floor of her study, next to her desk."

Hugh turned his head as if searching the room for an answer. Jack decided to let him stew a bit.

Jack looked over his shoulder as a gondola cabin shot out of the station and began its decent toward town. It made him think of the kid the night before. But there wasn't time for that now.

He turned his attention back to Hugh. "What was your mother's relationship like with Gordon Quinn?"

"She hated the man. Everyone does. Pompous little ninny." Hugh leaned his bulk into the chair, the smug look back on his face. "He tells everyone he's from Manhattan, but I have it on good authority that he's actually from the Bronx."

Only someone as spoiled as Hugh Sheppard would think that pulling yourself up by the bootstraps was a character flaw.

Jack didn't want to drag out the conversation any longer than necessary. "Why would she buy art from him?"

"Have you seen my mother's house? There's art everywhere. She buys from everyone."

"What about from the Lamston Gallery in New York?"

"Never heard of it." He indicated to the waitress he wanted another martini.

The two men sat in silence for a while.

"Where were you last night?"

Hugh looked indignant. "That's none of your business."

Jack lifted his hands from the table. "Just trying to cross you off the list."

"List of what? Suspects?" When Jack didn't reply,

Hugh continued. "You have some nerve. You know that?"

Jack noticed the top of his bald head glistening with a sheen of sweat. Was it nerves or just a fat man who was warm? Jack couldn't tell. He stared at Hugh, expecting a reply.

After several seconds, Hugh relented. "I was at home last night, not that it's any of your business."

"And your wife?"

"Eva?"

"Unless you have another one."

"I'm beginning to think your mission in life is to torment me."

"You were home alone?"

"I was. No one to corroborate my alibi. Is that what you're thinking?" When Jack didn't reply, he continued. "My wife was at one of her yoga classes. She's an Olympic athlete if you hadn't heard. Likes to stay in shape." He shot Jack a satisfied look. "Are *you* married, Detective?"

Jack knew the question was meant to be an insult. He also knew that Eva Sheppard hadn't gone to yoga the night before. She had been at Tomboy Tavern, dressed to the nines and flirting with him from across the table.

"Does she drive into town?" Jack asked, fishing for more information.

"She usually does, but the damn woman lost our car keys. She's been taking the gondola to town."

Jack knew that wasn't true. He was now certain that Eva Sheppard was cheating on her husband. God help the man she was cheating with.

"You only have one car?"

"Of course not," Hugh replied. "We keep one here, but we have three in California. Unfortunately, that's where our spare set of keys was for the G-Wagon. But we had one of the housekeepers overnight them to us. They came in this morning."

The waitress returned with the martini.

"Thank you, honey," Hugh said, taking the olive from his drink and tossing it into his mouth. He stared at Jack while he chewed. "Detective, what are you really doing here? Nobody is paying you to find my mother's killer. And nobody is going to pay you to find out what happened to those damn paintings."

When Jack didn't reply, he added, "The sheriff's office is investigating this. And I assure you, I won't have a moment's peace until someone pays for what they did to my dear mother." His declaration rang hollow.

Jack finished the beer and set the glass down on the table. "One last thing."

Hugh had been lifting his martini to his lips but stopped. "Thank God."

"I heard they found the missing suitcase." Jack saw him tense. "I understand it was in your possession."

Hugh Sheppard's face went crimson, and his eyes blazed. Was it from hatred? Or fear?

CHAPTER 65

BY THE TIME Jack reached the edge of town, he was exhausted. The sun hovered low on the western horizon, casting the sky in an eerie red glow. Probably half an hour before dark. As much as he'd like to fall into bed when he got to the trailer, he knew his day was far from over.

His next stop would be Quinn Gallery. Jack wanted to study Gordon Quinn's reaction when he asked him about the missing Bierstadts. He was sure Alice had purchased one of them from his gallery.

The paintings would have cost more than Jack had made in the last three years combined, but there was other valuable artwork in the house. The elks and the two landscapes were the only ones the thief had taken. Why?

Jack drove slowly through town, looking for an empty parking space, but there were none. As he approached Quinn Gallery on the south side of the street, he grew frustrated with the evening crowds. Large groups of people crossed at every intersection.

Pedestrians in Colorado have the right of way, so Jack had to stop at every crosswalk.

At each intersection, he looked up and down the side streets for a space. But it was mid-January, still peak winter season. He knew from his time in Aspen that parking would be nearly impossible.

After several blocks, he gave up and headed for the campground. It was almost six o'clock. Quinn Gallery wouldn't close for an hour.

As Jack wove his way to campsite twenty, he remembered how Hugh Sheppard insisted he didn't know how Alice's suitcase ended up in his closet. Jack had watched him closely as Hugh gave him the details about where the sheriff's men had found it.

Hugh had been indignant when Jack asked about his finances, referring to the financial information the sheriff's office had found in Alice's desk during the search. Hugh had ranted, wondering about how his mother had gotten ahold of the documents, even accusing Jack of somehow getting them for her.

But Hugh had finally calmed down and, when Jack pressed the issue, had admitted to being "financially challenged at the moment." Jack knew it was short-hand for conceding that he was broke.

But with Alice dead, Hugh Sheppard would likely inherit half her fortune. And that amount of money would go a long way in solving any financial problems he might have.

Jack pulled into the campsite and parked the truck beside the trailer. He thought of Lars Fremont. Lars would likely inherit the other half of his mother's fortune. But Tony Burns had said that Lars's alibi had checked out. A quick search of his phone records and credit card expenses verified that he hadn't gotten to Telluride until the day after his mother had gone missing. And although his fingerprints were found on the will, there wasn't enough to keep him in town. Jack agreed with Burns that it appeared Lars Fremont was innocent.

But one of Alice's sons had motive and means. Hugh. It would explain why there was no sign of forced entry. Hugh could have easily gotten into his mother's house, poisoned her, and then thrown her off the bridge.

But it didn't make sense. Jack didn't think Hugh would have hidden the body. It took seven years to declare a missing person dead. If he was after an inheritance, he wouldn't want to wait that long. Why dump Alice's body where she wouldn't be found until spring—if then? He'd want his mother found right away.

It didn't add up. Money was a strong motive for murder, but Jack knew it was far from the only one.

He let Crockett out of the trailer, pulled a folding chair from a compartment on the side, and sat down. As the dog loped through the snow, looking for something to chase, Jack's thoughts turned next to Buckley and Celeste Bailey.

Was it a coincidence Celeste was there when he'd found Alice's body? But Crockett had been the one that found her. And Celeste hadn't directed the dog toward the ravine. Jack thought about it for a moment, then decided that she had nothing to do with finding the body.

And what about Buckley? Why would he want Alice dead? He needed her money for his campaigns. He was an unethical politician—one many people loathed—but Jack didn't think he was a killer.

Gordon Quinn. Jack was sure the key to Alice's murder lay with the missing manuscript, the stolen paintings, and Gordon Quinn. He had an idea of how the three were related, but he needed to talk to Quinn to be sure.

He checked his watch. Six fifteen. Quinn Gallery would close in forty-five minutes.

Crockett suddenly stopped hunting and darted through the trees. Otto Finn waved at Jack, then bent to pet the excited dog.

Jack watched as the old man took something from inside the tent. The dog wagged his tail, then lay down and gnawed on whatever it was Otto had given him.

Otto Finn was an odd bird. Not quite a loner, he was someone who appreciated the company of others but preferred to live alone. There was something familiar about him. Then recognition hit Jack like a punch to the gut.

He watched as the old man sat down at the picnic table and pulled cigarettes from his coat. Crockett was lying at his feet. For a second Jack wondered if he was seeing a glimpse of his own future. He pushed the ridiculous thought aside.

Somewhere in the distance, a thundering sound rolled. Jack instantly recognized the roar of a Harley-Davidson. As it grew louder, Otto turned to look and Crockett lifted his head. By the time the bike emerged from the trees, the ground was rumbling.

The bike came toward them, then slowed as it approached campsite twenty. The rider was dressed in dark denim, a black helmet hiding his face. Jack stood up from his chair.

When he reached the campsite, the rider stopped the bike, dropped the kickstand, and pulled off his helmet. Jack immediately recognized the bald head and friendly face of Pastor Stan, Alice's preacher.

"I found you. Praise God." The pastor swung a leg over the bike and got off. He unlatched a leather saddlebag and pulled out a thick envelope. "Judith told me you'd be here."

Jack walked toward him and stuck out a hand. The preacher shook it.

"What can I do for you, Pastor?"

"I brought you this." He held out the envelope.

Jack took it from him. "What is it?"

"A copy of Alice's next book."

Jack was stunned. "How…?"

Stan offered a wan smile. "I heard that you found her." He shook his head. "I think she was always afraid something like this might happen. She brought this to me early last week, after she'd finished it. If she's in town when she finishes a book, she brings me a copy—for safekeeping."

"Why?"

Stan shrugged. "Didn't trust technology, I guess. She was old-school. Told me years ago that she typed her novels on paper, never used a computer. But it made her nervous to hand them off to her agent without keeping a copy for herself. Once the books were published, she'd get the copy back from me. She never said so, but I got the feeling she was afraid someone might break into the house to steal it if she kept it there." He shrugged. "So she started bringing them to me. But who really knows why Alice did any of the things she did?"

"Why *you*?"

He thought about it a moment. "Maybe because there wasn't anyone else she could trust."

"What about Judith?"

Stan nodded. "They were friends—you're right. But Judith has a reputation for being a bit of a gossip. Maybe she was afraid if Judith had the manuscript, she'd read it. It sounds harsh. Judith is a wonderful woman, but..." His voice trailed off.

Jack held up a hand. "I get it." He lifted the thick envelope. "Why are you bringing it to me?"

"Judith's suggestion, actually."

Jack frowned, confused.

"Let me back up," Stan said. "Alice told me that if anything ever happened to her and I had one of her manuscripts, to give it to the authorities—in this case, the sheriff. I was on a flight from Montrose to Denver on my way to a family reunion in Georgia when I got the message that Alice was found dead. In Denver, I caught the first plane back. I went straight to the church, got the manuscript, and went to see Judith at the café to find out more about what had happened. I told her the story of keeping copies of Alice's novels for her over the years and about what she said to do if anything ever happened to her. Judith suggested I bring it to you. She said that you were the only person concerned enough to look for Alice when she was missing. And that now you were the only one who could find out what happened to her."

Stan glanced down at the ground. When he looked up, there was pain in his eyes. "It couldn't have been easy being Alice Fremont. She was probably the most misunderstood person I knew. Most people thought she was callous, even heartless. I never read one of her books, but I heard stories. And Judith would tell me about the threats. Alice was even attacked twice. Did you know that?"

Jack nodded. "I heard."

Stan shook his head. "She was a very complex woman, but she was generous in her own way." He leaned and tapped the envelope to punctuate what he was saying. "She didn't deserve what happened to her. And I know it's asking a lot, but some of us would like to see someone brought to justice."

"She swore me to secrecy years ago, but I'm going to tell you: Alice was our largest donor." He glanced toward the mountains for a moment. "For some reason, the Scrooge image she projected didn't bother her, but having someone find out she was generous *did*."

The envelope suddenly felt heavy in Jack's hand. He realized the trust that Pastor Stan and Judith Hadley, two virtual strangers, had placed in him. Their sentiments only strengthened his resolve to find Alice's killer.

"I'll read it," Jack said, his hand closing tight around the envelope. "I'll see what's in it, and then I'll turn it over to Sheriff Burns."

Stan held his gaze a moment, then nodded. "Thank you."

Jack watched as the preacher thundered away. He then glanced through the trees at Otto. The old man was watching, probably wondering what the exchange was about. Jack wondered himself.

He carried the envelope into the trailer and set it down on the table, then rubbed at his eyes with his fingers. It was going to be a long night.

He would read Alice's book. But first he needed to get to Quinn Gallery before it closed.

Jack locked the door to the trailer, asked Otto to watch Crockett until he got back, and started for town.

He was sure the manuscript would help reveal Alice's killer. But as he walked out of the campground and onto the lighted street, Jack doubted that he needed it now at all. If his instincts were right—and they usually were—reading it would only confirm what he suspected.

Jack had a feeling he already knew who had murdered Alice Fremont.

CHAPTER 66

IT WAS A Friday evening in January, and the streets of Telluride bustled with activity. People were jostling for positions every which way on the sidewalk. The skis and snowboards that were held aloft earlier in the day were gone. No one marched around in ski boots. It was a night crowd.

Jack noticed a beautiful woman in a long fur coat with a small group of people collected around her. He was sure he'd seen her on some television show or in a movie. He walked past, having decided long ago that most celebrities weren't worth a second glance. During his years at the FBI, he had come into contact with several and concluded that nearly all, when the glitz and glamour were peeled back, were among the most *un*interesting people on the planet.

Jack started the incline toward Quinn Gallery. He glanced across the street when someone opened the door to Pandora Café and caught a glimpse of Judith Hadley inside. After he talked to Gordon Quinn, he'd stop in for dinner. He wanted to ask Judith about

Alice's manuscript and about her conversation with Pastor Stan.

As Jack turned his gaze back toward the gallery, something caught his eye. A lanky figure, dark hood pulled over his head, was keeping pace with him on the opposite side of the street. It was the kid. Jack wasn't going to let him get away this time.

Jack continued his climb toward the gallery but watched the kid from the corner of his eye. Then, just as a truck passed between them, blocking his view, Jack darted across the street and squatted behind the snow berm collected in the middle.

When the truck was gone, Jack peeked over the top of the snow and saw the kid stop and frantically look in both directions. He was standing under a streetlamp. Jack squinted but couldn't make out the face hidden in the shadows.

The kid started across the street. When he was only a few feet away, Jack jumped from behind the snow and was met with a forearm thrust out at lightning speed.

Jack's head popped back. He staggered, trying not to fall. A warm mercury taste filled his mouth. Blood. He knew instantly. He leaned forward and spat.

The kid had made it to the sidewalk and was pushing his way through the crowd.

Not again, Jack thought to himself and started after him.

Just before Jack was hit, he'd gotten a better look at his face. The kid wasn't much more than a boy. Something about him was familiar.

At the corner, the kid glanced over his shoulder and saw Jack following him, then bolted around the building and down the side street.

Jack ran, fogging the air in front of him as he struggled to breathe. Damn altitude. He'd never get used to the thin air.

When he reached the corner, he saw the kid standing at the end of the block, watching for him. It was downhill, but Jack was never going to catch him.

The kid bolted again, disappearing around the corner.

"Stop!" Jack called out, knowing damn well he wouldn't.

Jack bent at the waist to catch his breath. Then it dawned on him who the kid was and where he was probably headed.

Jack pushed off the side of the building and started to follow. The cross street was dark, and except for a woman walking her dog on the opposite side, deserted. At the alley, Jack took a sharp left and made his way carefully from building to building, shining the light of his phone onto each of the back doors, looking for the one he wanted.

When he found it, Jack dropped into the shadows and pressed his back against the wall.

It didn't take long. After only a couple of minutes, Jack heard someone coming. They were out of breath. When he reached for the door handle, Jack sprang from the wall, surprising him.

In the split second it took for the kid to figure out what was happening, Jack grabbed him and twisted him into a choke hold he'd learned at the academy.

The kid struggled. But Jack knew he finally had him.

"You busted my lip, you son of a bitch."

CHAPTER 67

STILL HOLDING THE kid by the neck, Jack reached for the door with his free hand. After several attempts, he got it open and pushed the kid inside Waggoner Mercantile.

The back room was empty.

Jack nodded toward the front of the store.

They found Ivy Waggoner straightening a stack of small rugs. Her mouth fell open as she looked from Sam to Jack. "Opal?" Her voice was high and tense.

Opal Waggoner had her back to the room as she flipped the sign in the window to indicate the store was closed. "What is it?" she asked, turning around. When she saw Jack and Sam, she froze.

Jack looked from one sister to the other. "I think you ladies owe me an explanation."

For a moment there was silence. Jack released the kid.

"We have no idea what you're talking about," Opal insisted.

"I think you're a liar," Jack replied.

Opal pressed down on her cane, stretching herself a fraction taller. "Well, I never—"

"Oh, yes you have," Ivy shot back, rolling her eyes. "And more than once."

Opal glared at her sister. "Know-it-all."

"Prune."

"That's enough." Jack held up his hands.

Opal turned her attention to the kid. "Get out of here, Sam. You forget this ever happened."

Sam looked from one sister to the next, then at Jack, unsure of what to do.

"For God's sake, Sam, move!" Opal stabbed the wood floor with her cane.

The kid jumped, then scurried from the room.

When Jack heard the back door close, he unzipped his coat and stuck his hands on his hips, flaring the sides. "All right. Now, what in the hell is going on?"

Opal Waggoner thrust out her chin. "I'm not sure I know what you mean," she said, feigning indignation again.

"Oh, shut up, Opal. It's time to tell the man the truth. If you won't do it, I will." Ivy took in and released a deep breath, thinking about what to say. "We've had Sam following you for a few days."

Jack frowned. "Why?"

"Because of Gordon Quinn," Opal said. "That's why. We wanted to know if the beastly little man was dragging us into his forgery mess."

Jack remembered his conversation with the director of Lamston Gallery in Manhattan. The FBI had called, asking questions about the Bierstadt she'd sold to Alice. She had put two and two together when they had asked about Gordon Quinn and his gallery in Telluride. "When the FBI asks questions about art," she had told Jack, "you know they're either investigating forgery or theft."

Jack turned to Opal. "So you know about Quinn selling fakes?"

"We had our suspicions. It seems now you have confirmed it."

Ivy explained. "We took two watercolors in on consignment—"

"*You* took them in," Opal corrected her.

Ivy rolled her eyes and continued. "*I* took them in—for Celeste Bailey. Then we started hearing rumors about Quinn Gallery being investigated. You know, word gets around fast in a small town."

"Get to the point," Opal said.

Ivy scowled at her sister before she continued. "We heard through the grapevine that Celeste had returned an oil painting to Gordon—a very expensive landscape. And the Baileys—Celeste, in particular—know a lot about art. So…"

Opal finished for her. "So we think she forced Gordon to take it back because she suspected it was a forgery. By then she had probably heard the rumors, too. She had already brought us the watercolors to consign. She probably decided to get rid of them and figured it was easier to bring them to us rather than ask Gordon to take them back."

"It's all speculation," Ivy said. "We don't know for sure."

Opal cleared her throat, annoyed by the interruption. "They're very nice watercolors but nowhere near as expensive as what she paid for the oil. We could never have consigned something like that for her. The landscape was something she would have to get Gordon to take back—no one else in Telluride sells anything that expensive. I would love to know how *that* conversation went." Opal chuckled, then shook her head. "Evil little man. Anyway, the next thing I know, Ivy went and sold one of the watercolors to Alice, of all people. Like Celeste Bailey, Alice is art savvy."

"Was," Ivy corrected her.

Jack was beginning to understand. "And you were worried the watercolor you sold Alice could have been a fake?"

"You are correct." Opal rapped the floor with her cane. "We don't know if it was or it wasn't. But *someone* found out about Quinn's forgeries and reported him. My suspicions tell me it was either Alice or Celeste. And now that Quinn is being investigated, we're concerned we could be dragged into the mess."

"But why have Sam follow me?"

"Because you were poking around, asking questions about Alice," she replied. "And then about Gordon Quinn. We wanted to find out what you were up to."

"You had Sam break into my trailer."

Opal had "guilty" plastered across her face. "He didn't *break* in," she said defiantly. "He said the door was unlocked. We had him looking for anything that would explain what you were up to."

"You thought I was working for Alice," Jack said. "Investigating Quinn." He understood now.

The sisters glanced at each other, then nodded.

"We did," Ivy said.

"We've heard rumors," Opal said. "About Alice's upcoming book. We've heard that it was going to be about people and scandals in Telluride. If she thought we had knowingly sold her a forgery…"

"She might include characters in her book that resemble the two of you."

Opal lifted her chin. "We are practically local legends."

Jack didn't doubt it.

"We don't know if the painting we sold Alice was a forgery or not," Ivy said quietly. "But it could have been. There's no way for us to know for sure."

"It was a mistake on Ivy's part," Opal said. "She should have never taken in Celeste Bailey's consignment, knowing it was possible she could have purchased it from that crook. Mark my words, if the rumors are true and Gordon drags us into his mess, I'll…I'll…"

"It's not going to happen," Ivy said.

Opal ignored her. "The next time I see him, I'll throttle the man."

Ivy rolled her eyes again. "I can only imagine his terror."

Jack checked the time on his watch. Quinn Gallery would be closing.

"Three paintings were stolen from Alice's house last night," he said. "One of them had Quinn's name written on the back."

"I knew it!" Opal said. "The man is toxic."

"Which paintings?" Ivy asked. "I hope one wasn't the watercolor."

"Something with elks and two landscapes by an artist named Bierstadt."

Ivy's eyebrows shot up. "That could be the oil Celeste returned to Gordon. Alice must have bought it from him."

"None of the three was a watercolor?" Opal asked.

Jack shook his head, and Ivy let out a sigh of relief.

Opal picked up her cane and pointed it at him. "You look into this, young man." She stabbed the air with her cane as she spoke. "That crook is trying to cover his tracks. My bet is that you'll find he's behind the theft *and* Alice's murder."

"Opal!" Ivy exclaimed.

"It may be a harsh thing to say, but it's probably true. You need to investigate that crook and find out." Opal lowered the cane slowly. The sharp edge to her voice was gone. "I can't say that I was fond of Alice, but she didn't deserve what happened to her. You talk to Gordon Quinn."

Jack zipped up his coat. "That's where I'm headed next."

CHAPTER 68

Saturday, January 15

JACK WOKE EARLY the next morning. Visions of Alice's frozen body and those of his grandparents had haunted his dreams.

He sat up and swung his feet to the floor, then dragged both hands down his face and massaged his eyes. But it was no use. He felt like he'd been hit by a truck.

The night before, by the time he'd left the Waggoner sisters and reached Quinn Gallery, it was closed. For some reason, Gordon had left early. Jack wondered if the FBI investigation had him rattled. Would he try to run?

Jack pulled his cell phone from the floor and checked the time. It was early, but he wanted to be at the gallery when it opened.

He pulled on the clothes he'd worn the day before, threw a clean set in a plastic bag, and opened the trailer door. He stood for a while, inhaling the frigid morning air and letting Crockett relieve himself.

The air stung his lungs, but it felt good and helped

wake him up, clearing his head. "All right," he told Crockett. "Get inside. I'll be back in a minute."

Jack closed and locked the trailer door, then set out for the public showers, scanning the campground along the way. He thought about the night before, about finally catching Sam and his conversation with the Waggoner sisters. It all made sense.

Inside the public bath, he undressed and stepped into one of the showers, the concrete floor cold on his feet. As the hot water spilled down on him, he went over the questions he wanted Gordon Quinn to answer. What was the story behind the Bierstadts that had sat on the floor next to Alice's desk? Where was he the night they were stolen?

Jack thought he knew the answers but wanted to hear them from Quinn.

The night before, he'd spent several hours scanning the manuscript. Nothing in it had surprised him. There weren't any revelations that Jack hadn't already suspected. But reading it had been entertaining. Identifying the characters was easy—Jack had met most of them already.

But parts of the manuscript were brutal. Alice had sacrificed friends—even family—for the sake of a sensational story. Maybe she was motivated by revenge. Jack didn't know and didn't care.

None of the characters resembled Judith Hadley or Pastor Stan. She also hadn't included anyone similar to Sally or Johnny Eagle. The ones she used were corrupt, people who cheated and lied, people with far fewer scruples than even Alice Fremont.

And Jack was almost positive he knew which one had poisoned her. The pieces to the puzzle fit. But he wanted to hear it from Quinn to know for sure.

After he showered and dressed, Jack went back to the trailer and grabbed the manuscript. He walked Crockett through the snow and found Otto outside smoking a cigarette.

"I've got a few errands to do this morning," Jack said.

The old man studied him for a moment, looking first at the manuscript Jack held in one hand, then at the bowl of dog food he held in the other.

Otto gestured toward town with his cigarette. "We'll be all right. You go take care of your business."

Jack nodded, then laid the bowl at Crockett's feet. "I'll be back."

On his way to the gallery, he stopped into the post office. He filled out a label with Douglas Townsend's address and slid the package across the counter to the clerk. Jack detested Alice's agent, a man motivated not by loyalty but by greed. But Alice would want her book published. When it came out, it would cause chaos, but then again, she would have known that—all of her books did.

Jack turned the corner. It was early, but Main

Street was already crowded with cars and tourists. There was a flurry of activity at the top of the hill, outside Quinn Gallery, and Jack quickened his pace.

As he got closer, he recognized the fleet of black Suburbans with government plates that blocked one of the lanes. FBI. Traffic was being directed around the block. Men were carrying furniture and art out of the gallery, loading it onto a box truck.

A young agent in a dark jacket, FBI emblazoned in yellow on the back and the sleeve, stood to one side, keeping pedestrians at bay.

As Jack got closer, the agent held up a hand. "The sidewalk is closed."

"Former Agent Jack Martin. Criminal investigations, Houston field office."

The agent removed his sunglasses to get a better look. "I've heard of you, Agent Martin."

"Good or bad?"

The agent stuck his glasses back on and continued to surveil the street. "Both."

Jack took a moment, then nodded. "Fair enough."

He knew it would be next to impossible to extract information about an ongoing investigation, but it was worth a shot. "Forgery investigation of Gordon Quinn?"

The agent didn't acknowledge the question but continued to scan the crowd. Just when Jack thought he'd struck out, the agent nodded once. It was all the information Jack was going to get.

Another agent came out of the gallery, wearing gloves and holding Alice's missing Bierstadts, one in each hand.

Jack pointed to them. "I'd tell him to be careful with those. They were stolen from a friend's house a couple of nights ago. Worth about a quarter of a mil each. At least the real one is."

The agent looked from the paintings to Jack.

Before he could reply, Jack spoke again. "Tell your supervisor to call me."

As he turned to leave, Jack saw Ryan Oliver coming toward him. Jack took several steps in Oliver's direction, then ducked into the adjacent doorway. Jack watched as Oliver looked up from his phone and realized what was going on at the gallery, fear registering on his face. Oliver pivoted and hurried back the way he'd come, throwing a last look over his shoulder before disappearing into the crowd.

Jack started for the campground. He threw a wave to the bewildered young agent still standing outside the gallery and was sure that he'd get a call from the kid's supervisor within minutes.

Now that Gordon Quinn was in the custody of the FBI, Jack knew he wouldn't be able to question him. But now he didn't need to.

Jack dug into his pocket and found his phone, then scrolled through his contacts for Sheriff Tony Burns.

It was time to trap a killer.

CHAPTER 69

AT ALICE'S ESTATE, Jack stood alone in the great hall, looking up at the painting of the dying elk. It haunted him, reminding him now of Alice, the mountain lion symbolic of the battle Alice had fought and lost. It was a battle of her own making—he knew that. Alice was both the elk and the lion. But he felt sorry for her.

He turned his attention to the corridor that led to the kitchen and waited for Alice's killer to arrive.

Several seconds earlier, he'd watched through a window as a car came toward the house, then disappeared around the corner. The murderer was comfortable on the property. Of course they'd use the back door.

It all made sense. The missing manuscript, the suitcase, the poison. Even the storm the night Alice went missing had played its part. Jack understood now why there was no evidence of forced entry the night the paintings were stolen and the night of the murder.

On his way to Trout Lake, he had called Tony

Burns and explained it all. But the sheriff had struggled putting the pieces together and pushed back,
unconvinced. Jack had grown frustrated but wasn't
deterred. His next call had been to Alice's killer.

And now the trap was set.

The house was deathly quiet.

He stood in the center of the massive room, the
ceiling soaring overhead. It was too open, the only
furniture hugging the dark paneled walls. He was vulnerable, but it was too late. Jack felt for the pistol
tucked into the waistband of his jeans. Satisfied he
was ready, he waited.

A door closed somewhere in the distance.

Soon the faint sound of footsteps echoed in
the hallway leading from the kitchen. As they grew
louder, Jack felt his heart rate speed up, recognizing
the familiar rush of adrenaline before confronting a
murderer.

It was go time.

Alice's killer rounded the corner and came into
the room.

Jack steadied his voice. "Hello, Eva."

She stopped when she saw him, her face softening with a sultry look. "Hello, Detective." Her Slavic
accent was thick but sexy as hell.

She looked stunning in tight jeans and tall boots,
her platinum-blond hair cascading down the front of
a black cashmere sweater. She took a leopard-print

coat that was draped over her arm and laid it across the banister.

Jack noticed she was wearing thin black gloves and fiddled mindlessly with the clasp of her designer purse. She was nervous.

"I came as soon as we hung up," she said. "You have information about what happened to my mother-in-law?"

"I do." Jack watched her closely.

"You said I was the only one who could help you find out who did this. But how? I do not understand."

"First, you can quit lying. I know the truth."

"Lying?" She frowned.

"I know you killed Alice."

"But that is ridiculous."

"Is it?" Jack took a step closer. "Somehow you found out what was in Alice's next book. And you didn't like it, so you murdered her."

Eva's lips parted, but she remained silent.

"You came the night of the storm, let yourself into the house—with your key, or maybe Alice let you in. But you poisoned her. Then you hid her body."

"It is not possible," Eva protested. She held an arm out. "Look at me. How could I drag a body across the bridge?"

"Alice was small. And you're an Olympic athlete. You made sure to tell me that night at Tomboy

Tavern. I believe your foot was on my calf at the time."

She glared at him. "That proves nothing."

"Maybe not, but I never said Alice's body was dragged across the bridge. Yet you knew."

She froze when she realized her mistake. "But everyone knows. The media…they reported…"

Jack shook his head. "There were postmortem bruises on the back of her head—likely from the crossties on the bridge when she was dragged out to the center. I advised the sheriff to keep the details a secret. The media wouldn't know that she was dragged. But her killer would."

"Even…even if it was possible, why would I?"

"The book," Jack replied. "Alice found out about the affair. It was with the artist, wasn't it? The one who forges paintings for Gordon Quinn. What's his name?" Jack watched her stew as he pretended to search for the name. "Ryan Oliver. Nice-looking fellow, but a bit young for you, don't you think?"

Her eyes raged.

Jack continued. "You were a bit effusive with your praises, Eva. He was *zee best in Telluride,* I think is how you put it."

"You are despicable!"

"I've been called worse."

"There was no affair."

"It was easy to figure out. The derogatory remarks

about your husband, the times you weren't at home, the yoga classes—including the one the night you were with *me*. I knew immediately that you were having an affair. But I didn't know it was with Ryan Oliver until after the Bierstadts were stolen from Alice's bedroom."

Eva's expression morphed from one of rage to one of confusion, and Jack realized she hadn't been involved with the theft. Until that moment, he hadn't been sure.

"Your car keys," he said. "The night they went missing, you must have been with the artist." She was thinking about it, and Jack continued. "He used them to break into the house and steal the paintings. That's why there were no signs of a forced entry."

"I do not know what you are talking about."

"Ryan Oliver took your keys, knowing you would have one to Alice's house. Maybe at some point during the affair, you *told* him you did." He could see her searching her memory, but Jack continued. "Then Oliver—or Gordon Quinn, I'm not sure which, but it doesn't matter—came out that night and stole the paintings. They were confiscated this morning from the gallery."

Jack watched as she processed the information, putting the pieces together. It would undoubtedly sting to realize that her boyfriend had stolen her keys to rob her dead mother-in-law. It had been a bluff.

Jack wasn't sure that was what had happened, but her response confirmed he was right.

But it didn't matter.

"Alice suspected the affair and put it in her book. Somehow you found out, so you murdered her. You've got a good thing going—married to Hugh and his family fortune, the affair on the side. The book would have ruined everything, wouldn't it?"

Eva's eyes bored into him as she searched for something to say. Jack knew he had hit a home run.

"It was my husband," she finally said. "Hugh murdered her. They found the suitcase in his closet."

Jack shook his head. "No. You set it up to look that way, but it wasn't Hugh. You took the suitcase and hid it in his closet, knowing the sheriff's men would find it." He jerked a chin toward the second floor. "You planted his financial documents with Alice's papers, too, knowing that when they were found, they'd know Hugh was broke and think he'd killed his mother for money. With Hugh in jail, he'd be out of the way. You could enjoy his houses and his money *and* spend more time with your boyfriend."

She stared at him, silent.

Jack had hit pay dirt again. "But there's a flaw in your logic. If Hugh killed Alice for the inheritance, he would've wanted her body found immediately— to start probate. It doesn't make sense to hide her where she wouldn't be found."

Eva's face was taut, her breathing shallow and quick. She was searching for an explanation, an excuse. Jack had seen the same look from perpetrators a hundred times before.

"It's over, Eva."

Her face relaxed with the realization she'd been caught. "Where is Sally?" she asked, glancing up at the second-floor landing.

"I told her and Johnny to go home. I wanted to talk to you alone."

"That was a mistake." Her eyes were hard. "Maybe you are very handsome, Detective, but you are not very smart like me."

She snapped open the purse and pulled out a gun. She pointed the pistol at his chest and took a step closer. Jack raised his hands. He glanced toward the closed doors of the parlor, then back. He was less than six feet from her but still too far.

"Guess whose gun, Detective?" A grin curled the corners of her mouth.

Jack knew immediately. "Hugh's." She was smart. She could kill him, leave the gun as further evidence against her husband. It was a brilliant move. He should have seen it coming. "Tell me about the eye drops."

"What is there to tell? It was simple."

"Most people don't know that tetra..." He dropped his hands, pretending to search for the name.

"Tetrahydrozoline."

"How did you do it?"

The question stroked her ego. A smug look came over her face. "It was easy. I came that night when I knew she would be alone. Alice always would be in the parlor at night, reading and having her bourbon. She was surprised to see me, but she had no clue. Stupid woman."

"You poured it into her drink."

"She didn't notice. All I had to do was wait." She was still smiling. "You understand now."

"I do. It was a brilliant plan." He had dropped his hands further and reached slowly for the gun at his waist.

"Up!" She jerked the pistol, sighting it on his chest again.

Jack froze, staring at the gun. He was running out of options. He needed to keep her talking. "Tell me about the manuscript. How did you find out what was in it?"

She looked at Jack like he was stupid. "There were rumors about the book. She had made comments to Gordon Quinn. I wanted to see."

"How did you find out what was in it?"

She shook her head at the question and let her hands drop slightly. "We came for dinner. I snuck away from Hugh and Alice and went upstairs. It was easy."

"You saw what was in it, so you came back and murdered her." She didn't answer him. "You took the manuscript with you."

"I burned it."

"What about the copy?"

She was quiet. "You are bluffing. There is no copy. We have talked enough." She raised the pistol again. "Goodbye, Detective."

The leather over her knuckle stretched as she started to pull back on the trigger.

Jack held his breath.

"I wouldn't do that if I were you."

Sheriff Tony Burns had quietly pulled back one of the parlor doors.

Eva swung around, and Jack lunged at her, throwing her off-balance. They both fell to the floor.

Burns rushed forward and kicked the pistol away, then wrestled with Eva and pulled her to her feet. Her beautiful face was contorted with rage. It was the face of a murderer.

Burns cuffed her.

Jack let out the breath he'd been holding and looked up at him. "What took you so long?"

Burns gave him a weak smile. His mouth quivered. "Looks like I was right on time."

Jack nodded his appreciation, then struggled to stand, pushing himself off the floor and feeling all his football injuries. "I'm getting too old for this," he said, smoothing the front of his jeans. He turned to Burns. "Well?"

The sheriff held Eva by the cuffs with one hand and tapped the shoulder mic fastened to his uniform with the other. "We got every word."

CHAPTER 70

TWO HOURS LATER Jack stepped into the warmth of
Pandora Café. It smelled of coffee and bacon and
made his stomach growl.

He let his eyes adjust, then scanned the late-morning crowd. Judith Hadley was refilling coffee for a
table of locals. Jack watched her talk to them. It was
an easy conversation. Something made her laugh,
and she slapped the shoulder of the man she stood
over. It was the kind of familiarity Jack missed after
leaving the people he knew in Texas. Judith saw him
and waved.

Jack took his table near the fireplace, shrugged
off his coat, and sat facing the door. The morning
had been a rush. There was no feeling like catching a
killer, but now he was beat. Every muscle in his body
ached.

He turned to the fireplace and watched the flames
lick at the gas logs, letting the heat warm his face.
The soft murmur of the crowd could have lulled him
into a trance if he'd let it.

Judith appeared at the table with coffee and

cinnamon rolls. She set it all down in front of him, then wiped her hands on her apron. There was something soothing about her presence.

"You look like hell, Jack. What happened?"

He pulled the coffee closer and blew over it. "Tony Burns just arrested Alice's killer."

Judith's eyes grew wide. She glanced over the café. "Give me two minutes. I want to hear all about it."

Jack watched her scurry off and say something to one of the waitresses. She pointed in his direction, and the girl came over. Without looking at a menu, Jack requested the largest breakfast they served. He didn't care what it included.

Several minutes later, Judith was back. She removed her apron and sat perched on the edge of a chair, resting her elbows on the table and leaning toward him.

"Tell me what happened."

For the next twenty minutes, between bites of scrambled eggs and pancakes and several slices of bacon, Jack gave her the details of what had taken place that morning. Judith sat with rapt attention, letting Jack talk.

When he finished, she slumped back in her chair and gazed into the fireplace. "Eva Sheppard," she said, shaking her head. "Poor Alice. Her own daughter-in-law."

Jack wiped his mouth with a napkin and laid it

back in his lap. "I guess it's better than it being one of her sons."

That brought Judith around. "Isn't that the truth? I was convinced one of those boys had something to do with it. I'm glad I was wrong." She paused. "Everyone was talking about Gordon Quinn this morning. You know the FBI arrested him?" Jack nodded, and she continued. "Locals are speculating that he had something to do with Alice's murder. I guess he didn't."

"Quinn didn't make sense." He told Judith about the stolen paintings. "Quinn, or someone working for him, took them. If he'd killed Alice to hide his forgery scam, he would have taken the paintings the night she was murdered. Why wait a week to do it?"

Judith was thinking about it.

"Plus," Jack continued. "There wasn't any evidence of breaking and entering the night Alice went missing. And she wouldn't have let Gordon Quinn in."

Judith blew out a breath. "No. She couldn't stand the man. But how did you figure out it was Eva?"

Jack told her about the affair, about the missing suitcase and Hugh's financial records.

"She planted them to make Hugh look guilty?"

Jack nodded. "She wanted Hugh out of the way."

"She wanted him in jail." Judith was putting the

pieces together. "So she'd get the houses, the money, *and* keep her lover,"

She had come to the same conclusion Jack had. Judith Hadley was a smart woman.

Jack knew that he was telling her more than he should, but he was too exhausted to care about procedure. Burns had Eva's confession—it should be an open-and-shut case. Besides, Jack liked having someone to talk to.

He finished the last of his coffee. "There was something else," he said, remembering. "Something about the way Alice was murdered."

"Poisoned?"

Jack hesitated, a tired frown creasing his forehead. The cause of death hadn't been released to the public. "How'd you know?"

"My cousin's boy, Monroe. He's a dispatcher with the sheriff's office." She must have noticed the puzzled look on his face. She added, "Word gets around in a—"

"Small town," Jack finished for her. "So I've heard." He laid his hands on the table and studied them while he spoke. "You know a woman is seven times more likely to kill someone with poison than a man? I remember the stat from the academy. It was a clue."

"Huh." She thought about it.

"Men almost never use poison to murder their

victims. They shoot them or stab them, even beat them to death, but they almost never poison them."

"So it's a woman's way to murder?"

"Sometimes," Jack replied. "It just fit. Everything pointed to Eva."

Judith motioned for the waitress to refill Jack's coffee.

When the girl left, she leaned closer, laying a hand on one of his. "You did a good thing, Jack Martin. Thank you." She saw the weariness in his eyes. "You're not getting paid for this one, are you?"

Jack took a sip of coffee. "Not this time," he said, setting the cup back on the table. But it didn't matter. Pay or no pay, he had wanted Alice's killer behind bars.

Judith gave him a moment. "So, what are you going to do now?"

"Take a nap." He knew she had meant long-term, but he was too exhausted to think.

Judith refused to let him pay for his breakfast and told him not to leave town without stopping in to say goodbye. Jack would miss her.

On his way back to the campground he got a call from Buckley Bailey. Buckley congratulated him on the arrest, sounding unusually exuberant, like he was relieved.

Buckley asked about the missing manuscript. Jack told him it hadn't been found, deliberately not mentioning the copy he'd mailed to Douglas Townsend. If the book was eventually published, Jack knew Buckley Bailey was in for another scandal.

Before the call ended, Buckley again threw out the offer to get Jack a job with the Texas Rangers. For a split second Jack considered taking him up on it but then declined.

"It's a standing offer," Buckley said, his cheerful voice booming through the phone. "You can take your time to think about it."

Jack pulled off Main Street into the campground and wound the truck through the trees. As he neared campsite twenty, he saw Otto and Crockett. The old man was sitting at the picnic table, throwing a stick for Crockett to fetch.

Jack pulled up next to the Airstream and parked. When he got out of the truck, Crockett rushed to him. Jack took the stick from his mouth and threw it back in Otto's direction, sending the dog running.

For several minutes, the two men threw the stick back and forth, Crockett dashing one way and then the other through the snow.

Jack heard an approaching vehicle and watched as a truck emerged from the trees. It pulled to the campsite and stopped. Sally Eagle stepped out of the passenger side, carrying a small bag. Johnny Eagle remained behind the wheel.

Sally approached him tentatively. Jack could tell

she was nervous. She pulled a jar from the bag and held it out for him, and he took it.

"We came to thank you, Mr. Jack Martin," she said, giving him a gentle nod. "For finding out what happened to Mrs. Fremont. Miss Hadley told us where to find you. She said we just missed you at the café."

Jack turned the jar over in his hand. There was a thick, yellow-brown liquid inside but no label.

"It is honey," she said. "The bees make it from the wildflowers of the mountains. We gather it in summer."

She dug into the bag again and pulled out something resembling a doll made of sticks. Scraps of fabric and yarn that bound the sticks together had been fashioned to resemble clothes. A crude face had been painted on tan cloth that was topped with something resembling horsehair.

"It is for Crockett," Sally said, nodding toward the dog that now stood at their feet, wagging its tail. "Johnny made it for him."

Jack glanced at Johnny. He was still sitting in the truck and gave Jack a silent nod.

"Thank you," Jack said, taking it from her.

As quietly as they had come, they left.

Jack tossed the stick doll into the snow that edged the river, and Crockett loped away to retrieve it. He then waved at Otto through the trees. The old man had been watching the exchange, probably wondering again what was going on. Jack would go over and talk to him, tell him about the things that had happened that morning he wouldn't have heard on his scanner, but not yet.

Crockett returned with the doll and jumped wildly at Jack's feet. He took it from him and threw it again, then stared up at the snowy slopes at the end of the canyon, everything frozen and blanketed in white. He could just make out the line of Ingram Falls, a ribbon of ice waiting for the spring thaw. He wondered how beautiful it must look in summer.

Jack drew in the cold scent of pine and clean air and thought about Santa Fe. He knew he should take Crockett and go. The heaviest snows would come in February and March, making the mountain passes too treacherous to pull the trailer. If he waited too long, he would be stuck in Telluride.

He dropped his gaze to the trailer. After only a week, the snow was already beginning to pile up around its sides. It was time to go.

But something held him there.

He'd grown to like Telluride—the town and its people. And he had a book to finish reading.

Crockett returned with the doll. Jack took it from him, then scratched him behind an ear.

"It's been one hell of a week, Crockett, hasn't it?"

The dog barked, and Jack laughed.

"But I kind of like it here." He stared up at the

mountains again. "How about if we hang around for a while and see what happens next?"

ACKNOWLEDGMENT

The Killing Storm depicts several real locations in and around Telluride and Mountain Village, but all events and characters are entirely fictional. Anything negatively portrayed is done so purely for literary purposes.

Living half the year in Telluride, I had a lot of fun weaving several of our family's favorite local places and restaurants into the story. Alas, Pandora Café is but a fictionalized version of my ideal eatery. I wish it were real!

Castle in the Clouds is also fictional but inspired by a fabulous historic estate outside of Redstone, Colorado.

Thank you once again to my fabulous editor, Kristen Weber. Working through your editorial comments is like taking a master class in creative writing!

Thank you to Susan Lilly with the San Miguel County Sheriff's office for answering questions on local procedures. All characters (including law enforcement) in The Killing Storm are completely fictional. Any mistakes regarding policy or procedures are my own.

Thank you to Mark Jacobs, my go-to friend for local geography since he's hiked more miles through the mountains around Telluride than I can count. I could never keep up, but thanks for letting my better half try!

And to my better half. Thank you Chris for once again indulging me while I bounced storyline and character ideas off you. Thank you for your patience the times I was lost in the story during meals, while we were traveling, while we were supposed to be watching television together, while you played golf, and on and on. Your support is my strength!

I would like to acknowledge my long-time author hero, Mary Higgins Clark, who famously said on more than one occasion: "When someone is mean to me, I just make them a victim in my next book." This brings me to the mean old lady from Oregon (who shall remain anonymous). Thank you for providing the inspiration for Alice Fremont!

And last but not least, to you, the reader. I appreciate every one of you. I can't thank you enough for continuing to read the Mountain Resort Mystery Series. I hope you enjoyed reading The Killing Storm as much as I enjoyed writing it. Thank you for all the encouraging messages, reviews, and comments on social media. There is nothing more exhilarating than hearing from you!